# EXPOSED

Visit us at www.boldstrokesbooks.com

# By the Author

Shots Fired

Forbidden Passions

Initiation by Desire

Speakeasy

Escapades

Sheltered Love

Summer Passion

Heartscapes

Love on Liberty

Love Down Under

Complications

Lessons In Desire

Hookin' Up

Score

Exposed

# EXPOSED

*by*

MJ Williamz

2018

---

**Credits**
Editor: Cindy Cresap
Production Design: Susan Ramundo
Cover Design By Sheri (hindsightgraphics@gmail.com)

# Acknowledgments

As usual, the first person I want and need to thank is my loving and supportive wife, Laydin Michaels, without whom I'd never get a book written.

I would also like to thank Sarah and Inger, my beta readers for their kind words and encouragement.

To all the people at Bold Strokes Books, Rad, Sandy, Cindy, Stacia, and all the others, thank you for helping me in my endeavor to be the best author I can be.

And, of course, thank you to you, the readers, whose feedback I cherish and for whom I live to write.

# Dedication

To my love and my life—Laydin

## Chapter One

Randi Hansen took a long pull on her beer and surveyed the scene in front of her. Women were moving on the dance floor to the beat of some great eighties music. She was in her element. She watched as couples moved together on the floor, then went off to separate tables. She sat back and admired all of the women. Randi felt each woman was beautiful in her own way. She was a lover of the female form and planned on doing some loving that night.

"Is this seat taken?" a voice said in her ear.

She turned to see a curvy brunette standing next to her.

"Help yourself," Randi said. "I'm Randi."

"I'm Melissa. Nice to meet you."

"Nice to meet you. Can I buy you a drink?"

"Are you always this forward?"

"Only with beautiful women."

Melissa blushed. Randi watched with great pleasure as the light pink worked its way up her neck to cover her face. She was quite attractive. And her low-cut top left little to the imagination. She had some bodacious breasts, and Randi decided she would be her bedmate that night.

"Would you like to dance?" Randi said.

"How about that drink first?"

"Oh, yeah. What would you like?"

"I'll have a gin and tonic.

Randi motioned to the bartender and ordered a drink for Melissa and another beer for herself.

"Do you ever drink anything stronger than beer?" Melissa said.

"Not very often. Sometimes I'll drink tequila, but I'm mostly a beer kinda woman."

Melissa nodded as she took a sip of her drink.

"This is really good," she said.

"Glad to hear it. Gin definitely isn't my thing."

"Why's that?"

Because my mother used to drink it until she was a royal bitch, Randi thought. She shrugged.

"I guess I just never developed a taste for it."

"Fair enough. Now, about that dance?"

Randi stood and offered Melissa her hand. Melissa's hand was soft and warm, and Randi was sure the rest of her would be as well. She made herself stop that line of thinking. One dance and a drink didn't necessarily mean Melissa would go home with her. But Randi seldom struck out.

They danced a couple of fast songs, but when Randi tried to pull Melissa in for a slow song, Melissa pulled away. She took Randi's hand and led her back to the bar. Too soon. Randi told herself to be patient.

Randi took a swig of beer.

"So, what do you do, Melissa?"

"I'm a clerk in the county office."

"Oh." It sounded boring to Randi, but she wouldn't let on. "Do you like it?"

"It's not bad. I've worked there since I graduated from college. It's a good job. What do you do?"

"I work for Animal Rescue."

"In what capacity?"

"If you see a wild animal or stray dog or cat, I'm the one you call to go get them."

Melissa laughed. It was an easy laugh, and it made Randi smile.

"Which are you more likely to see? A wild animal or a stray dog or cat?" she said.

"You'd be surprised," Randi said. "It's not uncommon to get called out because someone has a raccoon or a possum in their yard. Or even in their house sometimes."

"Wow. How do they get inside someone's house?"

"Dog doors, mostly."

"Excuse me?"

"People have those doggie doors for their dogs to go in and out. If the doors are big enough, critters of the night can get in looking for food."

"Oh, my God. That would terrify me if I found one of them in my house." Melissa laughed.

"No need to be terrified. You just call me. I come get them and release them back into the wild."

"So you don't kill them?"

"God, no. We take them back to the Everglades and let them loose."

"Well, that's decent."

Randi ordered two more drinks and leaned back and looked at Melissa. She was shorter than Randi with broad hips and large breasts and plenty of meat in the middle. She made Randi's mouth water. She wanted to run her hands and mouth all over her body.

"Oh, my," Melissa said.

"What?" Randi snapped out of her reverie and realized she'd been busted.

"You were practically drooling. I take it you like what you see?"

"I do. Very much. Now, how about some more dances?"

They made their way to the center of the dance floor and moved to the music. They danced three more fast songs, and this time, when a slow song came on, Melissa moved into Randi's arms.

She felt so good there. She fit so well. Randi fought every urge to kiss her right there in front of everybody. She'd rather wait until they had some privacy. They swayed together, and occasionally Randi would hear Melissa singing along with the song. She had a really nice voice. Just one more attribute to enjoy about her. Randi wondered how much longer they'd have to hang out before they could just go home.

When the song ended, Melissa took her hand again and led her back to the bar. This time, she grabbed her purse and kept walking toward the door. Randi's stomach flip-flopped. It was time for the fun to begin.

Once in the parking lot, Melissa turned to Randi.

"Your place or mine?" she said.

"Yours, if you don't mind." Randi didn't like to bring women home to her place. For one thing, she was a slob. For another, she couldn't just leave if she was at her own place.

"Sounds good. I drive that green Prius over there."

"That's my Frontier. I'll follow you."

Randi kept her focus on the Prius as she drove. She did not want to lose sight of it. She hadn't asked where Melissa lived. Melissa pulled up in front of a nondescript ranch house in a nice neighborhood. Randi parked against the curb out front.

"Nice house," she said when she walked over to Melissa.

"Thanks. It's not much, but it's home."

Melissa opened the door and invited Randi in. Randi stood with her hands in her pockets. She wanted to attack Melissa in a good way but was letting her set the pace.

"You want something to drink?" Melissa said. "I'm afraid all I have is wine."

"Red or white?"

"Red."

"I'd love a glass," Randi lied. She didn't want anything that delayed her from undressing Melissa and getting at that body.

Melissa served them and led Randi into the living room where she offered her a seat on the couch. Randi sat and Melissa sat next to her. Randi could feel the heat radiating from Melissa and knew she wanted this as badly as Randi did.

Randi looked around at the bold prints on the wall and the colorful carpet.

"You really like your colors, don't you?" she said.

"I do. They make me happy."

Randi thought of her own house, decorated in rustic style. She was happy, once again, that they'd agreed to go to Melissa's place.

She took a sip of her wine. Not bad. Not beer, but not bad.

"This is really good," she said.

"I'm glad you like it. It's my favorite."

Randi looked into Melissa's eyes and saw a combination of desire and fear in them. Oh, no. Had she made a mistake?

"What's wrong?" she said.

"What? Nothing. Why?"

"I don't know. You just seem a little on edge."

"I'll admit I'm nervous," Melissa said. "I'm not used to bringing home a stranger from a bar."

"Really?" Randi laughed softly. "It's not that hard."

Melissa laughed then, too.

"I take it you do this all the time?"

"Let's just say this isn't my first rodeo."

Melissa drew in a deep breath.

"Drink some more wine. You need to relax. Or you can tell me to leave if that's what you want."

"No. No. I don't want you to leave. I know that. I'm sorry. I'm not exactly helping set the mood, am I?"

Randi reached out and took Melissa's hand. She felt it relax in her own.

"See? That's nice, isn't it?"

"That's really nice. But I don't want to sit here holding hands with you all night."

"Don't worry. We won't."

Randi leaned in and gently brushed her lips against Melissa's. The touch sent shockwaves cascading over her body. She pulled back.

"Oh, that was nice," Melissa said.

"Good."

Randi set her glass on the coffee table and took Melissa's from her. She set it down and leaned in for another kiss. This one was still close mouthed, but it said more and lasted longer.

This time, when Randi attempted to pull away, Melissa reached her hand behind her head and pulled her back. She opened her mouth and welcomed Randi's tongue inside. Randi was quick to oblige. Her heart raced as their tongues danced together. She fought the urge to climb on top of Melissa right then and there.

When the kiss ended, they were both breathless.

"Come on." Melissa stood and offered her hand to Randi, who took it gratefully.

Randi stood on wobbly legs and let herself be led down the hall to Melissa's bedroom. Her gaze came to rest on the king-sized bed in the center of the room. Plenty of room for both of them. She smiled.

"What?" Melissa said.

"I like your bed."

"That's a good thing."

"That's a very good thing." Randi laughed.

She held Melissa in her arms and kissed her again. She kissed down her cheek to nibble on an earlobe before kissing her neck. Melissa moaned in delight.

Randi brought a hand up and cupped one of Melissa's full breasts through her dress.

"Get me out of this thing," Melissa said. Randi was happy to oblige. She unzipped the dress and helped Melissa step out of it. She quickly unhooked her bra and watched her breasts fall freely.

"My God, you're beautiful," Randi said as she watched Melissa step out of her panties.

"Your turn," Melissa said. "I want to see you in all your butch glory."

Randi stripped quickly and moved to take Melissa in her arms again. The feel of flesh on flesh made her lightheaded with desire. She held up one of Melissa's breasts and bent to lick the nipple. She felt it respond.

"I'm not going to make it on my feet," Melissa said. "Let's lie down."

Randi walked her back to the bed and eased her down. She climbed on top of her. She brought her knee up to press against her center as she kissed her hard on her mouth. Melissa was wet and warm, and Randi couldn't wait to get inside her.

She rolled off Melissa and bent to suck a nipple deep in her mouth. She took as much of her breast as she could with it. Her mouth full, she sucked hard and ran her tongue all over it. She skimmed her hand down the length of Melissa's body, over her curves to where her legs met. She slid her hand between them and found everything coated with a juice that made it easy to play.

Melissa's clit was hard and slick and Randi couldn't resist rubbing it until Melissa cried out in ecstasy. But Randi wasn't through. She moved her hand lower and dipped her fingers inside Melissa. She plunged them as deep as they would go before pulling them out again. She repeated this over and over. Melissa was arching off the bed, meeting every thrust. Finally, Melissa grabbed hold of Randi's wrist with both hands and held tight. Randi felt her clutching her hand deep inside her and stayed still until the spasms stopped.

Randi slowly withdrew her hand.

"That was amazing," Melissa said. "I don't know how many times I came."

"Good. You deserve to come as many times as you need to."

"You're a fantastic lover, Randi. You really are. I'm going to be hard-pressed to do you justice."

"Baby, I want you so bad that you're going to make me climax over and over again as well."

Melissa grinned at her even as she blushed.

"Then I'm ready to take my turn."

She nibbled Randi's neck and sucked on a nipple before she kissed her way down her taut belly. She spread her legs and climbed between them. She ran her tongue over Randi's clit and down to her opening. She licked as deep as she could inside Randi, who was writhing on the bed.

Randi felt like her clit was about to explode. She was all knotted up inside and needed relief.

Melissa moved her mouth back to Randi's clit and sucked it in her mouth. She rolled her tongue over it until Randi pressed her hand on the back of her head. Randi was so close. She needed just a little more, just a tiny bit more. And boom! Her world shattered into a million little pieces and floated to the ground.

Randi slowly opened her eyes and saw Melissa smiling down at her.

"That was fun," Melissa said.

"Yeah, it was."

"So now comes the awkward part."

"What part is that?" Although she already knew.

"The part where I don't know if you should stay over or not."

"Well, how do you feel about that?"

"Look," Melissa said. "I'm not kidding myself into thinking this was more than a one-night stand."

"Okay." Randi was relieved.

"So, I'm thinking it's just as well if you leave now rather than in the morning. Is that okay? Or do I sound cold and unfeeling?"

"No." Randi brushed a bit of hair off Melissa's face. "Not at all. It makes perfect sense. I'll get dressed and get out of here."

She quickly donned her clothes and stood looking down at Melissa's naked body. She'd been made to please, and Randi was glad she'd had the chance to do just that.

"So, I guess I'll see you around?" Randi said.

"Sure thing."

"Good night."

"Good night."

Randi let herself out into the night.

## Chapter Two

Eleanor Bremer stood at the front of her classroom.
"Don't forget, your papers are due Monday. Now put your homework on my desk and you're free to go. Have a great weekend."

She watched as her eighth grade class filed out. When the last student was gone, she sunk into the chair behind her desk. Thank God it was Friday. The kids were starting to accept her, but being a new teacher was never easy. Still, she was making progress and she had that to be thankful for.

She grabbed the homework the kids had put on her desk and began grading. She was on the last one when Ron Ferguson, a history teacher, popped his head in her room.

"Hey, Eleanor, a group of us are going to happy hour over at the Bull. You want to come with us?"

Every Friday since she'd been there, all four of them, she'd been invited to go out with the crew. Every Friday she'd declined. What was she so afraid of? She looked at Ron.

"Sure. I'd love to."

"Huh? Wow. That's great." He laughed. She laughed, too.

"Sure, what the heck? I don't know why it's taken me this long."

"Neither do I. Are you finished here? Do you want to ride with me?"

It was a simple question, but it made her gut churn. What did he mean? Did he assume she'd be going home with him? Or was it a simple offer? She chided herself to relax.

"I know where it is. I'm almost through here. I'll meet you over there."

"Great. See you then."

She tried to concentrate and was finally able to grade the last assignment. She stood, straightened her skirt, grabbed her purse, and left the building.

The Bull was a bit of a dive, but that's probably why the teachers liked it, she thought. It was dimly lit with two pool tables in the middle and booths around the edges. She easily found her group and waved to them as she walked up to the bar. The place was almost empty so it was easy to get the bartender's attention.

"Rum and Coke, please," she said. She took her drink and walked over to the table.

"You know everyone here, right?" Ron said as she took her seat next to Martina Sernova, the science teacher.

"Sure I do."

"I'm glad you finally came out with us," Martina said.

Better to come out with them than to them, Eleanor thought wryly.

"Me, too. It's just been so hectic. I'm glad you guys didn't give up on me."

"Never," Ron said. "The more the merrier as far as we're concerned. And we've been wanting to give you a proper welcome."

"I really appreciate that." Ron made her uncomfortable. He didn't wear a wedding ring. So either he was single or a slimeball. Neither of which appealed to her. He had big brown puppy dog eyes so she couldn't tell if it was just the way he was or if he was hitting on her.

"So, Eleanor," Martina was saying. "Where did you move from again?"

"California."

"All the way across country," Ron said. "That's a heck of a transplant. You're too young for midlife crisis, so may I ask what prompted the move?"

Because I found my wife in bed with another woman, she thought.

"It was just time for a change. I'd been looking for a while, and when I saw this opportunity in Florida, I had to take it. It was like a dream come true. My own personal adventure."

"Well, we've heard wonderful things about you," Martina said. "We're very happy to have you on staff."

"Thank you. I'm very happy to be here."

The afternoon turned into evening and Eleanor was actually relaxing. She shot a couple of games of pool. She lost both, but at least she tried. Finally, the gang started breaking up. Ron came over to her.

"Would you like to grab a bite to eat?" he said.

"No, thanks. I really need to get home and try to organize my things. I haven't even finished unpacking yet. But thanks."

"Sure. No problem."

Eleanor got into her car and drove through a burger joint to get dinner and went home. Alone in her house, she looked around at everything she owned and started to cry. Damn it, she thought she was past the tears, but sometimes the level of her loneliness was overwhelming. This was one of those times. It wasn't that she hated it here. Quite the contrary. Florida was beautiful. The people were nice. But why did she have to be alone? Didn't she deserve to be loved?

She knew the answer to that. She also knew she wasn't about to let anyone get close enough to love her. She'd been burned. Big time. And there was no way she was going to let anyone get close to hurting her again.

She finished her dinner and poured herself a glass of wine. She wished it was winter so she could start a fire in the fireplace. Then she remembered where she was. Winters would be warm and dry. Oh well, it was a lovely thought, anyway.

She sipped her wine and thought back to the happy years she and Sharon had shared. She had still thought them happy; had had no idea there was a problem. Until she came home one lunch hour to find Sharon in bed with someone Eleanor didn't even know. How had Sharon met her? Who was she to her?

Eleanor would never know the answers to any of those questions. She'd kicked Sharon out and wouldn't listen to any explanation. She sold the house, packed up her things, and moved to Florida shortly thereafter. And Florida had become home.

❖

Randi was in her garage lifting weights when her work cell rang. "Animal Control," she said.

"Yes. I need your help. I have a raccoon in my backyard and he's got my cat treed."

Randi smiled at the sound of fear in the older woman's voice. Surely the raccoon was as scared of the cat as the cat was of him, but she wasn't about to argue.

"Can you see the raccoon from where you are?"

"Yes."

"Good. Keep an eye on him. I'll be there in a few."

She got the woman's address, slipped her uniform shirt on, and headed out. She pulled into the driveway, and the elderly woman came out to greet her. Randi groaned inwardly. She'd asked the lady to keep an eye on the raccoon. Chances were it had taken off with her not watching it.

"He's still there," the lady said.

Randi followed her back to the backyard. There was no sign of the raccoon.

"He must have taken off," the woman said.

"Yes, he probably did." She tried to put things as softly as she could. "That's why I wanted you to keep an eye on him."

"I did. Right up until I heard you in the drive."

Her face dropped.

"Oh. I should have just stayed with him."

"It's okay. The only thing now is he might be back. If he comes back, call me again and I'll come out. But don't take your eye off him for a second, okay?"

"Okay."

They watched as the lady's frightened cat climbed down the tree and skittered past them.

"At least Fluffy's okay," the lady said.

"Yep. That's what's important. You have a good evening, you hear?"

Randi climbed back into her truck and drove home. She didn't mind being on call after hours. It was good money and things were usually quiet. As was the rest of that evening. She finished her workout, took a shower, and climbed into bed.

The next day was Saturday, and she didn't have to work. She turned her work cell off as soon as she woke up. She made herself some coffee and pondered what to do with her day. She decided to go fishing so she loaded up her tackle box and headed out. She made a quick stop at the mini-mart to pick up some beer and ice.

"Hey, Randi," the cashier, Veronica, said.

"Hey yourself. How you been?" They'd slept together on numerous occasions. Veronica was an excellent bedmate and never wanted anything more than sex from her. She always looked forward to their encounters.

"Good. What are you up to?"

"Goin' fishing."

"Great. What's biting?"

"I won't know till I get there."

"Fair enough," Veronica said. "Say, any chance of seeing you at Joni's tonight?"

Joni's was the women's bar. Suddenly, the prospects of the weekend were picking up.

"Sure, I'll be there."

"Buy me a drink?"

"You better believe it."

"Okay then," Veronica said. "Good luck and I'll see you tonight."

Randi parked her truck and hiked along the water's edge. She came to a spot where the water rippled nicely over a patch of rocks. She opened a beer, took a sip, and cast her line.

She enjoyed her quiet day in nature. She had no luck fishing. She didn't even get a bite, but she had a few beers and caught a few rays. Life was good. She packed up and drove home where she took a shower and dressed in cargo shorts and a green T-shirt to go out to Joni's. She seldom dressed up. It wasn't her style. She wore the occasional golf shirt, but that was only if she was looking to impress. And she figured that night Veronica was a shoo-in.

She had another beer from the six-pack she'd bought that morning and headed off to the bar. She got there a little after nine. The place was packed, but she easily spotted Veronica. Veronica always wore three-inch heels when she went out, so she stood above many of the other women there. Her bleach blond hair hung to her shoulders. As Randi cut through the crowd, she saw Veronica was wearing a micro skirt and a pink shirt with spaghetti straps. She looked like she was ready for action, and Randi had just the action she wanted.

"Hey, good lookin'," Randi said.

Veronica turned and looked at her. She greeted her with a big smile and kissed her cheek.

"Hey yourself," she said.

"You want a drink?" Randi said.

"Sure. I'll have a glass of Chardonnay."

"Coming right up."

"I'll walk to the bar with you."

Randi stood back to let her go first. She didn't know how she walked in those heels, much less looked so sexy doing it, but she was glad she did. She was easy on the eyes and made for lovin' up. Randi was already itching to get her out of there.

"Did you want to dance?" Randi said.

"Sure."

They cut through the crowd and found a spot on the floor. The other thing about Veronica was that she was a natural dancer. It was as if she became one with the music. She swayed and swerved, and Randi was mesmerized watching her. She was always disappointed when the music stopped.

She took Veronica's hand and led her back to the bar where they finished their drinks amid easy conversation.

"How was work today?" Randi said.

"Pretty busy. Made the day fly by. How was fishing?"

"Awesome."

"Did you catch anything?"

"I caught a few rays." Randi laughed. Veronica laughed as well.

"Very funny."

Randi ordered two more drinks and they sipped them. Well, Veronica sipped hers; Randi darn near chugged hers.

"You trying to get buzzed?" Veronica said.

"No. Just really thirsty for some reason."

"Okay. Because I need you awake and alert later on."

"Oh, don't you worry, honey. Nothing's going to slow me down."

She ordered another beer then led Veronica to the dance floor. They danced a few fast songs before a slow song started. Veronica moved into Randi's arms.

"You feel so good," Veronica said. "I love the feel of your arms around me."

"I love it better when we're skin to skin."

"Mm. Now you're talking."

"You ready to get out of here?" Randi said.

"Sure. Let's go."

The evening was warm and still as Randi escorted Veronica to her car.

"You remember where I live?" Veronica said.

"Of course. I'll see you there."

Randi fought the urge to kiss Veronica right then and there. She held back. She knew what pleasures lay ahead for her. She didn't need any public display of affection. She'd be fine waiting.

She drove to the apartment complex where Veronica lived. She knew the way perfectly as she'd been there so many times. She parked her truck in an open spot and crossed the lot to Veronica, who was waiting outside her door.

"I don't know if it's a good thing or not that you know where I live," Veronica said.

"Ah, you mean I've been here too many times? I don't think that's possible."

"I don't think it is either. Let's get inside."

She opened the door and Randi followed her inside. As soon as she closed the door behind her, Veronica was in her arms. She pressed against her, kissing Randi with a passion that met her own. Their mouths were open and their tongues played over each other. Randi ran her hands over Veronica's back, finally bringing them to rest on her firm ass. She pressed Veronica into her and ground her pelvis into Veronica's. She was sopping wet and ready to take her. She finally broke the kiss.

"Holy fuck, that was hot," Veronica said.

It took a moment for Randi to find her voice.

"Let's get to bed. I need you now."

Once in Veronica's bedroom, Randi kissed her again and attempted to strip her of her clothes. They broke the kiss so they could both finish undressing. Naked, they kissed anew, and Randi felt like she would burst into flame. She was burning with desire. She climbed onto the bed and invited Veronica to join her.

They rolled around on the bed, legs entwined and tongues dancing. Randi rolled on top of Veronica and kissed her hard. She kissed down her chest to suck on a pert nipple. She licked and tugged on it. Veronica had her hands in Randi's hair, holding her head in place. Randi continued to suckle her until Veronica cried out.

That's one, Randi thought. She released her grip on Veronica's nipple and kissed lower. She left little kisses all along her belly and finally came to rest between her legs. She dragged her fingers over the length of her.

"Don't tease me," Veronica said. "Please."

Randi laughed. It was an evil laugh.

"Please," Veronica said again.

Randi slid her fingers inside Veronica. She was wet and ready. And tight as hell. She felt so good, Randi almost forgot her need to taste Veronica. She bent down and ran her tongue over her while she moved her fingers in and out.

"Oh, my God, Randi. Holy shit. The things you make me feel. Oh, dear God. Don't stop. Please don't stop."

Randi had no intention of stopping. She focused her mouth on Veronica's clit. She sucked and licked it as she continued to move her fingers in and out, plunging them deeper with each thrust.

"Oh, shit," Veronica cried. "Holy mother of God."

Randi grinned to herself as she felt Veronica come over and over.

Veronica finally tapped Randi's shoulder.

"That's enough, hot stuff. I got nothing else in me."

Randi climbed up and kissed Veronica.

"You sure?" she said.

"Positive. Now it's your turn."

Veronica kissed Randi as she placed her hand between her legs. She wasted no time entering her. She clearly knew what Randi liked. She moved in and out of her until Randi's breathing became labored.

"Oh, God. Get me off," Randi said.

Veronica didn't need to be told twice. She brushed over Randi's clit with her thumb and that's all it took for Randi to catapult out of her senses.

"You ever going to let me have my fingers back?" Veronica laughed.

Randi opened her eyes and realized Veronica was still deep inside her.

"I'm sorry."

"Mm. Don't be. You feel really good in there."

"Yeah? You like it in there, huh?"

"Yeah, I do. But I think I'm going to need my hand. I'm going to try and pull out now, okay?"

"Yeah. Go for it."

She braced herself and Veronica was able to get her fingers out.

"You sure get tight," she said.

"Well, that's because you make me come so hard. So, it's not my fault."

Randi welcomed Veronica into her arms.

"Sex with you is always so much fun," Veronica said.

"Yeah, it is. But I should probably get going now."

"Oh, yeah."

Randi got dressed.

"Be careful driving home," Veronica said.

"I will. I'll see you next time, huh?"

"Count on it."

## CHAPTER THREE

Eleanor spent her Monday evening reading through papers. It would have been what she'd been doing if she were still in California, but she wasn't. She hated Sharon. No, she didn't. She'd catapulted her out of a dreadful routine and into a wonderful new life. Wonderful? Ha. Maybe not yet, but once she got her bearings about, she was sure she'd start having a blast.

Who was she kidding? She was a schoolteacher. They didn't have blasts. They worked their asses off all day to keep kids in line and spent their free time grading papers and the like. No wonder Sharon had looked elsewhere. Surely she'd gotten too boring for her. No. She refused to believe that. Eleanor was a fun loving person who was always up for something new. She wasn't a tired old worn out carcass of a woman. She was only thirty-three, after all.

She went to the kitchen to pour herself a glass of wine. She was out. That did nothing to improve her mood. She grabbed her purse and headed to the mini-mart down the street to pick up some wine.

Eleanor picked up two bottles of wine and headed toward the cashier. She stopped in her tracks when she saw the woman talking to the cashier. She was in a tan uniform of some sort. Her shorts showed off muscular legs, and her arms were tanned and toned. The way she leaned on the counter made it obvious she was flirting with the cashier. She struck Eleanor as some kind of rogue. She turned and looked at Eleanor, and Eleanor's breath caught at her green eyes and short, spiky blond hair. She was a very handsome woman.

Eleanor didn't appreciate the way she looked her up and down, as if assessing her.

The woman stepped away from the counter and let the next customer check out. She gave Eleanor one last look before leaving the store. Eleanor finally got to the cashier and paid for her wine. She was tempted to ask who that woman had been, but judging from the way they'd been talking she was probably the cashier's girlfriend.

She took the wine home and poured a glass. She got back to reading papers. She taught Accelerated English, so most of the papers were very well written. She was proud of her students. And grateful that the woman who had been teaching them before her had done such a good job.

Eleanor graded papers until her eyes began to cross. When she could grade no more, she climbed into bed, certain she would fall into a deep sleep. But sleep eluded her. Instead, she kept seeing bright green eyes and spiky blond hair. The vision danced in her mind until she fell into a restless sleep.

The rest of the week was uneventful for Eleanor. She worked during the day and graded papers at night. On Friday, she handed back the papers to the students and asked if anyone had any questions. Nobody did. They all seemed to accept their grades, which were mostly A's anyway.

She dismissed the class and had just grabbed her purse when Ron stuck his head in her classroom.

"Time for happy hour. You up for it?" he said.

"Sure," Eleanor said. "I even brought extra quarters for pool."

"Great. I'll see you there."

"I'm on my way."

She arrived to find the usual crew there. She bought a drink and sat next to Martina again.

"So," Ron said. "How was everybody's week?"

"You mean outside of the fire in my classroom?" Martina smiled.

"Oh, yeah. I heard about that," Eleanor said. "What happened?"

"Just kids being kids. I should have assigned groups instead of letting people choose their own groups. I've got one set of jocks that only want to goof off and see if they can blow things up."

"Bummer," Eleanor said. "How bad was the damage?"

"It was minimal. I have extinguishers all over the classroom. I had it out in minutes. But I did separate that group. They won't be working together again."

"Smart move."

The group moved to a pool table where they played several games. Eleanor even managed to win one. She was happy and having a good time. When people started gathering their things, Martina approached her.

"So, do you get out much, being so new here and all?"

"Nope. Happy hour is about the extent of it."

"Well, I'm starving and I know a great Thai place. Care to join me?"

Alarms started going off in Eleanor's head. Not as bad as when Ron had asked her out, but she wondered if Martina was a lesbian and if she had been giving off vibes. She told herself she was overreacting.

"Sure," she heard herself say. "That would be great."

She followed Martina to the Pink Orchid. It was a small, nicely decorated place in the middle of town. She and Martina were shown to a table in the back. It was quiet there. Eleanor was starting to feel uncomfortable again. She wished she wasn't so afraid. She'd been out, loud, and proud in California but wasn't ready for that here. For starters, she figured Florida would be much more conservative. And she wasn't ready to get involved with anyone again, and staying in the closet should insure that.

"What do you think of the place?" Martina said.

"I like it."

"The food's excellent, too. I hope you like spring rolls because I always get an order of them."

Eleanor laughed. Martina seemed easy to be with.

"Spring rolls would be great," she said.

Eleanor perused her menu. It all looked so good. And with the knots in her stomach slowly unwinding, she found herself very hungry.

"It all looks delicious," she said. "What do you recommend?"

"I've had it all. It's all good. You can't go wrong."

After they placed their orders, they sat back sipping their water.

"So, how are you acclimating so far?" Martina said.

"I think I'm doing okay. The kids are all performing very well. I haven't had any problems, nor have I seen any drop in their work, so I'm pretty happy."

"What about outside of school? There's lots to do around here. Have you checked the area out yet?"

"No. I confess I haven't. I've kept myself pretty busy with schoolwork. And setting up my house. I'll admit I still have boxes to unpack. But this weekend, I'm going to take a break and work on the outside of the place. The backyard is a jungle."

"Oh yeah? Well, that will keep you busy then. But don't forget to stop and smell the roses. Our little town has lots to offer, and I'd hate to see you miss out on the hotspots. Maybe I can be your tour guide some Saturday?"

Was she asking her out on a date? Eleanor's alarms went off again.

"Are you okay?" Martina said. "You look like you just saw a ghost."

"Oh, I'm fine."

"Was it something I said?"

"No. Not at all. And I'd love to take you up on that."

Dinner arrived and they ate with quiet, pleasant conversation. Eleanor was almost sad when it was over. She was no longer worried and felt like she'd made a new friend in Martina.

"Well, if you get tired of doing battle with your backyard tomorrow and want to go out for a drink or dinner or something, give me a call," Martina said as they left the restaurant.

Eleanor handed her her phone and Martina entered her number.

"Thanks," Eleanor said.

"No problem. It's always nice to have a friend in a new city, don't you think?"

"I do. And I really appreciate it."

"No problem. Don't work too hard tomorrow."

"I won't."

❖

It was Saturday afternoon, and Randi and her partner, Johnny, were sitting in their office at Animal Control. They had just gotten back from a drive around the city looking for strays that might be roaming the streets. It was a slow day, which was fine for Randi. She'd been out late the night before. She was hoping the rest of the day went easy for her. She was off on Sunday and planned on hitting Joni's that night for a little more fun and action.

They were in the middle of a game of chess when the phone rang. Johnny answered it.

"Animal Control. Yes. Yes, ma'am. Okay. Calm down and stay away from it. Okay. What's your address?" He wrote something down. "Okay, ma'am, we're on our way."

"What's up?" Randi said.

"Alligator in someone's backyard."

"What's the address?"

He told her.

"That's old man Winters's house. I thought it was vacant."

"No. The new middle school teacher lives there now."

"Oh great. We've got some school marm scared of an alligator. Let's hope she leaves it alone."

They arrived at the house, and a tall, thin woman in shorts that barely covered her ass and a tight T-shirt greeted them in the driveway.

"Oh, my God," she said. "I'm so glad you're here."

"Where's the gator?" Johnny asked.

"He's back here. Follow me."

Randi was happy to oblige. She didn't look like any schoolteacher she'd ever had.

"What's your name?" Randi said.

"Eleanor. Eleanor Bremer. The gator is right over there." She pointed.

Randi and Johnny walked slowly over to where the gator was lying in tall grass.

"You want the mouth or you want me to take it?" Johnny said.

"I'll take it. You just be ready."

"Okay. Be careful."

"Don't know any other way to be with a gator."

They approached the animal slowly then Johnny hung back and focused on Randi, who was circling it. The alligator followed Randi's every move, opening its huge jaws and clamping them shut. Randi circled it again. This time when the gator opened its mouth, she slid her hand under its lower jaw. She closed her thumb over the top of the gator's mouth, then grabbed it with both hands and squeezed like hell.

Johnny ran over and jumped on the gator and sat on it while Randi taped its large mouth shut. They secured its legs, picked it up, and carried it to the truck where they had a cage waiting. They wrestled it into the cage and locked it.

"Thank you both so much," Eleanor said from behind them.

Randi had forgotten about the beautiful Eleanor. She'd been so focused on the job at hand.

"No problem." Randi shrugged. "Just doing our job."

"I'd like to thank you somehow."

"You'll get our bill." Johnny laughed.

"No. I mean it. I'd like to do something nice for you."

"How about dinner tonight?" Randi saw a perfect opportunity. "I'm off at six and can meet you somewhere at seven."

"That sounds great," Eleanor only paused briefly. "I don't know my way around town, though. I'd have no idea where to go."

"There's a steak place out on the highway. You eat red meat?" Randi looked her up and down.

"Sure I do. I'll find it and I'll be there at seven."

"Sounds good. Now, we need to get this bad mamma jamma released. I'll see you tonight."

Randi and Johnny headed to the Everglades and carefully and cautiously released the alligator. When that was complete, they high-fived each other.

"Job well done," Johnny said.

"I'm just glad I didn't shit my pants," Randi said. "That's the biggest one I've ever wrestled."

"You were great. And the lady sure seemed impressed."

"And I got a steak dinner out of it." Randi winked at him.

"That you did. You are quite the smooth operator."

"Hey, she wanted to do something nice. I'll let her. Just giving the lady what she wants." She laughed.

The rest of the day was fairly uneventful. They picked up a couple of stray dogs roaming on the north end of town, but that was about it.

After her shift, Randi drove home, stripped out of her uniform, and took a quick shower. She drank a beer and got dressed. Tonight called for a golf shirt. She was out to impress Eleanor.

She arrived at the restaurant at exactly seven o'clock and found Eleanor waiting.

"I hope I'm not late," Randi said.

"No. I got here a little early since I didn't really know where I was going."

"Ah. Good idea. I suppose I could have offered to give you a ride."

"No. It's fine. I need to find my way around."

"How long have you lived here?" Randi said.

"A little over a month."

Randi took in the way Eleanor had dressed for dinner. Gone were the short-shorts. She was wearing a long blue skirt and a yellow blouse. The blouse brought out the blue in her eyes. Her long blond hair was loose now and fell to her shoulders. She was a sight for sore eyes.

"I remembered you while you were wrestling with that monster today," Eleanor said.

"Remembered me? Have we met?"

"No. I saw you at the mini-mart the other night talking to your girlfriend."

"Whoa. I don't have a girlfriend."

"Well, I saw you chatting up the cashier big time."

"Oh, yeah," Randi said. "Now I remember you. You were buying two bottles of wine. Must have been a rough night."

"I was grading papers."

"Enough said."

They laughed together.

They were shown to a booth in the back of the restaurant, which suited Randi just fine. She wanted to get to know Eleanor. She liked her. She wasn't sure what it was about her, but she was drawn to her. She got the vibe that Eleanor might be a lesbian, but she wasn't sure. She wanted to find out. And maybe even take her home that night.

They ordered dinner and sat back to chat.

"So, you're new in town," Randi said.

"Yep."

"Where'd you move from?"

"California."

"Wow. Major culture shock, huh?"

"Yeah," Eleanor said. "But I really like it here."

"What about the kids? Are they okay with you?"

"Yeah. No whoopee cushions or anything like that so far."

Randi laughed. Eleanor was funny. And she seemed smart, too. Two qualities she never really found out about the women she spent her time with. For her it was mostly caring about dancing and sex. That was about it.

Dinner came and they laughed and talked their way through it. The bill came and Eleanor reached for it, but Randi grabbed it first.

"What are you doing? I'm supposed to be paying you back for helping me out today."

"Nah. You heard Johnny. You'll get a bill. This will be my treat. As a way to welcome you to town."

"I don't know, Randi…"

Randi liked the sound of her name on Eleanor's lips. She hoped to hear it again soon.

"Nothing to know. My treat. Now, relax."

Eleanor seemed to relax a little, though she still seemed uptight. Randi didn't know why. All she knew was she'd had a great time and wanted to see Eleanor again.

"Well, thank you for dinner," Eleanor said.

"No worries. You know, if you ever want someone to show you around or anything, you can just call me."

She handed Eleanor her card. Eleanor smiled.

"Thank you," she said.

"Not a problem."

"Okay," Eleanor said. "I should get home. I've had a big day."

Randi hoped her disappointment didn't show on her face.

"Okay. I'll walk you to your car."

They stood at Eleanor's car for an uneasy minute. Randi wasn't sure what to do next. She wanted to kiss her. She wanted to very badly. But she didn't know enough about her yet. So she stood there, not willing to say good-bye because she didn't want the night to end. She was shocked when Eleanor wrapped her arms around her. Randi returned the favor and grew wet at how perfectly Eleanor fit in her arms.

"Thank you again," Eleanor said. "And I'll call you sometime."

"Okay."

She watched Eleanor drive away.

## Chapter Four

Eleanor drove home from dinner feeling lighter than she had in a long time. Randi had been so easy to be around. She was such a vibrant force. Eleanor would love to spend more time with her. But then she grew wary again. Did she want to spend time with her? What did Randi really want?

Randi was adamant that she didn't have a girlfriend. She almost sounded offended. Was that because she wasn't a lesbian or because she was a player? Either way, the farther she got from the restaurant, the more guarded she became. Sure, it was nice to have made two new friends in as many days. And Martina seemed like she'd be someone great to hang around with. But Randi? She wasn't so sure Randi would be good for her.

By the time she got home, she was chastising herself for ever going to dinner with Randi. Her type was always trouble. Good-looking, self-assured. She didn't need her in her life. She was glad she'd never have to see her again.

Sunday afternoon, Eleanor was cleaning house when her cell rang. It startled her since she didn't really know anyone there. She answered it.

"Hello?"

"Eleanor?"

"Yes. Who's this?"

"Oh. I'm sorry. We should have entered my number in your phone, too, so you'd know when I was calling. It's Martina. What are you doing?"

Eleanor breathed a sigh of relief. A friendly voice. How nice.

"I'm cleaning house," she said. "What are you doing?"

"I'm sitting here having a hankering for Italian food. Are you in the mood? I know a great place."

Eleanor paused. Italian sounded good. But she needed to get her house clean. Then she thought, why bother? No one was going to see it but her. She checked her watch. It was four thirty.

"Isn't it a little early for dinner?" she said.

"Sure. But I thought I'd give you time to get ready. And I like to get there early. You know, beat the crowds and all."

Eleanor hesitated again. How safe was Martina? Her reaction to Randi was still fresh on her mind. As a matter of fact, she'd thought of little else all day. But Martina seemed safe. She was her new friend.

"Okay. Give me a half hour to get showered and changed. Where should I meet you?"

"Why not give me your address and I'll swing by and pick you up."

"Sounds great."

Eleanor gave Martina her address and hung up the phone. She took a quick shower and perused her closet. What to wear? She hadn't asked what the attire should be. She opted for nice slacks and a blouse. That should be fine, she thought.

She put the vacuum, mop, and broom away just before the doorbell rang. She opened the door to find Martina dressed much the same as she was.

"Oh, good," Eleanor said. "I'm glad it's not a fancy restaurant. I wasn't sure what to wear."

"Nah. You look great."

I look great? What the hell is that supposed to mean? Eleanor thought. Clam down, she told herself. Martina was just being nice.

"Good. Shall we head out?"

"Let's do it."

Martina drove her to Tony's, a cute restaurant on the north end of town.

"You're going to love this place. Not only is the food excellent, but the wine selection is to die for. Oh, do you drink wine? I guess I should have asked."

"I love wine," Eleanor said. "Especially a good red one."

"Good answer. You're going to love it here."

They opened the door and the myriad smells had Eleanor's mouth watering.

"It smells delicious in here," she said.

"The smells' got nothing on the taste."

They were seated at a booth, and Eleanor's stomach growled loudly.

"I'm sorry. I just realized I haven't eaten all day."

"Oh, no. You should never do that. You should know better."

"I do. I just got busy cleaning and never stopped to think about it."

Still, before she looked at the food menu, she looked at the wine list.

"Choose anything you want," Martina said. "I'm buying tonight, and no bottle is too expensive."

"Really? I'd love a Rosso di Montepulciano."

"Sounds good to me."

They ordered a bottle and sat back to review the food menu.

"Oh, my God," Eleanor said. "Everything looks so good."

"You really can't go wrong. I'm telling you."

The waiter came and took their orders. They sat back sipping their wine.

"So, you mentioned you were going to do yard work yesterday," Martina said. "How'd that go?"

"Well, it was going great until I stumbled upon a giant alligator in my yard."

"Oh, no. I'm sorry. Though, I must admit, that's not unheard of."

"Apparently not. The animal control people were out there very quickly and made short order of catching him. And do you know? They don't kill them. They release them into the Everglades where they belong."

"That's fantastic. I'd hate to think of one of those beautiful creatures being put to death for being in the wrong place at the wrong time."

"Beautiful creatures?" Eleanor wasn't sure she'd heard correctly.

"Oh, yes. I love alligators. I collect them. Not live ones, of course. But statues of them and such. I love them."

Eleanor stared open-mouthed at Martina. The animal in her backyard had been terrifying. It was large and vicious. There was nothing beautiful about it.

"Well, there you go," she said when she finally composed herself. "Beauty is in the eye of the beholder."

Martina laughed.

"I suppose it is."

When dinner was over, they drove back to Eleanor's house. The familiar butterflies were in Eleanor's stomach. What should she do now? What did Martina expect?

"Would you like to come in for a drink?" Eleanor said.

"I'll have to take a rain check on that. It is a school night, after all."

"Oh, yeah. There is that."

"Thanks for coming to dinner with me," Martina said.

"Thank you. It was a lot of fun."

"Great. We'll do it again some time."

"I'd like that."

"Good night, Eleanor."

"Good night."

She climbed out of the car and let herself into her house. She closed the door and leaned her back against it. What was she thinking inviting Martina in? If she was straight, she'd probably just scared her away. If she was a lesbian, she'd probably just given her the wrong idea. Ugh. Why did life have to be so hard?

❖

Joni's was jumping the following Saturday night. It was Randi's weekend off and she was planning on celebrating. She took in the crowd as she made her way to the bar. Lots of familiar faces there, of course, but one or two new ones, as well. She'd always rather take her chance with a newbie. She ordered her beer, pulled up a barstool, and got comfortable.

As she scanned the dance floor, her gaze lighted on a tall, thin woman with shoulder length blond hair. Randi's thoughts went immediately to Eleanor. She focused on the woman, who eventually danced her way around until she was facing Randi. Randi felt the disappointment in her gut. No such luck.

She finished her beer and ordered another one. What the hell was she doing thinking about Eleanor at a time like this? Sure, she was hot. And, yeah, so okay, they'd had a good time at dinner. But she was on the prowl. No woman ever occupied her thoughts at times like these. She kept her mind and options open. She shook her head.

"You okay?" A woman had sidled up beside her to signal to the bartender.

"What? Oh, yeah, I'm fine."

"Okay. If you say so."

"I'm not a nut job or anything." Randi sounded more defensive than she meant to.

"Whoa. Easy, tiger. I was just checking."

Randi watched the woman walk off and checked her attitude. She needed to snap out of it and fast. She couldn't go biting women's heads off if she planned to get lucky. She ordered another beer and surveyed the room again.

The blonde she'd seen dancing was sitting in a group. Randi wondered if she was taken or not. She'd really like to dance with her, vertically and horizontally. She made her way to the table and was almost there when apparently, everyone's favorite song came on. They vacated the table and made their way to the dance floor.

Randi leaned against the table and waited for the song to end. It seemed to go on forever. But she really didn't mind. She enjoyed watching the way the music seemed to flow through the blonde. She was lithe and graceful and very easy on the eyes.

Just before the song ended, her gaze fell on Randi. Randi tried to look nonchalant, but almost burned up under the heat of it. She was interested. Randi felt it to her core. When the music died, the group returned to the table.

"Can we help you?" one of the group said.

"I was just hoping to ask your friend here to dance. That is, if she's not taken."

She never removed her focus from the blonde.

"Oh, I'm definitely not taken," the blonde said.

"Great. Then, shall we dance?"

"I need a drink first."

"Consider it done. What are you drinking?" Randi said.

"Piña coladas."

"Coming right up. Anyone else need anything?"

She took the orders and pushed her way through the throng to get to the bar. She juggled the drinks, but got them all back with minimal spillage. She walked around the table so she was next to the blonde.

"I'm Randi," she said.

"I'm Sally."

"Long, tall Sally, huh?"

"The very one."

Randi laughed and Sally joined her. It was soft and melodic. Oh, yeah, Randi thought. She had to have her.

They sipped their drinks and made casual conversation.

"So, what do you do, Sally?"

"I'm a city councilwoman."

Randi gulped.

"Oops. I suppose I should have known that."

Sally laughed.

"It's okay. As long as you voted for me, I don't care if you recognize me in public."

"That's quite a chance you take, coming to a women's bar, isn't it?"

"I'm out, loud, and proud. I refuse to hide my sexuality. I want to be a role model for others."

Randi let out a low whistle. Sally got better with every word that came out of her mouth.

"What was that whistle for?" Sally said.

"Nothing. Just color me impressed."

"Good. Now, come on. I love this song."

She grabbed Randi's hand and took her to the floor. They danced together until they both needed a break. They walked back to the table.

"You're quite a dancer," Randi said.

"Thanks. You're not so bad yourself. So often I've found butches seem awkward on the dance floor."

"Not me. I love to dance."

"It shows."

"How about another drink?"

"Let's cut to the chase. I want you and think you want me, judging from the way those green eyes burn holes into every inch of my body. So, why not just get out of here?"

"Are you sure?"

"Positive. Let's go. You can follow me to my place."

They left the club and stood in the parking lot.

"That's my BMW over there." Sally pointed.

"That's my truck parked a few cars down from it. Back out slowly and I'll follow you."

Sally led Randi to a gated community on the west side of town. Again, Randi let out a low whistle. She didn't realize council members made that kind of money. Or maybe Sally came from money. Either way, she was determined not to look as awestruck as she felt at the fancy digs.

She parked her truck next to Sally's car in the driveway and followed her to the door. Sally entered the code and the door unlocked. She pushed it open and let Randi enter first.

"Welcome to my abode."

"And what a nice abode it is," Randi said.

"Why thank you. It's home."

Randi looked around, unsure of what her next move should be. She wanted Sally and Sally wanted her. So, should she wait to see if

Sally offered her a drink? Or should she kiss her? For some reason, she felt unclear.

"The bedroom's this way," Sally finally said.

Randi followed her to a large bedroom with a desk, dresser, walk-in closet, and king-sized bed. She allowed her focus to remain on the bed. It was turned down, the satin purple sheets showing under the black comforter.

Sally moved into Randi's arms.

"I trust this meets with your satisfaction?" she said.

"Oh, yeah. I can't wait to get you on this bed."

Randi lowered her mouth to Sally's. The kiss was long and drawn out. Randi traced Sally's lips until Sally opened her mouth and allowed Randi in. Randi allowed her tongue to make lazy rounds inside Sally until she finally let it play with Sally's tongue. When their tongues met, she felt shock waves shoot down her body. Her knees went weak.

"Let's lie down," she said.

"Let's get out of these clothes first."

"Okay. You go first, though. I want to watch you undress."

Sally seemed happy to oblige. She slowly and deliberately stripped out of her outer garments until she was in her matching black lace bra and panties. She started to remove them.

"Wait," Randi said. "I'll get those for you."

She eased the bra straps off Sally's shoulders then deftly unhooked it. She held the perky breasts in her hands.

"They're beautiful," she said.

Sally blushed.

"Thank you."

"No. I mean it. They're really special."

Next Randi got on her knees and peeled Sally's panties off. She took her time as Sally's scent wafted to her and made her mouth water. She knew she'd be delicious and couldn't wait to taste her.

Naked, Sally stood before Randi and didn't seem the least self-conscious.

"I'm going to lie down now and watch you undress for me," she said.

Randi quickly disrobed and joined Sally in bed.

"Hey," Sally said. "You didn't give me time to fully enjoy you."

"Sorry. But I need you and I need you now. I can't stay away from your body a minute longer."

She rolled on top of her and kept most of her weight on her arms. She kissed her again, passionately, allowing all of her feelings to flow in that kiss. Sally kissed her back with equal fervor. Randi was getting wetter by the minute. She had to have Sally completely. She couldn't wait any longer. She kissed down her chest until she came to a pert nipple. She pulled it into her mouth and ran her tongue over it. Sally grasped hold of Randi's hair and cried out. Randi smiled to herself. She loved when a woman came during nipple play.

Randi kissed down Sally's smooth belly until she could position herself between her legs. She bent to taste her and knew she could stay there for hours. Sally was delicious. She ran her tongue all over her, and soon Sally was crying out again. She sucked on her lips and ran her tongue over them before taking her swollen clit between her lips. She'd barely gotten a grasp on it when Sally screamed yet another time.

"Okay, stud," Sally said. "Come on up here."

"I'm not through yet."

"I am. I've got no more in me. Now get up here so I can have my way with you."

Randi laughed as she lay next to Sally.

"Have at it," she said. She spread her legs wide.

Sally kissed Randi and Randi knew she was tasting her own orgasms on her lips.

"You taste wonderful, don't you?" Randi said.

"I do."

Sally continued to kiss her while she moved her hand down Randi's body and brought it to rest between her legs. Randi drew in a sharp intake of breath. She knew Sally would find her wet and ready and she moaned as Sally's fingers slipped inside her. Sally pulled her fingers out and plunged them back in. She repeated this until Randi could no longer hold her orgasm at bay. She cried out as her world went black, then exploded in an array of colors around her.

They lay together in silence for a minute before Sally spoke.

"I think you'd better get going."

"Are you sure?"

"I'm sure. We've had our fun. Maybe we'll see each other at the bar again and have a repeat performance, but for now, I think you should leave."

Randi dressed quietly, relieved not to have any awkward good-byes.

"Shall I see myself out?" she said.

"Please."

She kissed Sally and headed home.

## Chapter Five

It had been a hard week at school for Eleanor. The students were all growing restless with spring break only a week away. She was having a hard time keeping them focused and on track. Even their homework showed lack of trying. She'd had to give a couple of C's, which was a first for her at her new school.

So, when happy hour rolled around on Friday, she was more than happy to join the crew at the Bull. She did her usual when she arrived. She went to the bar for a rum and Coke, then walked over to the table. She was prepared to take her normal seat next to Martina, but stopped when she saw her place was taken. And not just taken. Taken by a stunning woman with short dark hair and piercing green eyes. The only available seat was across from the newcomer. She took it.

"Eleanor," Martina said. "This is Haven. She's been substituting in the math department this week. Haven, meet Eleanor."

"Nice to meet you," Eleanor managed.

"Nice meeting you, too."

Haven smiled at her, a knowing smile that sent chills to Eleanor's core. She got the vibe from Haven as soon as she'd laid eyes on her, but always hoped others' gaydars didn't work as well as hers.

Eleanor actually tried to engage Ron in conversation. Anything to avoid the deep, probing gaze of Haven. But it was no use. Haven seemed intent on getting to know her.

"What department are you in, Eleanor?" Haven's deep, rich voice washed over her.

"I teach Accelerated English."

"Impressive. Have you taught here long?"

"No. Only a couple of months."

"Really? Did you transfer from another school?"

Eleanor was struggling to maintain her composure. She wanted to melt under the extreme focus Haven was putting on her.

"Actually, I moved here from California."

"Whereabouts in California? I lived there for a while in my younger, wilder days."

"I'm from the San Francisco Bay Area. Where did you live?"

"Ever hear of Chico?"

Eleanor had to laugh. So Haven had attended a party school. She imagined Haven broke a lot of hearts in her younger, wilder days.

"Yes," Eleanor said. "I've heard of it. I had a lot of friends who went to school there. I've visited it on many occasions."

"Ah. So you know what a great place it is."

"Indeed I do. How long have you been in Florida?"

"Almost fifteen years now. And I love it. How are you liking it so far?"

"So far, so good."

Eleanor realized everyone else was around the pool table, and she and Haven were the only ones still seated at the table.

"Do you play pool?" Eleanor said.

"I used to be in a league. So, it's not really fair to play recreationally."

"Sure it is. It's all in fun. It's not like we play for money."

"I tell you what," Haven said. "I'll play you in a game. Loser buys the other dinner."

Eleanor knew Haven was dangerous. She could feel it to her bones. But she was hungry and one dinner wouldn't hurt anything. She knew she'd end up buying, but agreed to the game anyway.

"Sure," she said. "Why not?"

"There's the spirit."

Their group was crowded around one table leaving the other one empty.

"I'll even let you break," Haven said.

She racked the balls and handed Eleanor a stick.

"Knock yourself out," she said.

Eleanor felt butterflies in the pit of her stomach and she couldn't tell if they were nerves about the game, nerves about dinner, or just nerves from being around Haven. Either way, she had to force herself to hold her hands steady as she broke the balls. She got lucky and knocked three solids in. She tried to act like she'd meant to do it.

"Nice break," Haven said.

"Thanks." She felt all warm inside from the way Haven was looking at her. She tried to tell herself to remain aloof, but she knew that ship had sailed. She just needed to keep her head for the rest of the evening and she'd get out of it unscathed.

Eleanor made a couple more shots before handing the table over to Haven, who ran it. She sank the eight ball with ease and smiled a sexy smile Eleanor's way.

"I tell you what, since you have to buy, I'll at least be decent and let you pick the restaurant."

Eleanor laughed. Handsome and chivalrous. Yes, Haven was dangerous indeed.

"Unfortunately," Eleanor said. "I still don't know my way around town. I do know a great steak house out on the highway if you're into that."

"That sounds great. I'm starving."

Eleanor turned to say her good-byes and almost knocked Martina over.

"I was just coming to say good-bye," Martina said. "I have a seminar tomorrow, so I've got to get up early."

"Okay," Eleanor said, then got a great idea. "We were just going to grab a bite to eat. Would you like to join us?"

"I'd love to, but I can't. Thanks. Some other time."

Eleanor's body betrayed her as she felt relief that Martina wouldn't go. What was going on with her?

Haven agreed to meet Eleanor at the steak house, and Eleanor climbed into her car feeling scared and excited at the same time.

She was drawn to Haven. There was no denying that. But was Haven feeling the same? She seemed to be, the way her gaze burned Eleanor to her core. But what would Haven want from her? What did she want from Haven? She decided to relax and just see how the evening played out.

They pulled into the restaurant at the same time. Eleanor got out of her car and crossed the parking lot to meet Haven. She liked being close to her even as she felt the heat radiating off her. They walked in together and were taken to a table.

Dinner passed with easy conversation. Haven continued to be as easy to talk to as she'd been at the bar. They talked and laughed, and Eleanor was sad to see the evening coming to a close.

"I really like you," Haven said after the waiter had taken their plates.

"Thank you?"

Hayden laughed. Again, it warmed Eleanor all over.

"And I think you like me, too?"

Eleanor blushed. She knew there was no way to hide it. She felt it start at her neck and creep up. She took a sip of water.

"I do."

"So, look, I'm not looking for a relationship or anything."

"That's a relief."

"But I would like you to come home with me tonight."

Eleanor swallowed hard. Wasn't this what she wanted? Or was it? She wasn't looking for a relationship either. That was for sure. But was she the one-night stand type? How long had it been since she'd found comfort and pleasure with another woman? Too long, she decided.

"I think that sounds great," she said.

Haven exhaled loudly.

"Excellent. I was worried I'd blown it there for a second."

They sat in awkward silence.

"So," Haven finally said. "You ready to go? You can follow me to my place."

"Sounds good."

They got to the parking lot and Haven took Eleanor's hand.

"Are you nervous?"

"Very," Eleanor answered honestly. "It's been a long time."

"I hope to make it worth the wait."

"I'm sure you will."

Eleanor had butterflies in her stomach as she followed Haven home. She was so consumed with her own nerves, it took her a moment to realize she was in her own neighborhood. She followed Haven past her own house and around the corner to another nondescript ranch house. Haven pulled in to the driveway and Eleanor parked on the street.

When they got inside, Haven pulled Eleanor into a tight hug.

"Would you like another glass of wine?" she asked when she finally pulled away.

"That would be great."

"Have a seat there on the couch," Haven said. "I'll be right with you."

Eleanor sat on the couch and tried to relax. She felt like a virgin on her wedding night. She only hoped she wouldn't disappoint Haven. Surely everything would come back to her once things got started, right?

Haven returned with two glasses of wine. She handed one to Eleanor then sat close to her on the couch.

"What can I do to help you relax?" Haven said.

"Nothing. Really. You're wonderful. I just need to get out of my own head."

"Well, just sip your wine. We're in no hurry. We've got all night."

Eleanor told herself to just let it go. It would be fine. Her body definitely responded to Haven. She was a grown woman. There was no reason not to act on the response.

"Do you feel like you're cheating on someone?" Haven said.

"Oh, no. Nothing like that. It's just that it's been so long."

Eleanor looked at Haven and saw softness in her eyes along with longing. She knew Haven would know what she was doing. She just had to follow her lead.

They finished their wine.

"Would you like another glass?" Haven said.

"No, thanks. I don't think you want me passing out." She laughed nervously.

"No," Haven said softly. "Definitely not."

She took Eleanor's empty glass and set it next to hers on the coffee table. She slid her arm around Eleanor and pulled her close. Eleanor felt her skin come alive. She was covered in gooseflesh. It felt so good to be so close to Haven.

When Haven moved her mouth to Eleanor's, Eleanor's breath caught. She was going to kiss her. This was really going to happen. And suddenly, it was all she wanted. All she needed was Haven in every way, shape, and form.

Haven's kiss was soft at first, just enough to make Eleanor's nipples pucker. Then, she kissed her with greater fervor. Eleanor opened her mouth and felt Haven's tongue slip in. Their tongues did the dance of passion. Eleanor finally broke the kiss, breathless and dizzy with need.

"Are you okay?" Haven said.

"Oh, God, yes."

"Yeah?" Haven grinned.

"Yeah."

Haven stood and offered her hand to Eleanor. Eleanor allowed herself to be helped to her feet. She barely trusted her legs. They were shaking like leaves. Haven pulled her close and walked her down the hall to her bedroom. The room was sparsely decorated, which Eleanor didn't care about. It had a bed and that was all they needed.

Haven kissed her again. As the kiss deepened, she deftly unbuttoned Eleanor's blouse. She guided it off her shoulders and tossed it to the floor.

"Are you cold?" she said.

"Quite the opposite," Eleanor said. She felt like she could implode from the heat in her belly.

When she felt Haven's fingers at the button on her slacks, she shuddered. She wished she would hurry. She wanted to be naked with her. She wanted to touch her and be touched by her. She wanted Haven to make her feel things she hadn't felt in so very long.

Haven finally had Eleanor down to her underwear. Eleanor quickly shed them while Haven undressed. Eleanor took in Haven's fine form. She was tall and lean, but soft and supple. Her breasts would fit perfectly in her hands and Eleanor couldn't wait to play with them.

"Come on. Let's lie down," Haven said.

She offered her hand, which Eleanor took gratefully. She climbed onto the bed after Haven and moved into her arms. Haven ran her hand over Eleanor's body.

"You're so soft," she said. "I love your body."

"I like yours, too."

Haven kissed her hard, passionately. Eleanor worried that her lips might bruise. But she didn't care. She kissed Haven back, letting all the passion she was feeling come through in the kiss.

"Damn, woman," Haven said. "You just made my toes curl."

"I hope to be able to do a lot more than that."

"I'm sure you will. All in due time."

They kissed some more, and soon all Eleanor's hesitance was gone. She was ready for Haven. She'd do whatever she needed to do to please Haven the way she was sure Haven would please her.

"What do you like?" Haven asked.

"What do you mean?"

Haven laughed.

"You know. What would you like me to do to you?"

"I don't know." Eleanor felt her whole body blush. "I'm sure whatever you do will be wonderful."

"I hope so. But I want to know what really works for you."

Eleanor was too embarrassed to speak.

"I'm sorry," Haven said. "I don't mean to embarrass you. I just want to take care of you the best way possible."

She kissed Eleanor again and moved her hand all over her body, eliciting soft moans of pleasure from Eleanor. She brought it up and closed it over one of Eleanor's breasts. Her breast was too big for her hand, but she kneaded what she could then ran her thumb over her nipple.

"Do you like to have your breasts played with?"

"Yes," Eleanor managed. "Very much."

"Good. Because I love to play with breasts and yours are just perfect."

She lowered her head and ran her tongue over and around Eleanor's nipple before taking it in her mouth. She sucked hard and Eleanor mewled. She moved her hand lower and Eleanor spread her legs. She felt her clit swelling as she anticipated Haven's touch. When Haven's fingers brushed over it, she gasped.

"You're so big," Haven said. "You're so ready for me."

"I am. Take me, Haven."

"Oh, I will. Don't you worry about that."

Haven slipped her fingers inside Eleanor. She moved them in and out.

"More," Eleanor said. "I need more."

"Are you sure?"

"Yes. Please."

Haven complied and Eleanor felt full, just like she liked it. She moved on the bed, up and down, meeting each of Haven's thrusts. She felt amazing and knew she was close. Haven twisted and turned her hand deep inside Eleanor, and Eleanor could feel the pressure building inside her. She held her breath as the pressure built and let it out in a guttural moan as she reached a powerful climax.

"Oh, my God," she said when she could finally speak. "That was amazing."

"Mm. I'm glad you enjoyed it."

Eleanor fought to not show her disappointment when Haven finally withdrew her fingers. Until she felt them on her clit. Haven played her perfectly, and soon Eleanor was crying out again as another earth-shattering orgasm racked her body.

"Oh, my God, what you do to me," Eleanor said.

"I'm glad you enjoyed it."

Haven moved up and kissed Eleanor, whose nerves were back in full force. Gone was the bliss of the pleasure Haven had provided. It was her turn to please Haven, and she only hoped she would be able to return the favor.

She played with Haven's breasts, alternately kneading them and teasing her nipples.

"That feels great," Haven said.

Encouraged, Eleanor slid her hand farther down Haven's body until it came to rest between her legs.

"You're so wet," Eleanor said.

"That's all you."

"Yeah?"

"Yeah. You make me crazy."

"Good. That makes me feel good," Eleanor said.

She ran her hand over Haven's slick clit and listened to Haven's sharp intake of breath. She rubbed it hard and fast, and soon Haven cried out.

"You haven't lost your touch, if that's what you were worried about," Haven said.

"I'm glad you enjoyed it. You don't mind if I keep going, do you?"

"That's entirely up to you."

"I want to be inside you."

"I'd like that very much."

Eleanor moved her hand lower and teased Haven's opening.

"You like teasing me?" Haven said.

"I do." Eleanor laughed.

She slid her fingers inside Haven and felt her tightness draw her in. She ran her fingers over Haven's satin walls before plunging in as deep as she could get.

"You feel amazing," Haven said.

"I'm glad you like it. You feel wonderful in there."

Eleanor continued moving in and out until Haven grabbed her wrist and held her in place as she called out her name. Eleanor felt Haven close tightly around her. She smiled to herself, pleased that she had been able to have that effect on Haven.

"You ready for me to come out?" Eleanor said.

"If you have to."

"I can stay in for a little while longer."

"No. You can come out. I want to hold you."

Eleanor curled into Haven's arms and fell into a deep sleep.

## Chapter Six

Monday evening, Randi checked her refrigerator and found she was out of beer. She headed to the mini-mart to pick up a twelve-pack. Veronica was working and she looked good. Randi stopped to say hello on her way in.

"How you doin'?" she said.

"Hey good lookin'. I'm doing great. How about you?"

"I'm about to die of thirst. I need some brewskis."

"You've come to the right place," Veronica said.

"Don't I know it."

Randi made her way back to the cooler. She couldn't help but notice the blonde standing back there in slacks, a blouse, and practical shoes. Randi always noticed shoes. High heels turned her on no end. She moved so she could see the woman's face.

"Eleanor?" she said.

Eleanor turned and looked at her with surprise on her face.

"Hi, Randi."

"Hi. How are you?"

"I'm okay. But I'm hungry and nothing in this frozen food aisle is calling to me."

"How about I take you to dinner?" Randi heard herself say.

"What?"

"Well, you're hungry and I'm hungry. Why not go get some grub?"

"I don't know…" Eleanor said.

"Look, it's not like it'll be a date or anything. Just two people going to dinner."

"Okay. But we'll go Dutch."

"Fair enough," Randi said. "Dutch it shall be."

"I still don't know my way around," Eleanor said. "Can we just meet at that steak house again?"

"Sure. I just need to pick up some beer and I'll meet you there."

"Sounds good."

Randi watched her walk out of the store. There was something sexy about her, even in her schoolteacher clothes. Sure, the short-shorts the day she met her were hot, but even fully dressed, she couldn't contain her sexuality. It exuded from her. She wondered if she even had a clue.

She walked up to Veronica and paid for her beer.

"Why so quiet now, stud?" Veronica said.

"Oh, sorry. No reason." She wasn't in the mood to flirt with Veronica. Her thoughts were on Eleanor and Eleanor alone at the moment.

"Whatever."

Veronica rang her up and took her money.

"You going to Joni's next weekend?" she said.

"I'm planning on it. Will I see you there?"

"I'm planning on it, as well."

"Great. See ya then."

She took her beer and hurried to her truck. She didn't want Eleanor to wait too long. She mainly didn't want her to give up on her and leave. She was sorry to be so short with Veronica, but there was something about Eleanor. She was untouchable in some way. Which only served to make Randi want her more. She'd love to bed her, but she didn't seem the type for a one-night stand and Randi wasn't the type for anything else.

She got to the restaurant and found Eleanor had already gotten a table.

"Sorry it took me so long."

"No worries. It wasn't that long."

"Oh, good. Thanks for getting a table."

"They had one available, so I jumped all over it."

Randi imagined Eleanor spread out all over the table, naked, with Randi doing all kinds of fun things to her. She shook her head to clear her mind.

"You okay?"

"Yeah. Fine."

Randi sat across from Eleanor and almost lost herself in Eleanor's beautiful blue eyes.

"You've got really pretty eyes, you know?" she said.

"Are you hitting on me?"

"No. Just complimenting you."

"Well, then, thank you," Eleanor said. "Yours are such a deep green. They're quite unique."

"Thank you. I think."

"It was meant as a compliment, too." Eleanor laughed.

"Okay then." Randi laughed as well. She liked Eleanor's laugh. It wasn't high-pitched and annoying. Some women's laughter sounded forced. Eleanor's was easy.

After they'd ordered, Randi sat back against the booth.

"So, tell me, Eleanor. What's a middle school teacher do for fun?"

Eleanor smiled at her. It made her wet.

"As if there's any time for any fun. Being a middle school teacher takes a lot of time. More than you'd think."

"Well, I know you have to have some time off since you tear up your backyard looking for alligators sometimes."

Eleanor laughed again.

"Guilty as charged."

Randi smiled at her. Eleanor was so easy to be around.

"But seriously. You don't do anything in your spare time? No book clubs? Sewing circles? Nothing?"

Eleanor laughed heartily then.

"Is that how you see me? As an old-fashioned school marm?"

"I don't know. You tell me. Okay, so do you go clubbing?"

"Okay. No. I'm not the clubbing type."

"I didn't think so," Randi said. "Too bad. I go to a club on my weekends off. It's a lot of fun."

"I'm sure it is. But that's not really my scene."

"So, you never do anything fun?"

"Well, every Friday afternoon, I go to happy hour at the Bull."

"The Bull? Somehow I'm having a hard time seeing you there. It's kind of a dive," Randi said.

Eleanor laughed again.

"Several teachers from school meet there every Friday afternoon. Granted, it's not high class, but it's comfortable and we have fun."

"Do you ever shoot pool there?"

"Of course."

Randi raised an eyebrow.

"You're surprising me right and left tonight," she said.

"Am I now?"

Randi was glad. Eleanor seemed to be relaxing. She had seemed so uptight at the mini-mart. She was definitely letting her guard down a little bit.

Dinner was over and the table had been cleared. Randi wasn't ready to say good night. It was only eight o'clock. The night was still young.

"This has been fun," she said.

"It really has."

"I say we keep the fun going."

Eleanor visibly tensed. Whoa, Randi thought.

"I don't know," Eleanor said.

"Aw, come on. I just want to go play some pool at the Bull."

She watched as several emotions played across Eleanor's face. Finally, she smiled.

"That sounds fun," she said.

"Great. I'll meet you there?"

"Okay. Let's go. I must warn you, I'm not very good."

"That's okay. I won't play you for money."

"Gee, thanks."

They pulled into the parking lot at the Bull at the same time. Randi held the door open and followed Eleanor in. The place was empty, which suited Randi just fine. She didn't want to have to share a pool table with anyone but Eleanor.

Randi racked the balls and let Eleanor break. Eleanor broke and only knocked the cue ball in.

"I told you I'm not very good."

"Nonsense," Randi said. "It could happen to the best of us."

Randi took her shot and knocked in a solid, then missed.

"Can I get you a drink?" she said.

"Sure. I'd love a rum and Coke."

"Coming right up. Go ahead and shoot. I trust you."

Randi came back to find Eleanor had knocked in all the stripes and was ready to shoot the eight ball.

"Wow. I feel like I've been sharked."

Eleanor laughed.

"No. I just got lucky. Now to sink the eight ball."

Eleanor shot and knocked it in. She whooped with excitement and even hugged Randi. Randi loved the feel of her body against her and held her close for a moment too long. Eleanor seemed to come to her senses and disentangled herself from Randi.

"Sorry about that," she said.

"Nothing to be sorry for."

"I was just so excited. I don't win very often."

"Well," Randi said. "You deserved that one. Here, I'll rack 'em again."

They played several more games, and finally Eleanor looked at her watch.

"I need to get going," she said.

"Are you sure?"

"Yeah. It's a school night, after all."

"Oh, yeah. And middle schoolers are much harder to deal with than the occasional stray we encounter. Well, thanks for tonight. It's been fun."

"It really has."

"I'd like to see you again sometime, if that's okay."

Against her better judgment, Eleanor took Randi's phone and entered her number in it. She wasn't sure what she was doing. She reflected later that it might have been the alcohol, but she knew better. Randi was fun. Dangerous, but fun. She would love to hang out with her again.

She handed her phone to Randi.

"You'd better enter your number in mine, so I'll know if it's you when you call," she said.

"Good idea."

Phone numbers exchanged, they walked out into the warm night air.

"You okay to drive?" Randi said.

"Oh, yeah. I didn't have that much to drink."

"Okay. Just checkin'."

Eleanor drove home with a smile on her face. Another lonely night at home had been replaced by dinner and pool with a charming woman. She was bothered how much her body responded to Randi, as she was certain she was not her type. And when she'd hugged her? Electrical currents had flown throughout her body. She'd had to pull away quickly lest she explode.

What happened to her lying low and keeping to herself? So far, in the last week or so, she'd had dinner with Martina, slept with Haven, and gone out with Randi. She was becoming a social butterfly. And it felt good. It scared her, to be sure, but deep down, she liked being around people.

Back home in California, she and Sharon had settled into their routine of going to work and coming home and being together. They hardly socialized. Their work schedules essentially prohibited them from doing that. Oh, once in a while, they'd get together with friends, but for the most part it was just the two of them. Which had suited Eleanor just fine. But now she found she liked going out with people. It was good for her.

She got home to her empty house, but even that didn't bother her. She wasn't looking for a partner. That much she was sure about. She thought about Randi with her cropped blond hair and deep green eyes. Eleanor wanted her. There was no doubt. But she'd just slept with Haven. Was she really looking for another one-night stand? She could get a reputation. What would that do to her job?

No. She needed to cool her jets. She could hang out with Randi, but she couldn't go falling into bed with her. Besides, who said that's what Randi wanted? But she knew better. She could tell. Randi was the type to bed anything in a skirt. Eleanor had better keep her cool.

She climbed into bed and tried to sleep, but she kept replaying the fun she'd had that evening. Who knew a trip to the mini-mart could be such fun? She finally fell asleep smiling.

Eleanor woke late the next morning. She had slept through her alarm. She had to hurry through her shower and didn't have time for coffee. It was going to be a long day. She got to her classroom with fifteen minutes to spare before her students got there. She needed to be more careful when she went out on school nights.

The first four periods were frustrating, as had become the norm. With spring break the next week, keeping kids on task was practically impossible. Finally, fourth period was over and she went to the teacher's lounge for lunch.

Unconsciously, she searched the room for Haven and felt a twinge of disappointment that she wasn't there. Sure, she was a substitute, but Eleanor would have liked to see her again. She was about to sit by herself and feel sorry for herself when Martina called to her from across the room.

Eleanor joined her.

"How are your kids?" she asked.

Martina rolled her eyes.

"Don't even ask. Yours?"

"I feel like I'm working in a flippin' day care. Not an Accelerated English class."

"Well, look at it this way. We have all next week off."

"I'm half tempted to give them all papers to do over the break," Eleanor said.

Martina laughed.

"That would be cruel and unusual punishment. Especially to you. You'd have to grade them all after."

"Too true."

"So," Martina said. "Do you have any plans for the break? Are you going back to California?"

Eleanor turned cold inside. She'd never go back to California. There was nothing for her there. But she couldn't tell Martina that. She quickly regained her composure.

"No. I plan to simply decompress. You?"

"Nothing special. A group of us are renting a houseboat for a couple of days on the lake. You're welcome to join us."

Eleanor fought the urge to ask if Haven would be one of those people.

"Maybe. I don't know. I think I'll probably just hang out at home. Thanks, though."

"No problem. I'll call you before we go, though, just in case you've changed your mind."

Lunch was over and Eleanor dragged herself back to her classroom. She was exhausted already and had two more periods to get through. She managed without having a complete meltdown and excused her final class then breathed an air of thanks that she'd made it through the day.

As she left the school, she performed a mental inventory on what she had at home to make for dinner. Nothing. She contemplated going by the mini-mart to pick something up. And maybe see Randi in the process, but knew that was irresponsible. She had to go to the grocery store and do some major shopping.

When she was finally home, she put away her groceries and slipped out of her work clothes. What she needed was a hot soak in her tub. That would ease away the troubles of the day.

The warm water and soothing scent of lavender was working perfectly to relax her. Her mind drifted first to Haven and then to Randi. What had gotten into her all of a sudden? She felt like a player and knew that wasn't in her nature. She allowed her focus to stay on Randi. She closed her eyes and could picture her perfectly in her mind's eye. She was a very handsome woman and probably knew it. She remembered how strong her arms were when she'd hugged her after winning at pool. She was quite a woman.

As she thought of Randi, she moved her hands to her breasts and played with her nipples. She knew what she was doing, but couldn't stop herself. She felt herself growing wet and breathless. She slid her hand between her legs and felt how slick she was. She imagined Randi's hands on her as she moved her fingers inside herself. She brought them back out to tease her clit. In no time, she clenched her eyes shut and came, thoughts of Randi swimming in her mind.

## Chapter Seven

Friday afternoon, Eleanor dismissed her students with a sigh of relief. She had survived. It was spring break. No kids for nine days. She collapsed into her chair. She felt she could fall asleep right there. It had been a hard week. But she gathered up her things and was heading out the door when Ron stopped by.

"The Bull?" he said.

"I'm on my way."

"Great. See you there."

Eleanor drove to the bar, excited to see her coworkers and let off steam. She walked in to find them all at a table, with a rum and Coke already sitting there for her.

"I figured you'd need this," Martina said.

"Thanks. You're so right."

Eleanor sat down and fought the urge to pound the drink. She sipped it. It tasted good.

Martina raised her glass.

"To surviving the last week before spring break," she said.

"Hear, hear," the others said.

They all clinked their glasses, and Eleanor sat back and relaxed. It felt good to have camaraderie. She truly appreciated these teachers and believed they appreciated her, too. They sat at the table longer than usual, but finally, one by one, they got up to shoot pool.

"Are you joining us at the pool table?" Martina said.

"Sure."

She walked over and put her quarters on the table and ended up challenging Ron. Ron was usually far superior to her, but she got lucky on the break and knocked in four balls. Ron knocked in two balls before missing and Eleanor ran the table after that.

There were congratulations all around. She felt happy, in her element. She didn't want happy hour to end. But people slowly bid good night and left to start their vacations.

"How about dinner?" Martina said. "We deserve a nice dinner out, don't you think?"

Eleanor barely heard her. She'd caught movement out of the corner of her eye and turned to see Randi walking in. She waited a moment to see if anyone was with her. Nobody was.

"Eleanor?" Martina said. "Are you with me?"

"Oh, I'm sorry. I just saw a friend walk in. I think I'll go over and visit with her. Thanks for the offer, though."

Martina arched an eyebrow.

"I'm glad you're making friends," she said.

"Slowly but surely."

"Okay, then," Martina said. "I'll call you over the break. Enjoy your time off."

"You, too."

Eleanor watched Martina walk off and then crossed the bar to where Randi stood. As she walked, she wondered if Randi had come there looking for her. She had told her she was there every Friday. Had Randi paid that much attention?

She sidled up next to Randi at the bar.

"Hey, stranger."

Randi looked at her and smiled. It was a crooked smile that could mean anything from hello to I want you.

"Good to see you. Fancy running into you here."

Eleanor didn't know what to say. She knew she'd told Randi she was there every Friday afternoon.

"And what are you doing here?" she said. "Shouldn't you be working?"

"It's six o'clock," Randi said. "How much have you had to drink?"

"Not that much." Eleanor laughed. "I guess time does fly when you're having fun."

"Can I buy you a drink?"

"Sure."

"Rum and Coke?"

"Please."

Randi ordered and Eleanor stood there, not certain of where to look or what to do. She was beginning to second-guess her decision to stay. She knew what effect Randi had on her. She wondered if it was wise to see her again.

"Here you go." Randi handed her her drink.

"Thank you."

"You okay? You seem nervous."

"I'm fine," Eleanor lied.

"Good. How about some pool?"

Eleanor wasn't sure she'd be able to focus on pool, but she bravely nodded and followed Randi to the table.

"So, what's new in the world of teaching?" Randi said.

"It's spring break. Finally. I get a whole week off."

"Right on. That's most excellent. What are you going to do with yourself?"

"I have no idea." Eleanor laughed. "But I'm still looking forward to it."

"How's the backyard coming along?"

"It's not. Not to sound like a damsel in distress, but seeing that alligator put an end to my yard work. I suppose I should get back to it, but I'll admit, I'm scared."

"How about I come over tomorrow and help out? I'm off and I'm not scared of hard work."

Had Eleanor heard right? More time with Randi. What was Randi trying to do, ingratiate herself to her? Maybe Randi really did like her. Doubtful. Still, she could really use the help in the yard.

"That would be great," she said.

"Just say when and I'll be there."

"Let's say ten o'clock?"

"Let's say we decide on the time based on when we get out of here." Randi laughed.

Eleanor laughed with her.

"That sounds fair."

They shot pool and drank and talked until Eleanor decided she'd had enough. She was hungry and needed to get food.

"I need to go home and feed myself," she said. "I'm starving and these drinks aren't filling me up."

"Let's go get some Italian," Randi said. "Have you been to Tony's yet?"

"Oh, my God. I have. It's delicious."

"Let's go, then."

"Sounds great. I'll meet you there."

Randi smiled to herself as she drove to Tony's. She'd taken a chance by showering before heading to the Bull, but was glad she had. She had spotted Eleanor as soon as she walked in, but didn't let on. She'd let Eleanor come to her. There was something about Eleanor that called to her. She couldn't stop thinking about her. She was hoping after the drinks at the bar and a good meal, she'd be able to take her to bed. That should stop her from being on her mind night and day. It would get her out of her system, she was sure.

Not that she wanted Eleanor drunk to be with her. That was not the case. She wanted all her senses keen so that she could enjoy Randi to the fullest. Because Randi planned on pleasing her like she'd never been pleased before.

They got a quiet table near the rear of the restaurant.

"Doesn't this place smell amazing?" Eleanor said. "I love it here."

Randi fought a pang of jealousy that she'd been there before with someone else.

"When have you been here before?" she said.

"One of the teachers brought me here. She's been so nice welcoming me. She's taken me to a few places for dinner."

Randi wondered if there was something between the two women.

"Is she an English teacher like yourself?" she said.

"No. She teaches science."

"Oh, wow. Major braniac, huh?"

Eleanor laughed. She had such an easy laugh. It made Randi's boxers wet.

"I suppose so. I don't know her from her classroom, though. I only know her through happy hours and dinners. I do know she's pretty darned good at pool, though."

"Yeah? I wonder if there's any correlation."

"I have no idea."

They ordered their dinner.

"So," Randi said. "What exactly do we need to do in your yard tomorrow? I want to mentally prepare myself."

"Really, I just want to pull up dead shrubs and the like. The yard looks like an overgrown wasteland and I want to replant it with local plants to make it lush."

"Sounds easy enough. So, I'll bring gloves and a shovel. Anything else?"

"Nope. That should do it."

Dinner passed with pleasant conversation. Eleanor was so easy to talk to. And Randi loved the way her eyes lit up when she smiled or laughed. Hell, if she was honest, she liked everything about Eleanor. This was strange, forbidden territory for her. So, why didn't she just cut and run? She wished she knew the answer.

After dinner, Randi walked Eleanor to her car. She wanted to invite her home in the worst way, but the words just didn't come out.

"You sure you're okay to drive?" she said.

"Oh, yeah. I'm fine. You?"

"No problem here."

"Good."

They stood in awkward silence.

"So, I guess I'll see you tomorrow, then?" Randi said lamely.

"I guess so."

Still, they stood there. Finally, Eleanor moved toward her and Randi wrapped her in a long hug. It felt nice. Eleanor fit perfectly in her arms. She never wanted to let go.

Eleanor finally backed away.

"See you at ten?" she said.

"I'll be there."

Randi drove home with all sorts of feelings coursing through her body, not the least of which was pure desire for Eleanor. She got home, stripped out of her clothes, and climbed into bed. But sleep escaped her. Thoughts of Eleanor filled her mind. The way she'd felt in her arms, the way her hair smelled of lavender shampoo. Randi finally fell into a restless sleep and woke at eight o'clock the next morning.

She poured herself a cup of coffee and sat on her patio contemplating the day ahead of her. It was going to be a lot of hard work, but at least she'd be with Eleanor. She took in the sight of her own backyard. It could use some maintenance itself. She needed to mow the lawn and trim some hedges. But she was in no hurry. Today was all about helping Eleanor. And maybe, just maybe, she'd be rewarded for her troubles.

She showered and dressed in old cut-offs and an old faded T-shirt. She didn't look her best, but she didn't want to show up all decked out to tear out Eleanor's backyard. She paced back and forth in her house, waiting impatiently for the clock to show it was time to leave. When it was finally ten to ten, she jumped in her truck and headed to Eleanor's.

She knocked on the door and was greeted by Eleanor wearing short-shorts again, a tight T-shirt, and her hair pulled back in a ponytail. Randi thought she'd never looked better. When she turned to let Randi follow her in, Randi enjoyed the sway of her ass, just visible in her denim shorts. Randi's mouth was watering.

"Can I get you a cup of coffee?" Eleanor said.

"That would be great."

She poured them each a cup.

"Let's go look at the backyard while we drink these," Eleanor said.

"Sounds good. Lead the way."

She admired the view as Eleanor led her through a small dining room and out the sliding glass doors to the backyard. She tore her gaze away from Eleanor to survey the yard. Eleanor was right. It needed a lot of work. She let out a low whistle.

"Wow. We've got our work cut out for us."

"Listen." Eleanor placed a hand on her arm. It was warm and soft. "You really don't have to do this if you don't want to."

"No worries. I said I would and I will. I'm not afraid of a little hard work."

"Good. And knowing you're not afraid of alligators helps."

Randi laughed.

"Not afraid? True. Willing to wrassle one on my own? No, thanks."

"Wrassle?" Eleanor laughed. "Is that what you call it?"

"I do indeed. Wrestling isn't a strong enough word."

"Fair enough. Well, let's hope we don't see one today."

They finished their coffee and Randi continued to survey the disaster area that was Eleanor's backyard while Eleanor took their cups inside. This would be an all-day affair. Maybe more than one day. Randi could live with that.

Eleanor was back and putting on gloves. Randi went out to her truck to get her gloves and a shovel.

"Where shall we start?" Randi said.

"I think over there." Eleanor pointed to a section of yard that had probably once been a flowering hedge, but which was now a line of brown bushes.

"Okay. I'll shovel and you haul away. Sound fair?"

"Works for me. And then we can switch, if you need to."

Randi knew she wouldn't give up her shoveling no matter how bad her back hurt. She was too butch for that.

They worked until one o'clock when Eleanor decided it was time for lunch. Randi stretched out her sore back and followed Eleanor to the back door. She put her filthy gloves on the patio table.

"I'm not sure you want me coming in. I'm covered in dirt," Randi said.

"Nonsense. I can clean the house later. Come inside and cool off."

Randi stepped inside and felt immediate relief in the cool, air-conditioned house.

"Would you like a beer? I bought some for you," Eleanor said.

"I'd love a beer. Thank you."

"No problem."

Eleanor handed Randi an ice-cold beer. Randi took a big swig. It felt so good on her parched throat. She watched as Eleanor poured herself a glass of ice water. She thought how nice it was that she'd bought beer for her.

They ate sandwiches that Eleanor made for lunch before heading back into the heat to finish the row they were working on. They worked until four when Eleanor pleaded exhaustion.

"I can't go another minute," she said. "I don't know how you are managing."

Randi didn't want to admit she was beyond fried.

"You give me a job to do and I'm going to do it," she said.

"Well, color me impressed. You were a maniac today. Thank you so much for all your help."

Randi shrugged.

"My pleasure," she said.

"I'd like to do something nice for you," Eleanor said.

Images of the two of them naked danced in Randi's head.

"That's not really necessary," she said.

"Still. You know, I never bought you dinner. Choose a place and we'll go tonight. My treat."

Randi almost held her breath. She was close to winning. She could feel it in her gut.

"Okay. If you insist."

"I do. Where would you like to go?"

"After all the work we did today, I'd like a thick, juicy steak."

"That can be arranged," Eleanor said.

"I'll go home, shower, and pick you up at six?"

"Sounds great. I'll see you then."

## Chapter Eight

Eleanor was so sore after her hard work, she could barely raise her arms to wash her hair. She couldn't believe how much they got done. She would have called it quits at lunch, but as long as Randi was willing to keep going, she was determined to keep up. She was sore at the moment and knew it would only be worse the next day. Still, that time with Randi had been nice.

She still wasn't sure she fully trusted her, but she'd been the perfect gentlebutch while she was there. She'd worked her ass off and didn't flirt or even look at Eleanor wrong. Eleanor felt momentarily disappointed. Maybe she didn't want Eleanor, after all. Eleanor shook it off. It didn't matter to her. But she knew she was lying to herself. She wanted Randi, eventually, and hoped that Randi felt the same.

She stood in her closet, looking at all her clothes, trying to decide what to wear. She wanted to look nice, but not overly so. She chose a denim skirt that fell to mid calf, a sunflower yellow blouse, and some flats. Randi wasn't overly tall and she didn't want to tower over her. She knew she was giving it too much thought, but couldn't help it. She was into Randi. She could no longer deny it. She sipped a glass of wine while she waited for Randi to arrive. She had made up her mind to sleep with Randi, but not that night. She was too tired.

Her doorbell rang at five minutes to six. She opened it to see Randi in khaki cargo shorts and a black golf shirt. Her short hair was spiky and her eyes deep green. The crooked smile she always wore was firmly in place.

"Hi," Eleanor said.

"Hello."

"Would you like to come in and have a beer before we go?"

"Sure. I was thinking we should call and see if we can make reservations."

"For what time?" Eleanor said.

"Seven?"

"Sounds good to me." Her heart fluttered in her chest. An hour to just sit and visit with Randi sounded wonderful.

Randi called and made the reservation, then Eleanor led her to the living room. Randi chose a wing chair and Eleanor, confused, sat on the couch alone.

"So, how are you feeling?" Randi asked.

"Oh, my God. I'm so sore." Eleanor laughed.

"I hear ya. My arms are screaming."

"I'm sorry to torture you that way."

"No problem. It feels good. Makes me know I worked hard."

"I could barely lift my arms to shampoo my hair," Eleanor admitted.

Randi laughed.

"Then I'm the one who should be apologizing. I shouldn't have pushed you that hard."

"No. I appreciated your help. We got so much done. I was just admiring our handiwork."

"I'll come over tomorrow and drag all the dead stuff to the curb for you."

"Thank you," Eleanor said. "But you've done enough. You don't need to do that."

"But it'll be easier for me than you. And I've got no plans tomorrow. I'll be here at ten again."

"Okay. But the way I feel, I can't even guarantee I'll be out of bed by then." She laughed.

"Oh, you will be. Especially if you know I'm coming over. You wouldn't want me to catch you in your nightie."

Eleanor blushed a deep red. She'd like nothing more than for Randi to see her in her nightie. Or in nothing for that matter. She looked down at the wineglass she was holding, hoping Randi didn't see the blush.

If she noticed, she didn't let on. Again, quite the gentlebutch.

"You're right," Eleanor finally managed. "That wouldn't be cool."

Randi leaned back in her chair and appeared to relax. That made Eleanor feel good. She wished she could relax in Randi's presence, but it was no use. She was a bundle of sexual energy that kept her constantly on edge.

"So, if you don't work weekends," Eleanor said. "How did you end up coming out to my place to wrassle that alligator?"

"I work every other weekend. I'm working next weekend, then I'll have two days off the following week."

"So you have to work seven straight days?"

"Yep. It's not so bad. I love my job. The bummer is being on call at night. We rotate that, but usually end up on call two nights a week."

"Do you generally get called out when you're on call?" Eleanor said.

"Generally? No. But I have to be available just in case."

"That's a drag."

"Yeah, but we're paid more when we're on call, so I can't really complain."

"Fair enough."

An uneasy silence fell between them. At least it was uneasy for Eleanor. She searched her mind for something to say.

"So," she said. "Are you from here?"

"Born and raised. Went to the University of Florida, then moved back home."

Eleanor nodded. She had nothing else to say.

"And you? Where did you go to school?"

"Berkeley."

"Ah. A liberal."

Eleanor laughed hard at that.

"At least you didn't call me a hippy."

"Nah, you're not a hippy. You shower."

"Oh, wow."

"I'm just teasing," Randi said. "I've got nothing against hippies. Nothing at all."

"Good. Because, you're right, we had our fair share of them at Berkeley."

"I bet. So, why did you leave California?"

Eleanor froze internally. She slowly thawed. Could she trust Randi? Did she want her to know?

"It was just time for a change," she said.

Randi arched an eyebrow at her, looked like she would say something, but only nodded.

"Fair enough."

"Do you need another beer?" Eleanor said.

"Sure, but stay there. I know where the kitchen is."

It warmed Eleanor that Randi felt so at home in her house. She liked that she didn't need to be waited on, too.

"Do you want some more wine?" Randi called from the kitchen.

"Yes, please."

"I'll bring the bottle."

Eleanor smiled. She wouldn't have more than another glass, but it was nice of Randi to bring the bottle to her rather than making her get up. There was certainly more to her than met the eye.

Seven o'clock neared and they decided it was time to leave. Randi followed Eleanor and enjoyed the sway of her hips under her skirt. The skirt was loose at the bottom, but fit fine around her shapely ass. It took every ounce of Randi's self-control not to reach out and grab it.

She'd been on her best behavior so far that day. She'd worked her ass off earlier and then made of point of sitting away from Eleanor when she'd arrived that evening. Sitting too close to her would have tested her too much. She wanted Eleanor and thought Eleanor wanted her, too, but she still wasn't absolutely sure. This confused her. Normally, she could tell if a woman was into her. Oh well, only time would tell.

Randi opened the truck door and helped Eleanor in. When their skin touched, she could feel the currents shoot through her. She told herself to calm down and keep it together. She drove to the restaurant and helped Eleanor out of her truck again. She was showing a chivalrous side that even she hadn't known she'd had.

They were taken to their table and Eleanor looked at her.

"Did you want a beer?" she said. "I'm buying, you know."

"So you said. And yes, I'd love a beer."

"I think I'll have a half carafe of red wine."

"Why not get a full carafe? I'm driving."

"Are you trying to get me drunk?" Eleanor laughed.

Randi laughed with her. Getting her drunk was the last thing she wanted. Although, she had a feeling that tonight wasn't the night to take her. They were both exhausted.

"No. Of course not. I just…well…truth is I don't know that much about wine. I don't know how much either of those is."

"Well, if I order a full carafe, will you help me drink it?"

Randi thought for a moment. Why not? Red wine went great with steak.

"Sure, I will," she said.

"You will?" Eleanor seemed surprised.

"Yeah. I don't mind wine. Especially with a good steak. I'll have a beer then switch to wine."

They ordered their drinks then perused their menus. Randi knew what she wanted. She knew it would cost Eleanor a pretty penny, but she'd offered to take her to dinner. And she was starving. The rib eye was just what she wanted.

"Are you ready?" Eleanor said.

"I am. I'm flippin' starvin'," Randi said.

"Me, too. I could eat a whole cow."

"You?" Randi laughed as she looked up and down Eleanor. "I can't imagine you could eat that much. You didn't even finish your dinner the first time we were here."

"I was still in shock from that alligator." Eleanor laughed.

"Okay. I'll buy that."

They kept the conversation light as they ate, but every moment had Randi wanting Eleanor more. She wondered that Eleanor hadn't burst into flames with all the heat coming off her. And the wine had mellowed her mood, making her braver. Almost brave enough to ask Eleanor home. Almost.

Dinner ended, but Randi wasn't ready to take Eleanor back to her place.

"I know a great pie place," she said. "Did you save any room for dessert?"

Eleanor thought for a long moment. Randi held her breath.

"Sure. A piece of pie sounds great."

The diner was almost empty when they arrived. Randi led them to her favorite table.

"What's good?" Eleanor said.

"Anything. I'm a huge fan of the apple, but their chocolate is to die for, as well."

Eleanor read over the choices.

"I'm having the peanut butter cheesecake," she said.

"Oh, now that sounds yummy."

They ordered their pies and sat back against the booth.

"I've really enjoyed today." Randi finally got up the nerve to say.

"So have I. Not the yard work so much." She laughed. "But this evening has been a lot of fun."

"I even enjoyed the yard work. I like hard work."

"You're crazy."

"Thanks."

Their pie arrived and they dug in.

"Oh, my God," Eleanor said. "This is delicious."

"I'm so glad you like it. I love this place."

"I can see why."

When they'd finish their pie, Randi reluctantly scooted out of the booth and offered her hand to Eleanor. She helped Eleanor slide out of her side. She didn't release her hand and Eleanor didn't pull away. Good sign.

They walked to the truck hand in hand. Randi was disappointed when she pulled up in front of Eleanor's house.

"Would you like to come in?" Eleanor said.

Randi's heart skipped a beat. She was beyond tired, but wasn't going to pass up on this opportunity.

"Sure. For a little bit."

"Yeah. Just for a beer?"

"Sounds good."

They walked inside and Randi took her place in the chair. Eleanor walked out of the kitchen with a glass of wine and a beer. She sat on the couch.

"You know, you could always come join me on the couch," she said.

Randi thought about it. Did she trust herself? Did she care?

"Okay," she said.

She walked over and sat next to Eleanor, who moved closer to her. Randi could feel the heat again and got dizzy with need. She put her arm around Eleanor, who didn't seem to mind.

"Are you serious about coming over tomorrow to move all that crap to the curb for me?"

"Of course."

"I meant it when I said you don't have to."

"And I appreciate it. But I helped make the mess and I'll help clean it up."

"You know," Eleanor said. "You're a lot different than what your first impression showed."

"How's that?" Randi laughed.

"The first time I saw you was in that mini-mart and you were flirting hard core with the cashier."

"Oh, Veronica? She's an old friend."

"Still. I thought for sure you were a player."

Randi stared down at the beer in her right hand. She didn't say anything.

"So you don't deny it?"

"I've had my days," Randi said.

"But you're not anymore?"

"I don't know," Randi answered honestly. She could see herself settling down with Eleanor. At least she thought she could.

"Oh, well," Eleanor said. "You're a very nice, chivalrous, person. And I really like you."

Randi brought her head up until her gaze met Eleanor's.

"I like you, too."

The moment seemed to drag out forever. She moved her gaze from Eleanor's eyes to her lips. They were parted slightly, as if inviting her. She lowered her head and lightly brushed her own lips over Eleanor's. The kiss, however brief, sent chills down her spine. Her boxers were wet. If she kissed her again, would she be able to stop?

She didn't have a choice in the matter. Eleanor pulled her close and opened her mouth, allowing Randi's tongue to enter. The tips of their tongues met and Randi shuddered. Her crotch clenched. This was what she had wanted for so long. She moved her tongue in farther and danced with Eleanor's. Her need was overwhelming. She pressed against her and felt the swell of Eleanor's breasts against her own.

Somehow, she became aware that she was about to spill her beer and pulled up, off of Eleanor.

"I'm sorry," she said.

"For?"

"I almost got carried away."

Eleanor pressed her lips together.

"And I almost spilled my beer," Randi added.

Eleanor laughed.

"Oh, well. I would have cleaned it up."

"I appreciate that."

There was an awkward moment.

"I should get going," Randi said.

"Okay. If you insist."

"I do. I'll see you in the morning?"

"I'll be here."

Eleanor walked Randi to the door. Randi pulled her close and kissed her again. Her head was swimming when the kiss ended.

"Good night, Eleanor."

"Good night."

## CHAPTER NINE

Eleanor closed the door behind Randi and leaned against it. Randi had kissed her and she'd liked it. She'd wanted more of it. Why had Randi stopped? Did Randi not want her as badly as she wanted Randi? Had Eleanor done something wrong?

The questions whirled through her mind as she relived their day together. And their evening. Oh, their evening. The things she felt when she was with Randi made her question her morals. She'd just slept with Haven and now was pining over Randi. She didn't know what had gotten in to herself.

But the more she got to know Randi, the more comfortable she was that Randi wasn't after just one thing. She could have had it just then. Eleanor had made it more than apparent to Randi that she was ready and willing. Yet, Randi had left. Certainly, she was more chivalrous than Eleanor had originally thought.

She pushed herself away from the door and set about cleaning up after them. Randi had left half a bottle of beer in her hurry to get out. Maybe Eleanor had done something wrong, after all. With everything cleaned up, she stripped out of her clothes and lay on her bed. The sheets touched her and she imagined Randi's hands on her. She had it bad.

Eleanor woke the next morning, tired after a restless night, yet excited about the day ahead. She cleaned her house from top to bottom and had just gotten out of the shower when she heard Randi's truck pull up. She pulled on shorts and a T-shirt and hoped she looked seductive enough.

Randi knocked on the door. Eleanor opened it to see Randi in much the same outfit she'd had on the day before.

"You ready to get to work?" Randi smiled her crooked grin.

"Ready as I'll ever be."

"I brought some heavy duty trash bags. I figured you didn't want just the dead stuff all out in front of your house on display."

"Good thinking. Thank you."

"No problem."

"Did you want to come in and have a cup of coffee first?" Eleanor said.

"Sure. That would be great."

Randi seemed at ease. She leaned against the kitchen counter while Eleanor filled two cups of coffee. Eleanor could feel the heat radiating from Randi and wanted her right then. Maybe if she played her cards right, today would be the day.

"You okay?" Randi said.

"Yeah. Fine. Why?"

"You seem a little uptight. Do we need to talk about last night?" Eleanor blushed.

"No. I mean, why would we?"

Randi placed a finger under Eleanor's chin and forced her to look her in the eye.

"Because you're being weird. And I don't want you to be," Randi said. "I mean, I don't want things to be weird between us."

Eleanor fought to maintain eye contact. Randi's gaze was so intense and all Eleanor wanted to do was look away. She finally did.

"Things aren't weird," she said.

"Good."

Randi took her in her arms and kissed her lightly.

"I really enjoyed last night," she said.

Eleanor fought to keep her balance. Her legs were shaking.

"So did I."

"You're shaking," Randi said. "Are you sure you're okay?"

"Yes. I'm just responding to you."

"Oh, yeah?" Randi arched an eyebrow.

"Yeah. And don't go getting all cocky now."

Randi laughed out loud. She pulled Eleanor closer and hugged her tight. She kissed the top of her head.

"Me? Cocky? Never."

Eleanor relaxed enough to laugh with her.

"Now, let's get to work," Randi said.

"Okay. Let's do it."

They worked well together. Eleanor raked everything into a pile and they both loaded the garbage bags. But Randi insisted on being the one to carry the bags to the curb.

"It's just a butch kinda job, so I'll do it," she said.

Eleanor laughed at her.

"If you insist."

"I can't have you breaking a fingernail."

"Hey, I can hold my own. It's not like I'm a high femme or anything."

"True. And that's just one of the things I like about you." Randi threw over her shoulder as she walked around to the front of the house.

Just one of? Eleanor thought that sounded like a good thing. She was still contemplating it when Randi came back and saw her just standing there.

"Earth to Eleanor," she said.

"What?"

"You were zoning out. I'm just making sure you're okay."

"I'm fine."

"Great."

Randi took the last bag to the curb. She came back looking hot and sweaty. And completely doable.

"Would you like a beer?" Eleanor said.

"That would be great."

Eleanor popped the top of two beers and took them out back. She found Randi sitting at the patio table, looking perfectly at home. She liked what she saw. She walked over and handed Randi a beer then sat down herself.

"You're having a beer?" Randi said.

"Yeah. Why not? I'm thirsty, too. And there's still plenty of beer here."

"I just didn't think you were a beer drinker."

"I'm not, normally. But I wanted something cool and refreshing, so here I am."

Randi sat back and surveyed the yard while she drank her beer.

"So, what's next on your yard work agenda?" she said.

"Oh, I don't even know. And I don't want to think about it today. Thank you so much for your help the past couple of days."

"Don't mention it. I was thinking we should pull up all that dead grass over there." She pointed to the back left section of the yard. "We can replant with fresh seed."

We, Eleanor thought. *We?*

"We?" she said out loud and laughed.

"Sure. Why not? I'm already invested in the yard. Why stop now?"

Eleanor shook her head.

"Okay. If you insist."

"I do."

The silence that followed seemed to drag on forever. Eleanor searched for something to say.

"Would you like another beer?" she said.

"I would, except I'm starving. Let's go grab a burger."

"I could make you lunch here."

"No, thanks. I'm jonesin' for a thick, juicy burger. And I know just the spot. You game?"

"Of course."

"Great. Let's go. We'll take my truck."

Excellent, thought Eleanor. We're taking her truck. So, we'll have to come back. Maybe something will happen when we get home.

Randi was ecstatic that Eleanor was allowing her to take her out again. She followed her to the truck, admiring, as usual, the little bits of ass cheek peeking out below her shorts. She knew she'd never had a teacher as hot as Eleanor and wondered if Eleanor ever worried about running into students or their parents dressed like that. Not that she cared. Eleanor was eye candy and she was happy to enjoy it.

She drove to a little burger joint on the outskirts of town. It was one of her favorite places and she hoped Eleanor would like it, too. They asked for a table on the deck that overlooked the Everglades.

"I hope you'll be okay if you see a gator," Randi said.

"As long as it stays there where it belongs, I'm fine."

Randi laughed and Eleanor joined her.

"Fair enough," Randi said.

They ordered their burgers and sat back to enjoy the scenery.

"So, what else is on tap for today?" Randi said.

"I don't know. I hadn't really made any plans. I didn't know how long the yard work would take, but you made pretty short order out of it. What about you? Any plans?"

Only to spend the day with you, Randi thought.

"Nope. I just need to get some sleep sometime tonight since I work tomorrow, unlike you."

"Still, I'm sure I'll be getting some sleep, too."

Hopefully, we'll be doing so together, thought Randi.

The waiter brought their burgers and they dug in.

"Oh, my God. This is delicious," Eleanor said.

"I know, right?"

They finished their burgers. Randi had been starving, so it didn't surprise her that she'd finished, but she gaped at Eleanor's empty basket.

"What?" Eleanor said.

"I don't know. I'm just blown away you could eat that whole burger. And the fries."

"I was famished. I may not have carried the bags to the front yard, but I still got a workout this morning."

"Fair enough."

Randi continued to shake her head in dismay. She loved a woman who wasn't afraid to eat. And clearly, Eleanor was not. She'd seen her put away several meals now and she hoped she wasn't bulimic. Because she kept her figure nice and tight and that made Randi happy.

Their meals gone and appetites satisfied, they sat in the sunshine on the deck and watched the life in the water.

"I love it here," Eleanor finally said.

"I'm glad to hear that. It's been home for me forever, as you know."

"I do know. And I can see why you came back here after college. It's such a warm, wonderful place."

"That it is."

They sat in silence for a few more minutes.

"I should probably get you back home. You've probably got lesson plans or something like that to do," Randi said.

Eleanor smiled softly at her. It made her insides melt again.

"I'm on vacation. None of that pesky stuff until next Sunday."

"Oh." Randi wondered how she could suggest they spend more time together.

"I do need a shower, though," Eleanor said.

Randi's heart sank. Their time together was over.

"Okay. I'll drive you back home."

There was tension between them on the drive back to Eleanor's. Randi felt it and wondered if she'd done something wrong. She drove along in silence and wished she could read Eleanor's mind. They got to Eleanor's house.

"Did you want to come in for another beer?" Eleanor said.

Randi smiled. She was so relieved she could have screamed, but decided to play it cool.

"That would be great," she said.

"Awesome. Come on in."

Randi's palms itched to touch Eleanor. She knew Eleanor enjoyed her company. She figured she liked her kisses. All that was left was to find out how far she'd let her go. Randi was in the mood for a little afternoon delight and hoped Eleanor was, too.

She followed Eleanor to the kitchen and stood as close to her as she could without touching her. Her whole body was alive with need. Gooseflesh covered her. She had ice-hot chills flowing through her veins.

Eleanor turned to her with a beer and bumped into her.

"I'm sorry," Eleanor said.

"Don't be."

Randi used her free hand to wrap around Eleanor's waist. She looked deep into her eyes and saw a longing that matched her own. Yes, today was the day. She was sure of it.

She lowered her head and tasted Eleanor's lips. They were soft and warm and Randi needed more. She ran her lips along Eleanor's and Eleanor opened her mouth and welcomed Randi in.

The kiss went on for what seemed like hours. When it ended, Randi was dizzy with need. Eleanor leaned into her.

"I can't stand up much longer," Eleanor said.

"Yeah, that was some kiss."

"You are such a good kisser."

"So are you, Eleanor. I could kiss you all day."

"Shall we move to the couch?" Eleanor said, still somewhat out of breath.

"I don't want to sit on your nice furniture in my filthy clothes. I tell you what." Randi paused. She knew she was taking a leap of faith here. "Why don't you join me in a shower?"

Randi was holding her breath. She knew the answer Eleanor gave would affect their relationship in a huge way. Not that they had a relationship, really. Or did they? She wasn't sure.

"That sounds really nice," Eleanor said, even as she blushed.

"Are you sure?"

"I'm positive."

"Okay." Randi exhaled. "Okay, then."

Eleanor laughed.

"You're as nervous as I am, Randi."

"Yeah. I guess I am."

"That's so cute."

"Why?" Randi laughed.

"I don't know. You just seem so sure of yourself. It's nice to know you get nervous, too."

"I like you, Eleanor. I don't know what it is about you, but I like you. I don't want this to be a one-time thing. Am I blowing it by telling you this?"

"No, Randi. Not at all." She took Randi's hands. "I'm glad to hear that because I'm definitely drawn to you, too. But I'm not the one-night stand type of girl."

"I get that from you. I'll admit, I totally am. But I'm willing to try to fix that so I can be with you."

"I'd appreciate that."

"It won't be easy," Randi said. "And it'll require patience on both our parts, but I will try."

"I get that it won't be easy. And I get that you'll try hard. But believe me, if we're going to make this work, the first time you're with another woman, we're through."

Randi swallowed hard. She wanted Eleanor so desperately. And she liked her so much, which was odd for her. But could she give up her womanizing ways for her? Was she worth it?

"Randi?" Eleanor said.

"Yeah," Randi said. "I understand. I won't need to be with any other woman as long as I have you."

"I hope you mean that."

"I do. I totally do."

Eleanor moved into her arms again and Randi grew damp at the feel of her long, lithe body against hers. She kissed her hard to let her know she meant business. Eleanor returned the kiss in kind.

Randi pulled away.

"Why don't you lead the way to that shower? I think I'm ready for it now."

"Me, too," Eleanor said.

She led the way down the hall to a small bathroom. There was a claw foot bathtub and a separate shower. With the toilet and the sink in there, there was barely room to move to turn around.

"Sorry it's so small," Eleanor said.

"No worries. We don't need a lot of room, do we?"

Randi stood awkwardly wondering what to do. Should she undress first? Should Eleanor? And why was this so hard? Usually, everything came so naturally to her. Why was she overthinking everything?

She moved to Eleanor and kissed her again. As the kiss intensified, she unbuttoned Eleanor's shorts. She felt her skin ripple in response to her touch. She unzipped the shorts and slid them off Eleanor's legs.

She pulled away to let Eleanor step out of them, then took her T-shirt off. Eleanor stood there in her underwear. It was nothing fancy, cotton panties and a sports bra. But Randi had never been so aroused. She quickly took off her own clothes while Eleanor stripped out of her underwear and soon they were naked.

Randi pressed against Eleanor in another deep kiss. The feel of Eleanor's skin against hers had her on fire. She was filled with an overwhelming need, and she was glad she was close to quenching the fire that had been burning since she'd first laid eyes on her.

Eleanor turned the water on and they stepped into the tiny shower together. Randi was glad it was so small. There was nowhere for Eleanor to go except against her. This worked for her.

She lathered up a bath sponge and rubbed it all over Eleanor's body. She hung it up and ran her hands over Eleanor's firm breasts, lathering them up even more. She kissed her hard as she ran her hands down her body and stroked her between her legs. She felt Eleanor's fingernails digging into her back as she fought to maintain her balance.

Randi pressed Eleanor up against the wall and continued to kiss her until Eleanor buried her face in Randi's shoulder and cried out as she came.

"Oh, my God. I guess I was ready for you," Eleanor said.

"I like that." Randi grinned her crooked grin.

"Yeah? So now it's your turn."

"Why don't we finish getting clean and take this to your bedroom?"

"What an excellent idea."

## Chapter Ten

It was with shaky legs that Eleanor got out of the shower and allowed Randi to wrap a towel around her. She dried quickly and watched Randi's muscles ripple as she did the same. She felt weird for a moment, unsure of her body. Randi was so muscular and tight, while she was soft. She hoped that wouldn't be a problem for Randi.

Randi was looking at her when she had finished drying off. The look in her eyes said Eleanor's body was just fine. Eleanor moved next to her and let Randi pull her to her. Randi kissed her and all worries were gone. Nothing mattered but that moment. The kiss, the desire, and all that it promised.

"Now, about that bedroom?" Randi said.

"Follow me."

Eleanor felt Randi's gaze on her naked body. It felt like it was burning a hole through her. She wondered if the evidence of her arousal was visible as it ran down her leg. She wanted Randi again. The shower had just been a warm up, she was sure.

She led them to a small bedroom that held a king-sized bed, a dresser, and a walk-in closet. That was it. That was all she needed. But all they needed was the bed. She walked over to it and lay down. She tried to look as inviting as she could as she stared up at Randi, who was staring back at her.

Randi approached the bed slowly, as if drawing the moment out. Eleanor pleaded with her eyes. She needed to be taken again. And again, probably. And then maybe one more time.

She moved over to allow Randi to join her. Randi lowered herself on top of Eleanor, supporting herself with her arms. Their bodies fit together so well. Eleanor arched off the bed to be closer to Randi, to become one with her.

Randi kissed Eleanor with a long, drawn out kiss that made her toes curl. It also had Eleanor dripping wet. The more Randi pressed their pelvises together, the wetter Eleanor got.

"I thought it was your turn now," Eleanor said when the kiss finally ended.

"Not yet," Randi said. "Soon, but not yet. I need to have you again. The shower was just the beginning."

She kissed down Eleanor's body until she reached her breast. She took her time with it. She licked all over it before she ran her tongue over her nipple. She pulled up and blew on it. She watched it harden even more as Eleanor shivered.

"You like that?" Randi said.

"It was cold."

"But your nipple puckered big time."

"Good."

Eleanor was glad Randi was enjoying her body, but she was ready for more. She was a hot, horny mess and needed relief. But she didn't want to hurry Randi. She was sure the wait would be worth it.

Randi sucked on her nipple a little longer and Eleanor's breaths were coming in short gasps. She felt like she could come, but that had never happened. Not from just someone suckling her. But she was close, so very close. She felt the energy build at her core. She clenched her hands in Randi's hair so she wouldn't move. She closed her eyes and focused on nothing but the sensations Randi was creating. Suddenly, she could hold off no longer. She cried out as she came.

"Wow," she said.

"Hm?"

"I've never done that."

"Done what?"

"Come from someone sucking my nipple."

"Well." Randi smiled. "I'm happy to be the first."

She kissed down Eleanor's body until she came to where her legs met. Eleanor was trembling with need, even though she'd just come. She was eager to see what other pleasures Randi could bring with her tongue. She knew she was in for a treat.

Randi ran her tongue all along Eleanor. She sucked her lips and dipped her tongue between them. She found her opening and slipped her tongue as deep as it would go, running it along Eleanor's satin walls. Eleanor fought to keep from coming too soon, but it was no use. She climaxed again and again.

But Randi wasn't through. She slid her fingers inside Eleanor where her tongue had just been and stroked her nice and deep. She took her swollen clit between her lips and ran her tongue over it. Eleanor pressed her face into her and cried out her name as another orgasm washed over her.

Randi kissed up Eleanor's body and settled against her.

"You're an amazing lover," Eleanor said.

"You're very easy to love."

They lay there in silence with Eleanor still trying to recover and simply enjoying the feel of Randi's hand lightly strumming up and down her back.

"Careful," she said. "You're going to put me to sleep."

"Nothing wrong with a little nap."

"True. And maybe we'll take one later, but I want at you first."

"Whenever you're ready. I'm not going anywhere."

Eleanor kissed Randi softly and tentatively. She felt like a schoolgirl again, unsure of what to do. It hadn't been that long since she'd been with a woman. Haven had only been a couple of weeks before. She shouldn't be this nervous. What was going on?

But deep down, she knew what it was. She really wanted to please Randi. It was more than just sexual. She wanted her to feel a connection with her. She wanted to be good enough to make Randi want to come around some more. She wanted it to be perfect.

She drew a deep breath when the kiss ended.

"Relax," Randi said. "Take your time. I'm in no hurry."

Eleanor merely nodded. She didn't trust her voice. She moved her mouth to one of Randi's pert nipples and pulled it into her mouth. She loved the feel of it pressed against the roof of her mouth and continued to lick and suck on it until she'd had her fill.

She kissed down Randi's muscular belly.

"I love your body," she said.

"It's sure lovin' what you're doing to it."

Eleanor dragged her hand up one inner thigh of Randi's, then the other. She felt her quiver and had to restrain herself from diving right in. She wanted to drag this out, to make Randi beg. Or close to it, anyway.

"You're making me crazy," Randi said. "I'm not going to last much longer. I may come without your participation."

Eleanor laughed.

"Where's the fun in that?"

She finally settled between Randi's legs and breathed deeply. Randi smelled delicious. There was the light scent of soap, but beneath that was a deep, rich smell that was all Randi. Eleanor lowered her mouth to taste her. Her breath caught. Randi was delicious. Eleanor decided she could stay there all day. She licked and sucked Randi's clit until Randi issued a guttural moan as she climaxed.

Eleanor continued to play with Randi's clit as she slid her fingers inside. She plunged them as deep as she could. Randi arched off the bed and met every thrust. It wasn't long before Eleanor felt Randi clamp down on her fingers and heard her cry out as her next orgasm hit. She tried to remove her fingers so she could move up next to Randi, but Randi had a firm grip on them.

"You're not going to let me go, huh?" Eleanor said.

"Sorry. Give me a minute. I'll de-clench."

"Mm. No hurry. You feel so good in there."

"So do you."

Eleanor moved her fingertips against the soft spots inside Randi.

"I've got nothing left," Randi said. "You can try all you want, but those were two powerful orgasms you gave me. I'm wiped out."

Eleanor smiled to herself. She was quite proud of herself. She'd brought Randi to not one, but two orgasms and Randi said they were powerful. Yes, Eleanor was feeling quite good indeed.

When Randi had finally relaxed enough to let Eleanor have her hand back, Eleanor climbed up next to Randi and snuggled into her arms.

"You see, that's the glory of afternoon sex," Randi said.

"What is?"

"You take a nap after, then wake up and do it all over again."

Eleanor smiled broadly.

"That sounds wonderful," she said.

"Good. I'm glad you think so. Now, let's get some sleep."

Randi woke first and lay there watching Eleanor sleep. She was so beautiful. Her blond hair was mussed and she had a faint smile on her face. Randi wondered if Eleanor was dreaming of her. She hoped so. She hoped she brought a smile to her face just thinking about her. She knew Eleanor had that effect on her. She had thought of little else since the moment they'd met.

Eleanor woke and took a moment to focus on Randi lying there watching her,

"Hey there, sleepyhead," Randi said.

"Hey. How long were we sleeping?"

"A couple of hours. Do you need more sleep?"

"No. I think I'm good."

"Good."

Randi kissed her.

"What do you want to do now?"

Eleanor blushed. Randi watched the pink start at her chest and work its way up.

"Oh, believe me. That can be arranged."

Randi moved between Eleanor's legs and ran her tongue over the length of her. She could taste her earlier orgasms and thought she could stay there for hours just savoring Eleanor. She took Eleanor's clit between her lips and flicked it with her tongue. Eleanor cried out.

Randi climbed up next to her in bed.

"I love how easy you are."

"I should be embarrassed."

"No, you shouldn't. It's wonderful."

"Are you sure?" Eleanor said.

"I'm positive."

"Okay. If you say so."

"It means I turn you on," Randi said. "How can that be a bad thing?"

"That's true. And you do. Big time."

"Most excellent."

"So, now it's my turn again?" Eleanor said.

"No, thanks, baby. I'm fine for now."

"Are you sure?" Eleanor looked so disappointed.

"Sorry, but I don't think I have another one in me right now. Maybe later?"

"Okay. I'll hold you to it."

"Please do."

Randi rolled over onto her back and pulled Eleanor against her.

"I can't believe I'm going to say this," Eleanor said. "But I'm starving."

Randi laughed out loud.

"Well, you've been getting quite a workout."

"I know, but we just ate that ginormous burger."

"That was several hours ago. Let's get dressed. I'll take you out for dinner."

"I'm going to get as big as a house if I keep going out for meals."

"Nonsense," Randi said. "You look great. We'll get Italian again, okay?"

"Sure."

"I need to go home and change. Give me a half hour and I'll be back."

"Sounds great."

True to her word, Randi was back in thirty minutes, looking dapper in her cargo shorts and golf shirt.

"You know," Eleanor said. "It would have been easier to just take me to your place and leave for dinner from there."

"Ah, yes," Randi said. "You see…well…that is…my house isn't really ready for a femme to see it."

"Oh, come on. How bad can it be?"

"It's horrible. But I promise to spend some time cleaning it so you can come over sometime."

"That would be nice, but you don't have to clean on my account."

"Oh, believe me, I do."

"If you insist. At any rate, Tony's is calling me."

"Me, too," Randi said. "Let's get going."

After they had ordered, Randi looked hard at Eleanor. She so enjoyed her company and wanted to spend every minute with her. But could she do that without giving up her social life? She knew she wouldn't be sleeping around anymore and was fine with that, but what about going out and having fun?

"What's up?" Eleanor said. "You look very serious."

"Do you like to dance?" Randi said.

"Sure, why?"

"There's this great women's bar I go to. They play great music." Eleanor shook her head.

"Oh, no. I'm sorry, Randi, but I can't."

"Why not?"

"I can't be out yet here. I'm not ready."

"What? How can that be?"

"I don't know," Eleanor said. "But I just feel as a teacher, I need to stay in the closet."

"That's crazy. These aren't the dark ages."

"Look, Randi, I'm willing to date you. I'll go out in public with you whenever you want. And you know I'm willing to sleep with you. But I can't be seen at a women's bar."

Randi was frustrated. What was the big deal?

"Look, Eleanor. I'm out, loud, and proud. I don't believe in closets."

"So, what are you saying?"

Randi looked at Eleanor. She looked scared. Randi didn't want to hurt her. She didn't want to lose this new thing between them. She wanted to see where it would go.

"I'm saying I love to dance and would love to take you dancing with me. I usually hit the club on my weekends off."

"But you didn't go this weekend."

"No. I didn't. Being with you was more important. And I'm sure it will continue to be. But every so often I might want to go dancing. If you won't go with me, it won't be as much fun, but I still might have to do it. Are you going to have a problem with it?"

"Will you be taking anyone home with you?" Eleanor said.

"No. I've already given you my word that I won't be with anyone but you now that we're together. I just need to know if you'll be okay if I go out once in a while. If you'll trust me."

"If you say I can trust you, I will."

"I say you can."

"Then there's no problem."

Randi sat back against the booth. She didn't even know if she would want to go dancing without Eleanor. She wanted to see Eleanor move and groove with the tunes. She was sure she would be an excellent dancer. But dancing was so much a part of her life. But was it the dancing or the scoring that was important? Would she really need to go to the club now that she had Eleanor? She shook her head. Too many thoughts.

"What?" Eleanor said.

"What, what?"

"You shook your head. Is our conversation continuing in your brain?"

"No. Not really. I've just got a lot to sort through. This monogamous thing is so new to me."

"Why is that, Randi? Why hasn't some hot young thing scooped you up and taken you away?"

"I have been in relationships in the past. Let's just say they never ended well. And after the last one, I swore off them. So while I really like you and want things to work between us, please don't freak out if I get cautious or wary. It's in my nature now."

"Oh, believe me, I understand."

"And what about you, Eleanor? What big secret is hiding in your past? What made you move to Florida in the first place?"

"I suppose we both have a lot to learn about each other, don't we?" Eleanor said.

"I suppose we do."

"But isn't that what the whole beginning of a relationship is? A getting to know you phase?"

"Yeah," Randi said. "And I can't wait to get to know you better. I'm sure crazy about the part I know so far."

"Thank you. I really like you, too."

## Chapter Eleven

Eleanor was silent on the drive back to her house. She was lost in thoughts about Randi. She wished she could go to the club and dance the night away with Randi. She liked that she was her new girlfriend. And having a girlfriend practically outed her just in concept. How could she have a girlfriend if she was straight?

But who would know she had a girlfriend? She thought about that seriously. In a small town like theirs, that kind of news would travel fast. And how could Randi explain to all her friends that she had a girlfriend if Eleanor wouldn't let her mention her name?

"You're awfully quiet," Randi said. "Penny for your thoughts?"

Eleanor sighed heavily.

"I'm just wondering how closeted I can stay. I mean, I figure you're going to want to tell your friends about us, and if I'm going to stay in the closet, I can't have you telling anyone my name."

"That is tricky," Randi said. "But it's doable. Believe me. I'll do whatever you need me to do. Just ask, baby, and it's yours."

"Thank you. I'm beginning to wonder if I deserve you."

"I think, somehow, on some level, we deserve each other in a big way. I suppose just how and why will surface over time."

"I suppose so."

Randi pulled up in front of Eleanor's house.

"Did you want me to come in?"

"Of course. Oh, wait. We're out of beer. Let's go to the mini-mart and pick some up."

"Great. I can run in and you can wait in the truck, if you want."

"Sure."

They pulled into the parking lot and Eleanor noticed the same woman was working the register as the night she'd first seen Randi. She felt herself growing jealous.

"I can run in if you want," Eleanor said.

"No. I've got this. You wait here."

Eleanor watched carefully to see if she could detect any flirtation between Randi and the cashier. She saw Randi wave to her as she walked back to the beer section. She watched Randi pay and walk out. There seemed to have been a brief conversation as she paid, but nothing major. And nothing in Randi's body language indicated flirting. Eleanor felt bad for worrying.

Randi opened the car door and handed Eleanor the beer, then climbed in.

"Wasn't that your friend working tonight?" Eleanor said.

"Yeah. Veronica. She asked where I was last night." Randi laughed.

"Did you have a date?"

"Date? Oh, God, no. She had just expected to see me at the club."

"Something tells me your reputation is going to be harder to change than mine is to keep."

"Nah. I'm not worried about it. People will get used to the fact that I've settled down eventually. Yours, however, will be much harder to keep from the piercing minds and wagging tongues of our town."

Eleanor took in Randi's words. What would be better? To attempt to stay in the closet and hope for the best or to come out and let the chips fall where they may? No, she didn't know how the middle school would take to her being a lesbian. But was Martina? She didn't know for sure. And that's how she'd have to live. Not letting anybody know for sure.

They got back to the house and Randi put the beer in the refrigerator.

"Do you have wine?" she said.

"I do. And I'd love a glass, please."

"Coming right up."

Eleanor was sitting on the couch. Randi came over and joined her. She handed her the wine, which Eleanor took gratefully.

"You okay?" Randi said. "Did I do something wrong? You're really spending a lot of time in your own head. I wish you'd talk to me."

"It's just this whole closet thing. I wish I could be like you, but I'm not sure how the school would take having a gay or lesbian teacher. It's so conservative, you know?"

"You mean you haven't met any yet?"

"Not that I know of."

Randi laughed.

"Maybe your gaydar is broken. There are a lot of teachers there. Someone's gotta be queer."

"That would be me. I'm the token. And I don't want the others to know."

"Oh, come on. No one's been nicer to you than anyone else?"

"Well, there is one teacher. From the science department. But I think she's just been nice because I'm new to town and all."

"And you got no inkling she might like you?"

"I don't know. I wondered, but then thought she was being nice."

"Well," Randi said. "There's no point arguing the issue. You'll stay in the closet until you're ready to come out. And not a moment before."

"Thank you for understanding," Eleanor said.

"Don't mention it."

Randi kissed Eleanor then and Eleanor knew that everything was all right. Randi still liked her and wanted her. She was okay with Eleanor's request and Eleanor needed to stop worrying. She let her cares go and lost herself in the kiss.

"That was nice," she said when the kiss ended.

"Yeah, it was. I want more."

They set their drinks down and resumed kissing. Soon Eleanor was on her back on the couch and Randi was on top of her. Eleanor wrapped her legs around Randi and pulled her close against her.

Randi ground her hips into Eleanor and Eleanor almost lost it on the couch.

She broke the kiss.

"We should go to bed," she said.

"I think you're right."

Randi stood and offered her hand to Eleanor, who took it and stood up. Eleanor held her hand as they walked back to the bedroom. As soon as they were near the bed, Randi had her arms around Eleanor and was kissing her again. Every inch of Eleanor was alive and begging for Randi's touch.

She stepped back and quickly removed her clothes. She needed to be naked for Randi. She wanted her to be able to get to every spot. She watched in pleasure as Randi took off her own clothes. Soon, her glorious naked body was on display and Eleanor was shaking with desire.

Randi kissed Eleanor as she eased her back on the bed. She climbed on top of her and brought her knee up to press against her center. Eleanor ground into it and lost herself in the feeling. She closed her eyes and cried out as she came on Randi's leg.

"You're so hot," Randi said before she kissed her again.

Eleanor ran her hands all over Randi's body. Her back was muscular and it was such a turn on to touch her. She rolled Randi over and climbed on top of her. Randi smiled as Eleanor left a trail on her belly as she slid lower.

Randi held Eleanor's hips as Eleanor slid her hand between her legs. Randi could see her swollen clit and watched Eleanor stroke it. Eleanor moved lower and continued to work to get herself off, but this time she was stroking Randi as she stroked herself.

"Oh, my God," Randi said. "Oh, my fucking God, you're amazing."

Eleanor was breathing heavily. She needed to come. She was ready to come, but she wanted Randi to come with her.

"Are you close?" she said.

"Oh, God yes. I'm so close."

"Come with me, Randi," she said. "Please come with me."

Eleanor could wait no longer, but she heard Randi cry out as her own world split into a million tiny pieces.

She collapsed on top of Randi, then slid off and curled into her arms.

"Oh wow," Randi said. "You've got a few tricks up your sleeve, haven't you?"

"I've read about that before and always wanted to try it to see if it would work."

"Well, now we know. And you're welcome to do that again any time you like. Watching you touching yourself is hot enough, but when you started stroking me, as well? Oh, dear God, it was all over but the crying."

"Hold me while we sleep?" Eleanor said.

"Gladly."

Randi woke up the next morning, stretched, and admired Eleanor sleeping next to her. She carefully rolled her onto her back and spread her legs. She ran her fingers over her clit and teased her lips. She lowered her mouth and sucked on a nipple.

"Mm," Eleanor said. She opened her eyes. "Good morning to me."

Eleanor was instantly wet and Randi easily slid her fingers inside. Eleanor rode her fingers briefly before crying out as wave after wave of orgasm cascaded over her.

"I don't know how you do what you do, but I'm glad you do it."

"Good. As long as you enjoy it."

Randi rolled over and looked at the clock.

"Oh, shit. I need to get going," she said. "I'm going to be late for work."

"You can shower here and go."

"No. I need my uniform, so I'll have to go home and get it."

"Okay."

"I'm sorry to have to rush out of here," Randi said.

"It's okay. I understand."

Randi kissed Eleanor on the mouth.

"Can I come over after work tonight?"

"I wish you would."

"Great. Have an awesome day."

Randi got home, showered, changed, and made it to work only five minutes late. There was a spring in her step and a smile on her face and she didn't try to hide either.

"You're late, Hansen," Johnny said.

"Did I miss anything?"

"No, but it's the principle. You're always the first one here."

"I overslept this morning."

"Okay. I'll give you that. How was your weekend?"

"Awesome. How was yours?"

"Not bad," Johnny said. He looked at her out of the corner of his eyes. "Did you go to the club this weekend?"

"Nope. I didn't make it."

"Then what's got you so flippin' happy on a Monday?"

"Life's just good, buddy boy. Life's just good."

"Oh, yeah? Who was she?"

"Nobody."

"Nobody?" Johnny said. "Just another nameless bimbo in your endless string of women, huh?"

Randi's insides roiled. Eleanor was anything but a bimbo, but she couldn't say anything. Eleanor had been right. This was going to be hard to do. She wanted to shout it from the treetops, to tell the world that she had a girlfriend who was the most amazing woman Randi had ever met. But Eleanor wouldn't allow it. Not yet, anyway. She hoped she'd come around eventually.

Work was uneventful, and Randi couldn't have been happier when five o'clock rolled around. She finished up the report she'd been working on and put her things away.

"I'm outta here," she said.

"Right behind you," Johnny said.

They locked up the building and Randi set off to Eleanor's house. She glanced over at the overnight bag she'd packed before leaving her house that morning. She hoped she wasn't being presumptuous in thinking she'd be staying the night again.

She knocked on the door and waited for what seemed an eternity. Finally, Eleanor answered it in an ankle length blue dress. She looked amazing.

"Come on in," Eleanor said.

Randi stepped inside and kissed Eleanor on her cheek.

"You look beautiful," she said.

"I just got out of the shower."

"Ah, so I'm too late? I should have driven faster so I could have joined you."

Eleanor smiled at her, a warm smiled that melted Randi to the core.

"Easy there, Turbo," Eleanor said. "Come on in and rest a while. I'll grab you a beer. How was your day?"

"Mellow. It was mostly a paperwork kind of day. Nothing too thrilling."

"No? No alligators to wrassle?"

"Not a one. Which is just as well. That's not an easy thing to do."

"You sure made it look simple."

Randi laughed.

"I'm not sure how I did that, but thank you."

Randi was sitting on the couch when Eleanor walked out with her beer.

"Are you going to join me?" Randi said.

"Of course."

Eleanor sat next to Randi. Randi put her arm around her and pulled her close. She smelled fresh and clean.

"You always smell so good," Randi said.

"Thanks. You do, too, you know. You have a rugged smell to you that I really like."

"Rugged, huh?"

"Yep."

"Okay. I guess I'll take that. Even last night? After I used your soap?"

"No. Last night, not so much."

"Maybe I'll have to buy a spare set of toiletries to leave here," Randi said tentatively. She held her breath and waited for Eleanor's response.

"That would probably be a good idea," Eleanor said.

Randi exhaled loudly.

"What was that about?" Eleanor said.

"I just worried that you'd say no."

"And why would I do that? I like you sleeping over here. At least until you can get your house cleaned up enough for me to see." She grinned.

"Oh, yeah. It's on my to-do list. But I plan on spending more time here than there for a while, so it's not gonna happen any time soon."

"Fair enough," Eleanor said. "I'm patient."

"Good. I'm not, though."

With that, Randi bent to nuzzle Eleanor's neck. She was warm and soft, and Randi wanted more.

"You'll have to be," Eleanor said. "Dinner is ready, so we'll have to eat first, then we can get on to more fun endeavors."

"Right. Food. I'm famished. I didn't know you could cook."

"But of course."

"Well, the night I saw you at the mini-mart, you were looking for frozen food to eat, remember?"

Eleanor laughed.

"Of course I remember. Just because I know how to cook doesn't mean I always want to cook."

"Yeah. That makes sense."

"But I was in the mood to today, so you reap the benefits."

"Most excellent. It smells delicious."

"It's no Tony's, but I hope you'll like it."

"I'm sure I will."

Conversation was easy during dinner, but all Randi could really focus on was dessert. Eleanor was simply stunning in her dress with her hair loose and her skin radiant. Randi needed her in a big way.

After dinner, Randi offered to do the dishes. She wanted to make short order of them so they could get to bed.

"Don't worry about them," Eleanor said. "I can do them in the morning."

"Are you sure?"

"Yeah. I'm off tomorrow, so it's no big deal. Besides, I believe we had some plans."

"I believe we did."

Randi opened her arms and Eleanor stepped into them. Randi tipped Eleanor's chin up and looked into her eyes. She lowered her mouth and captured Eleanor's with it. The kiss was tender but conveyed everything Eleanor was feeling. She felt passion, yearning, desire, and caring all in that one kiss.

She took Eleanor's hand and led her to the bedroom.

"You even changed the sheets?" Randi smiled.

"I had time. Don't expect that from me every day." Eleanor grinned.

"I won't."

Randi kissed Eleanor again and reached around to unzip her dress. She stepped back and let it fall to the floor. Randi admired Eleanor's body anew. She was the picture of perfection. Not too thin, not too fat. She had meat on her bones and Randi loved that about her. And as she rubbed her hands over her shoulders and back, she loved how every inch of her responded to Randi.

Randi's body was responding on its own, as well. She quickly stripped out of her clothes and lay in the bed. She pulled a naked Eleanor on top of her.

"You feel so awesome," Randi said. "I love to feel your skin against mine."

"Oh, God, don't I know that. It's pure heaven."

Randi kissed Eleanor again before rolling on top of her. She took one nipple between her thumb and finger as she sucked on the other one. Eleanor cried out almost immediately. Randi ran her hand down her body and placed it between her legs.

"Oh, God," she said. "You're so wet."

"I need you, Randi. Please."

Randi smiled at her, then continued to watch her face as she plunged her fingers inside her. She loved how tight Eleanor was, yet how easily she took her in. She watched Eleanor struggle to keep her eyes open and finally give up the battle. She saw the look of determination on her face as she rode Randi's hand. Randi finally saw the look of complete bliss as Eleanor climaxed on her hand then settled back to reality.

## Chapter Twelve

Eleanor opened her eyes and saw Randi watching her. She blushed.

"Have you been watching me this whole time?" she said.

"I have."

"Why?"

"Because you're beautiful."

"Whatever. Kiss me, please?"

Randi kissed her and Eleanor felt the heat coursing through her body again. She wanted to continue to lay herself bare for Randi's pleasure, but she wouldn't be selfish. She knew Randi needed attention, too.

"If you need more, just say the word," Randi said, as if reading her mind. "I could make love to you for days on end, if I had the chance."

Eleanor smiled at her. She hoped her smile conveyed everything she was feeling—gratitude, appreciation, a deep, powerful emotional attraction.

"I would love that, too," she said. "But I do believe someone's been asking for it since before dinner."

Randi blushed.

"Oh, my God. I didn't know you could do that," Eleanor said.

"What?"

"Blush." She laughed.

The blush deepened and Randi looked away.

"I'm sorry. I don't mean to make fun of you. It's rather endearing."

"Yeah?"

"Yeah. Now come here."

Eleanor wrapped her arms around Randi and pulled her to her. She kissed her hard on the mouth. She pried her lips open and made her way inside. Randi welcomed her and their tongues frolicked together until, breathless, Eleanor broke off the kiss.

"Damn," she said.

"I hear ya."

"Roll over and let me have at you."

Randi rolled onto her back and Eleanor gazed at her body appreciatively.

"You are such a fine specimen," she said.

"Thank you?"

"Mm. Oh, yes. That's a compliment."

Eleanor licked one of Randi's nipples before sucking it as far into her mouth as she could. She ran her tongue over it and felt Randi's hand tangled in her hair. She smiled inside. She was pleasing Randi. It seemed that's all she wanted to do anymore. Please her and be pleased by her.

She kissed lower, down her taut belly. She spread Randi's legs and settled between them. She dipped to taste her and felt her own clit swell at Randi's distinct flavor. She licked and sucked before she slipped her fingers inside. She loved how tight and responsive Randi was. She kept moving her fingers in and out while her tongue played with Randi's clit. In no time, Randi was calling her name.

Eleanor stayed where she was and tried to coax another climax out of her.

"Sorry, baby," Randi said. "That one was soul rocking. I don't have another one in me right now."

"Mm. Okay. You just taste so good. I don't ever want to stop."

Eleanor waited until Randi had stopped clenching her, then withdrew her hand. She slid up next to Randi.

"So, I brought some extra clothes with me. I'll just shower here in the morning, okay? I'll try to be quiet and not wake you."

"You can wake me the way you woke me this morning anytime."

"Oh, you liked that, did you?"

Randi kissed Eleanor then. She nuzzled her neck and teased her nipple until Eleanor cried out again. Eleanor curled into Randi's arms and allowed herself to enjoy the perfect moment of peace.

"By the way," she said. "I might be late getting home tomorrow night."

"Oh, yeah? Why's that?"

"I guess several of the teachers from my school rented a houseboat on the lake for a few days. They invited me to go with them, but I told them I'd just go out for the day."

"And is one of those teachers the science teacher you told me about?" Randi said.

"Yep."

"Hm. I'm not sure how I feel about that."

"What? Oh, wait. Are you jealous?"

Eleanor rolled over so she could face Randi.

"There's nothing to worry about. I'm yours."

"Still, she doesn't know that. And what if she invited a bunch of lesbians instead of other teachers? It would be a feeding frenzy."

"Randi, you need to trust me. I will trust you. I've already told you that. But you need to trust me, too."

Randi's eyes were a color Eleanor hadn't seen before.

"I don't like it," Randi said.

"I have to interact with these people every day at the workplace."

"But a boat isn't the workplace. There will be drinking and who knows who might hit on you?"

"But I won't respond. Don't you see? There will always be women hitting on you, too, Randi. You're too hot for me to believe otherwise. But I trust that you won't respond or be tempted by the flirting and all that."

"I see what you're saying," Randi said. "I'm sorry. I don't mean to be insecure. It's just that I don't think you realize how attractive you really are. And I worry you might consider someone just being kind when they're actually hitting on you."

"I'm a big girl. I can take care of myself. No one's going to hit on me. And if they do, I won't flirt back. Believe me. Trust me, okay?"

Randi exhaled loudly.

"I suppose I don't have any choice."

"Thank you for understanding."

"So, you'll just call me when you get home then?"

"Yeah."

Eleanor woke up to Randi sucking on her nipple. She grabbed hold of her short hair and held her there, lost in the feelings until she felt her insides turn into a giant ball of energy. The ball exploded as she crested on the climax and rode it to its end.

"Thanks," Eleanor said.

"My pleasure. I need to hit the shower now. Care to join me?"

"I'd love to."

They lathered each other up and took their turns pleasing each other. Satisfied, they dried off. Randi put on her clean uniform and made her way to the front door.

"I'll see you tonight?" she said.

"I'll call you when I get home. I shouldn't be too late."

"Okay, baby. I'll see you then."

Eleanor made herself some coffee then dressed in shorts and a T-shirt. She'd told Martina she would try to be there around ten. She drove to the lake. She called Martina to have her send a motorboat to take her out to the houseboat.

She climbed up to the top deck where she saw several people she recognized. She asked where Martina was and was told she was on the second floor. She climbed down the ladder and saw her over by the barbecue.

"Hey, you," Eleanor said.

Martina turned and took her in her arms.

"Eleanor. So good to see you."

"Good to see you, too." She tried not to bristle at Martina's touch. She wondered again if Martina was a lesbian. She chided herself. People hugged all the time. There was no reason to read anything into it.

Martina pulled back and extended her arm.

"You remember Haven don't you?" she said.

Eleanor swallowed hard.

"Of course." She offered her hand. "Nice to see you, Haven."

"It's wonderful to see you, too. Are you staying for the three days?"

"Oh, no," Eleanor was nervous in her presence. "I'm only here for the day."

"That's too bad." Haven smiled.

Eleanor felt the heat cover her face. So, this was what it was like to be hit on when you're in a relationship that you can't tell anyone about? It wasn't fun. That much was sure. She got herself together.

"Yeah. I have too much to do to stay away for days at a time. But I'm sure you'll all have a great time."

"Oh, yeah. No doubt about that. Can I get you something to drink?"

"Sure. That would be wonderful."

Haven wandered off. Eleanor watched her walk away. She remembered that night they'd spent together. She'd thought it would be awkward to see her again, but it hadn't been bad. It was just like they'd been friends. She was glad Haven was behaving herself. She'd be fine, she told herself.

Haven was back with a beer for Eleanor.

"We only have beer at the moment. Hard alcohol should get here later."

"Beer is fine. I don't usually drink at this hour anyway." She smiled.

"I hear ya."

The stood in silence for a moment.

"Well, it's a beautiful day to be on the lake," Eleanor said.

"That it is. We're supposed to have fine weather the whole time. I'm really excited. Martina has done this the last few years. It's always a good time."

They were interrupted when Ron walked up.

"Why, hello, Eleanor. I didn't know you were going to be here."

"I'm only here for the day."

She watched his face fall.

"That's too bad. You'll miss most of the shenanigans that way."

Eleanor made herself laugh.

"I'm sure I'll see enough shenanigans today to last me."

"Have you gotten the tour yet?" he said.

"I was just about to show her around," Haven said.

"Great. Well, I'll see when you resurface."

"Thanks for that," Eleanor said when they were out of earshot.

"Not a problem. I've seen the way he looks at you. Like he'd stand a chance." She laughed.

Eleanor shivered.

"He gives me the heebie-jeebies."

"Yeah, well, I wasn't going to let you be alone with him wandering the place. I wouldn't trust him."

"Neither would I."

Haven took Eleanor on a tour that covered all three floors.

"This place is amazing," Eleanor said.

"It's pretty cool. We have a lot of fun with it."

"And you come every year?"

"Yep. Martina's really good about inviting me, even though I'm just a substitute," Haven said.

"That's really nice of her."

"Yeah. She's a good person."

They made their way back to the second floor to find people serving up lunch. There were burgers and hot dogs, potato salad, and chips and dip.

"There you are," Martina said. "I wondered where you'd disappeared to."

"Haven just gave me a tour of the boat."

Martina beamed.

"Isn't it great? I love this boat. And I love doing this three-day party for faculty and friends. I'm still sad you can't stay the whole time."

"I wish I could," Eleanor lied. "But I really do have too much going on."

"Really?" Haven said. "Your social calendar has filled up now?"

"Oh, no," Eleanor said. "Nothing like that. I just really need to get my yard in order and put some boxes away. Things like that. No social life for me."

She was growing more uncomfortable by the moment. She just wanted to tell them she was seeing someone. Surely, they'd be safe, right? No. She couldn't trust anyone. Not even them. Sure, Haven knew she was a lesbian, but she trusted her not to discuss their night together with the others. But if she let slip she was in a relationship, who knew whose tongues would wag?

"Wow," she said. "Lunch smells fantastic."

"Lunch today is courtesy of Martina," Haven said. "We all have a meal we're responsible for."

"Serve up," Martina said. "Help yourself. Take as much as you like. I always overdo it and prepare way more food than is necessary."

Eleanor got in line with the others and relaxed as she served herself her lunch. The food was great and she enjoyed it with a music and a PE teacher. She didn't know them well, so it was good to get to know them better.

She stood and made her way to the trash can.

"Did you enjoy lunch?" Haven said.

Eleanor jumped at the sound of her voice. She really felt the need to distance herself from her now. She'd let her give her a tour just to get her away from Ron, but now, she felt like she was being unfaithful to Randi every moment she was with Haven.

"Are you okay?" Haven said softly.

"Yeah, sure, why?"

"You seem edgy, like you can't relax. I hope I'm not the cause of that."

Eleanor sighed deeply.

"I'm sorry, Haven. It's been so long. I guess I don't know how to act after…"

"No worries. I'm not going to try to bed you again right now." Haven laughed. "Though I can't promise I won't try in the future. That is, if someone hasn't snatched you up by then."

Eleanor smiled.

"That's very kind of you," she said.

"So, will you relax and have fun?"

"I will."

The rest of the day passed pleasantly for Eleanor. She watched people jump off the boat into the lake, although she hadn't brought her suit so couldn't participate. It looked like fun.

And there were pool tables and foosball tables onboard, so she engaged in several games of each. Finally, she looked at her watch and decided she'd had enough fun for one day. Enough fun without Randi, anyway.

She said her good-byes, got dropped off at the pier, and drove home. She figured she might be able to get there before Randi got off work. Randi. The knot that had been in her gut all day, albeit somewhat more relaxed after talking to Haven, slowly unwound. She'd had fun. She had to admit that. But being around that many people always took its toll on her. She was not a social butterfly. She could hold her own in small groups, but the amount of people on the boat took a lot out of her.

She pulled into her driveway and pulled out her phone.

## Chapter Thirteen

R andi was just pulling out from work when her phone rang. "Hello?" she said.

"Randi?"

"Hey, baby. Where are you?"

"I'm home. You can come over whenever you want."

Randi gave a silent whoop of excitement and changed her direction. She was happy she wouldn't have to cool her jets at her place. She hadn't looked forward to that in the least.

"Great. I'm on my way," she said. "I'll see you in a few."

She arrived fifteen minutes later. The joys of living in a small town, she thought. Everything was nearby. She knocked on the door and Eleanor answered wearing decent length shorts and a loose T-shirt.

"No short-shorts today?" Randi grinned.

"Very funny. Not around faculty members."

"Ah. That makes me feel better."

"You're so funny," Eleanor said. "You'll notice I not only came home alone, but came home early to spend more time with *you*."

"I do see that," Randi said. "And I thank you for that."

She pulled Eleanor in for a hug and a kiss.

"How was today, anyway?"

"Not bad. Okay. Kind of fun."

"Well, okay then. Glad you had such a rip roarin' time."

Eleanor laughed and Randi couldn't resist. She kissed her again.

"But," Eleanor said, "I did just get home, so didn't have time to make dinner. Where would you like to go?"

"Let's get a steak."

"Do you ever get your cholesterol checked?" Eleanor said.

"Funny. I'm in great health. I just love red meat."

"Why don't we go pick up a couple of steaks and barbecue here?"

"That would be great."

"I'll go pick them up while you shower."

Randi made a show of sniffing her armpits.

"Am I that bad?" she said.

Eleanor laughed.

"No. I just thought you'd like a shower."

"I would. See you in a bit?"

"Count on it."

Randi went out to her truck and brought in yet another overnight bag. This one had more than just one change of clothes in it. She unpacked it, admiring then moving out of the way, some of Eleanor's delicate underthings. She took her shower and got out just as Eleanor was coming in.

"Well, well," Eleanor said as Randi peeked her head around the hallway wall. "Are you indecent?"

"Yeah, but give me a sec."

Eleanor hurried to her.

"Oh, no you don't."

She ran her hands over Randi's naked body.

"No chance we're going to waste this opportunity," she said.

"But what about the steaks?"

"Let's work up our appetites."

Eleanor walked Randi backward until she was in the bedroom. She playfully pushed her onto the bed and climbed between her legs.

"What about you?" Randi said.

"There'll be plenty of time for me later."

Randi relaxed and let Eleanor have her way with her. Her tongue was talented and it wasn't long before Randi cried out as the climax tore through her body.

Eleanor moved up and kissed Randi. She could taste her orgasm on Eleanor's tongue.

"You're all sorts of worked up," Randi said. "That must have been some party you went to."

Eleanor's demeanor changed. She seemed to stiffen. She climbed off Randi.

"You'd better get dressed or we'll never eat."

Randi quickly pulled on some shorts and a T-shirt and walked out to join Eleanor in the kitchen.

"Was it something I said?" she said.

"Hm? What?"

"You went from hot mama to ice princess in the blink of an eye back there."

"I'm sorry. I just got hungry. I wanted to get dinner started."

"Okay. If you say so."

Eleanor seasoned the meat while Randi fired up the grill. Eleanor brought the meat out.

"Do you want to talk about it?" Randi said.

"There's nothing to talk about. Honest."

"So, who all was there? Anyone exciting?"

"They were all faculty members and some friends, so no, it was pretty tame."

"Look, baby. I know we're still getting to know each other and all that," Randi said. "But I think I can tell that something's eating you. I'm a pretty good listener."

Eleanor sat in a patio chair.

"There was someone there."

Randi felt the hair on the back of her neck stand up. Had someone hit on her? She told herself to play it cool.

"It was nothing. I mean, I don't know why I'm even telling you," Eleanor said.

"Well, you haven't told me anything yet."

"It's just that there was a woman there. One I went out with one night."

"Did you sleep with her?" The words were out before she could stop them.

Eleanor was silent for a few minutes. Randi knew the answer before she said anything.

"Yes."

"Okay." Randi didn't know what to say. She was feeling all sorts of emotions at the moment. Mostly unfamiliar and unwelcome. First and foremost, she was feeling jealousy. This was new to her and she knew she'd better tread softly or she could blow this thing they had by being unreasonable. "So, how was it seeing her today?"

"It wasn't bad. I thought it would be all awkward and stuff seeing her, but it wasn't at all. I think it's because I know I'm with you now. She was nice, though. But I didn't spend all my time with her, if that's what you're worried about. I don't even know why I'm telling you this. It really shouldn't matter."

Randi was seething inside. She felt like she'd had to share Eleanor that day and she didn't like it at all. She kept her head, though.

"Look, babe. It was before us, so it doesn't matter. I'm not going to lie and say it doesn't bug me a little. Okay, a lot. But I have no right to get jealous. You didn't even know me when you slept with her. And God knows, I've slept with women before you. So, it's no biggie. I appreciate you telling me it, though. I knew something was on your mind."

"Yeah. I mean, not while I was making love to you, it wasn't. Believe me."

"Good. I'm glad to hear that." She smiled.

Eleanor got up and walked over to her. She moved into Randi's arms and Randi simply held her for a long while.

"So, we're okay?" Eleanor said.

"Yeah, we're okay."

Eleanor breathed a sigh of relief. The whole day had been too much for her. She just wanted to be with Randi and now she was. Yet, for some reason, she'd felt guilty about the time she'd spent with Haven. And now she didn't have to. She'd told Randi about it and she was fine.

"We'd better get these steaks off," Randi said. "Or we'll be eating leather."

Eleanor got a platter from the kitchen and Randi put the steaks on it.

"I'm starving," Randi said.

"Me, too."

"Did you eat at the party?"

"A little. But eating you really worked up my appetite."

She blushed furiously. Randy simply grinned her crooked grin at her.

"Is that right?"

"Yeah."

"Should we start keeping midnight munchies by the bed, then?"

"Maybe so. Except you wipe me out after you've had your turn with me."

"Color me proud," Randi said.

They ate their dinner and after, Randi helped her do the dishes. With everything put away, they sat together on the couch, each enjoying their beverage of choice.

"Thank you for telling me about your day," Randi said. "I know it couldn't have been easy."

Eleanor moved closer to her on the couch, reveling in the warmth that radiated from her body.

"It wasn't. I didn't know if I should. I mean, it didn't matter, but somehow I felt like you should know."

"Well, like I said, I'm glad you did."

They cuddled together for a while, not saying anything. Eleanor wondered what Randi was thinking.

"Penny for your thoughts?"

"I don't know if you want to know."

"Of course, I do."

"I was just thinking of how jealous I was," Randi said. "How insanely jealous I got when you told me."

Eleanor turned to face her on the couch.

"You didn't seem insanely jealous."

"That's because I chose my words and kept my head. I didn't want to blow it with you, but I was jealous, believe me. And that's so unlike me."

"Well, I'd like to think it's unlike you because you haven't been with anyone like me."

"I never have," Randi said.

She kissed Eleanor then. It was a soft, sweet kiss but said so much.

"I'm crazy about you," Eleanor said.

"The feeling is mutual."

Eleanor set her wine down and leaned into Randi for a deep kiss. Her whole body was alive with passion and emotion. The feelings she was feeling were so fresh and unexpected still. She hadn't expected to fall so hard for Randi, but she had. The fact that Randi felt the same only fueled the fire burning inside her.

Randi eased away and set her beer on the table. She took Eleanor back in her arms and kissed her again. Eleanor was burning with desire. She needed Randi to take her and take her soon.

She pulled away from Randi and stood. She offered Randi her hand and she took it. Randi's grip was strong and certain. Eleanor liked that about her. She was confident and sure of herself. Both very attractive qualities.

Eleanor led Randi back to her bedroom and quickly undressed. She needed to feel Randi's touch all over her. She needed her so desperately.

"I need you, Randi. Take me. Please."

Randi stripped and climbed into bed with Eleanor.

"Yes, ma'am," she said.

"I'm yours," Eleanor said. "Make me yours."

"You are mine. Never forget that."

Randi kissed her hard on her mouth and Eleanor let her tongue wander into Randi's mouth. She savored her taste, the feel of her and craved even more, if that was possible.

Randi ran her hand down Eleanor's body and Eleanor spread her legs for her. Randi ran her fingers lightly over Eleanor's swollen clit.

"More," Eleanor said. "I need more."

Randi circled her clit, teasing her. Eleanor opened her eyes and saw Randi staring down at her. She pleaded with her eyes and Randi stopped teasing her. She pressed into Eleanor's clit and rubbed hard. Eleanor closed her eyes again and watched the light show that played out as first one, then another orgasm rippled through her body.

Eleanor opened her eyes to see a smile on Randi's face and pure lust in her eyes.

"Do you need more?" she said.

"Yes. Please."

Randi slid her fingers inside Eleanor, who arched to take them in.

"More," she said again. "Please. More."

Randi slipped another finger inside and Eleanor moaned.

"That feels so good," she said.

"Good. I want to make you feel better than you ever have."

Eleanor thrashed her head from side to side. She was so close to cresting again. She knew she wouldn't last long. Randi swiped her clit with her thumb and that was all it took. Eleanor soared into orbit and slowly floated back to earth.

She was breathing heavily and it took her a moment to find her voice.

"That was amazing," she said. "Unbelievably fantastic. Thank you."

"My pleasure."

They lay in silence for a while. Finally, Randi broke it.

"I like when you say you're mine," she said.

"I like being yours. I'm glad you don't mind me saying that. I was a little afraid at first. I thought it might scare you off."

"It's too late in the game to scare me off, baby. I'm in this to see where it goes. Don't worry about that."

"Good. I'm glad."

Eleanor had gained her strength back and lay there looking at Randi's fine form lying next to her. Her desire flared anew. She rolled over on top of Randi and kissed her passionately. It was her turn to claim Randi and she was going to enjoy it so much.

She kissed down to her small breasts which she licked and loved on. She sucked a nipple into her mouth and teased it with her tongue. She loved the feel of it as it responded and grew larger in her mouth.

She moved her mouth lower and plastered Randi's muscular stomach with myriad kisses before she took her place between her legs. She got comfortable, intent on loving Randi long and slowly.

Eleanor ran her tongue over Randi's lips, occasionally sucking them into her mouth. She licked her juices off and swallowed them greedily. The more she licked, the juicier they became.

"You're driving me crazy," Randi said.

But Eleanor didn't reply. She'd been taught not to talk with her mouth full. She moved her tongue to Randi's clit and lapped at it while she slid her fingers as deep as they would go.

"Oh, yes," Randi said. "Oh, dear God, yes."

Eleanor stayed focused, even as Randi's hand on the back of her head was making it difficult to breathe.

"Oh, God, baby," Randi cried out. "Oh, God, yes!"

Eleanor continued to lick and suck until she felt the spasms deep inside Randi subside. She kissed her way back up Randi's body until she was snuggled against her.

"We've got something good, don't we?" Randi said.

"Yeah, we do."

"I'm glad we found each other."

"Me, too."

Eleanor fell asleep feeling happier than she had in a long time.

## Chapter Fourteen

Randi lay awake and listened to Eleanor sleeping. It had been a pretty intense day for her. For them both, she supposed. She wished she'd been able to go to the party with Eleanor, but she knew she'd probably have punched the dyke she'd slept with before her. Even though, she knew it wasn't right, she was still jealous. She wondered when they'd slept together. How long had it been before they'd gotten together? No, she told herself. It didn't matter. She'd been with another woman two weeks before they got together, so she had no room to be jealous.

And yet, if she let the jealousy go, there was a feeling of such contentment inside her. She was so happy with Eleanor. Who knew another woman could make her that happy? She'd been happy once, but that seemed like ages ago now.

She finally drifted off to sleep and dreamed of happy things like forever with Eleanor. She awoke late to the smell of coffee. She turned over and looked at the clock.

"Holy shit. I'm late."

She rushed out to the kitchen.

"How could you let me sleep this late?" she said.

"I'm sorry. I wasn't sure what time you had to get up. Would you like a cup of coffee?"

"Sure. Let me go put my uniform on. I'll be right back."

Randi came back and took her coffee from a rumpled looking Eleanor. She looked so cute, she had to kiss her nose.

"You look beautiful this morning," she said.

Eleanor smiled.

"You are such a charmer."

"I mean it. You look adorable."

"Even if I let you oversleep?"

"Oh, shit, that's right. I've got to go. I'll see you tonight?"

"Count on it," Eleanor said. She moved into Randi's arms for a quick hug and a kiss and Randi was out the door.

The work day dragged on interminably for Randi. She hated being away from Eleanor. She figured it would be easier when Eleanor was back at work, but knowing she was at home alone drove Randi crazy. She wanted to be there with her, holding her, loving her.

No woman had ever excited her as much as Eleanor did. Sure, it had been a long time since she'd been with a woman for more than just one night, but still. Eleanor had her grip on Randi and Randi didn't care. She never wanted her to let go.

"What's got you so silent today?" Johnny said.

"Hm? Oh, I don't know. Guess I'm just bored."

"Well, let's drive around for a while. Maybe pick up a couple of strays or something."

"Sounds good to me."

They cruised around town, up and down the streets with no luck. They decided to drive out to the outskirts of town to a spot notorious for people dumping animals. They saw a black mama kitty and her litter of kittens crossing the street.

"That's not safe," Johnny said.

"No. Let's take them in, give them some food and water, and see if we can find homes for them."

Randi put on her thick leather gloves and quietly approached the area under the bushes where the cats had disappeared. Johnny went around to the other side. Randi heard the hiss before she felt the scratch on her face. Seeing black cats in a dark space was clearly not easy. She reached her hands in and closed around the mama cat.

"I've got some kittens," Johnny said.

"I've got the mama."

She dragged the cat, who was biting her gloves, out from her hiding place. She tried to get her hand on the scruff of her neck, but was unsuccessful. Mama kitty scratched with her back claws and tore open Randi's forearm. They finally got them all in a cage in the back of the truck.

"How bad did she get you?" Johnny said.

Randi examined her wounds.

"Not too bad. We'll treat them at the office."

"That one on your face is pretty nasty. It'll leave a scar, I bet."

"Oh, well. Scars add character."

They drove back to headquarters and took the cage out of the truck. They placed it on a shelf. They carefully put a bowl of water, a bowl of milk, and some food in the cage with them.

"I feel good," Randi said. "They could have been killed or starved to death or who knows what out there on the streets."

"I agree. Now let's get you cleaned up."

Randi gritted her teeth as Johnny washed her arms, applied medicine, and wrapped them. She grinned and bore it when he washed the gash on her face.

"I'm serious, Randi. That's going to leave a mark."

"Not much I can do about it now. I got too close. It was my own damned fault."

"Okay, well I put some Neosporin on it, which should help it heal."

"Thanks."

Randi volunteered to fill out the paperwork that went with the collection of the cats. It took her a while, though her mind did drift occasionally to Eleanor. She wondered what she'd do when she saw Randi all beaten up from fighting with a little cat. She grinned to herself. Randi figured she could play it up for sympathy. Or she could act like she was trying to butch up, which should also get her sympathy. Either way, she liked the idea of Eleanor fussing over her much more than she did Johnny.

She finished up the paperwork and filed it away.

"You ready to call it a day?" Johnny said.

Randi looked up and saw it was just after five.

"Heck yeah. Let's get out of here."

She got out the nightlight they used when they had animals in the office and turned it on to keep the cats from being any more traumatized than they already were.

Randi drove to Eleanor's house. Her face throbbed, though the scratches on her arms only stung. She lightly fingered the gash and winced. She checked it out in the rearview mirror. Yeah, she was going to get some sympathy, for sure.

She knocked on Eleanor's door and waited impatiently for her to answer. When she did, the look of shock on her face made Randi feel guilty about wanting sympathy.

"Oh, my God," Eleanor said. "What happened to you?"

"I got in a fight with a stray cat. It's no biggie, honest."

"It looks like a biggie. How long have you been doing this? How is it that you're not shredded to pieces already?"

"I'm usually pretty careful. I just got my face too close to the mama cat. She was protecting her kittens. And I put my face right in their den. Not smart."

"Is there anything I can do for it?" Eleanor said.

"Nope. Johnny put some stuff on it at work."

"It won't last forever, though. Come with me."

Eleanor took Randi's hand and led her to the bathroom where she opened the medicine cabinet.

"I have Neosporin. Will that help?"

"That'll be perfect," Randi said. "But I don't need any now. I could really use a beer, though."

Eleanor went to the kitchen and got Randi a beer. She turned to find Randi inches from her.

"I never got my hello kiss," Randi said.

Eleanor looked into her eyes and lost herself. She forgot about the awful gash that ran the length of Randi's left jaw. All she saw was desire and hers rose up from deep within her. She reached her hand behind Randi's head and pulled her close. Their lips met and Eleanor's knees went weak.

"That's better," Randi said.

She took the beer Eleanor handed her and waited while Eleanor poured herself a glass of wine. They went to the living room.

"So, tell me about your day," Eleanor said. "I mean any parts that don't involve you being attacked by a wild animal."

"Not wild, baby, feral. And she was only protecting herself and her babies."

She took a long pull off her beer.

"Outside of that," she said. "It was pretty much status quo. How was your day?"

"I worked in the yard a bit. And bought some plants and flowers. I'm really excited about making my yard what I want it to be."

"Good. I hope you're not trying to do too much. I'll be able to help again this weekend. Or I should."

"Yeah? With your arms all torn up?" Eleanor said.

"They'll be all better by then."

"We'll see."

"Yeah. Besides, I'll be on call, so who knows how busy I'll be."

"I thought you said on call weekends were usually slow," Eleanor said.

"They are. But watch, the one time I make plans, I'll get called out."

"We'll see."

Eleanor moved closer to Randi. She loved the smell of her and the feel of her closeness. She'd missed her big time that day. There was no reason for it. Well, maybe there was. They'd been pretty open discussing their feelings the night before. It made Eleanor feel closer to Randi. She only wondered if Randi felt the same way.

"So, did you get in trouble for being late?" Eleanor asked.

"No. Johnny didn't get there that much before me."

Eleanor thought about Johnny. He was obviously very important to Randi. Eleanor felt she deserved to meet him, then remembered her vow to keep herself and their relationship in the closet. It could prove harder than she expected.

"Whatcha thinking about?" Randi said.

"Oh, nothing."

"Well, you looked pretty serious for not thinking about anything."

"I was thinking about Johnny, if you must know."

"Johnny?" Randi blinked. "Why on earth would you think of him? Do you even know Johnny?"

"No, I don't. I mean, I saw him when y'all came out and wrassled that alligator, but I don't know him."

"Well, then why are you thinking about him?"

"I don't know," Eleanor said. "It's just that you talk about him all the time. He's such a part of your life. I feel like I should know him."

"He's part of my work life. You're part of my personal life. There's no reason for the two to intersect."

"Aren't you even curious about my coworkers at school?"

"Sure. Where is this going?"

Eleanor sat quietly. She didn't know where it was going. She had made her decision and things wouldn't change.

"I don't know," she said. "Keeping this relationship a secret is going to be harder than I first thought."

"Ah. We don't have to, you know. You just say the words and I'll shout it from the rooftops."

Eleanor laughed.

"If only it was that easy."

"It could be. You just have to be strong."

"Are you calling me weak for wanting to stay in the closet?"

"Not weak, really. But scared. And it's going to take some herculean strength to overcome that fear."

Eleanor didn't respond right away. She thought of all she could lose if she came out in Florida. She could lose her job, her friends. And probably more she couldn't think of off the top of her head. And what could she win? The ability to be open about Randi.

"No," she said. "It's just not worth it yet."

Randi pulled her close.

"And that's okay, baby. You'll be ready when you're ready. And I'm not pushing you. You'll know when it's time."

"I appreciate that, Randi. So very much."

Eleanor allowed herself to be held for a few minutes before she turned in place and looked into Randi's eyes.

"What's up?" Randi said.

"Just want you to know how much I appreciate you."

"I think I have a pretty good idea," Randi said.

"I hope so."

Eleanor jumped up.

"What's up?" Randi said.

"Dinner's going to burn. I forgot all about it."

She managed to save dinner and they ate in peaceful quiet. When the dishes were done, Randi took Eleanor in her arms.

"I think it's time for me to show you how much I appreciate you," she said.

"Oh, Randi. With your face like that? Won't it hurt?"

"It shouldn't. Now come on."

Their lovemaking that night was tender and gentle. Not just because they were being careful of Randi's face. It just felt right to take things slowly. There was no rush for either of them. They kissed for what seemed like hours before Randi finally skimmed her hand over Eleanor's body. Eleanor felt her skin ripple in response. Her whole body was alive, every nerve ending in tune with Randi's touches.

Randi lowered her hand to rest it between Eleanor's legs. Eleanor spread them wider in a silent plea for more. Randi ran her hand along the length of Eleanor, touching and teasing her. Eleanor closed her eyes and enjoyed the sensations. She vowed not to hurry Randi, to let her take her time until Eleanor could no longer stand it.

Finally, Eleanor said something.

"Please. I can't take the teasing any more. I need you to take me. Hard and fast. Please. Do it."

Randi slid her fingers deep inside Eleanor. Eleanor moved up and down against her, driving her deeper and deeper with each thrust. Randi put her mouth on Eleanor's nipple and played over it with her tongue while she continued to work inside her.

Eleanor felt the orgasm building. A ball of energy filled her center. She focused on nothing else until the ball exploded, sending currents of white heat soaring throughout her body. She was just about to float to earth when there was another explosion. And another. She lay spent and was only vaguely aware of Randi pulling out of her and lying next to her.

"That was incredible," she said finally.

"Mm."

"Give me a minute and I'll take care of you."

"There's no hurry," Randi said.

When Eleanor's breathing had returned to normal, she returned the favor and slowly and meticulously made love to Randi. She, too, took her time and made sure no part of Randi was left unkissed. She spent a long time sucking and licking Randi's nipples before moving down between her legs.

She ran her tongue all over her before dipping it inside to taste her excitement. She finally took Randi's swollen clit between her lips and flicking her tongue over it, driving Randi to one orgasm after another.

Eleanor climbed up into Randi's arms and, feeling safe and secure, fell into a deep sleep.

## Chapter Fifteen

The rest of the week passed uneventfully for Randi. She was keeping Neosporin on her gash and it seemed to be healing for the most part. Her days were spent at her job and her nights were wonderfully spent with Eleanor. She was happier than she had been in a long time and owed that entirely to Eleanor.

Friday night, she went to her own house to shower and pick up some weekend clothes to take to Eleanor's. She called Eleanor when she was on her way over.

"Hello?" Eleanor said.

"Hey, baby. I hope you didn't make dinner tonight. I want to take you out."

"That sounds wonderful. I'm in the bath now. Where are you?"

"I'm almost there."

"The door's open," Eleanor said. "Just come on in. I'll be getting ready."

Randi's crotch clenched at the thought of Eleanor in the bath, all naked and slick from the oils she used. But she would see her soon enough and later, she'd be able to enjoy all her nakedness for her very own.

She let herself in and could smell the lavender and vanilla from Eleanor's bath hanging in the air. She grabbed a beer and a glass of wine then walked back to the bedroom.

"Hey, baby." She kissed her. "How was your day?"

"Not bad. I'm bummed, though."

"Why's that?"

"I have to go back to work on Monday."

"Oh yeah," Randi said. "That is a bummer."

"But I've had a great week off, so there's that."

"Yeah, there is."

"So," Eleanor said. "Where are you taking me to dinner?"

"Tony's. I want Italian. Sound good to you?"

"Sounds great."

Eleanor took the glass of wine from Randi gratefully.

"You didn't have to pour me a glass. I'd get one eventually."

"But I wanted you to have one now."

"You're so sweet."

Randi kissed her again.

They walked out to the living room and sat while they sipped their drinks.

"So..." Randi began hesitantly.

"Yes?" Eleanor raised an eyebrow.

"I've kind of been hanging out here all week."

"Yes. And?"

"Well, I was kind of wondering..."

"Yes?" Eleanor said again.

"I was wondering if I could use your washing machine to do some laundry."

Eleanor laughed.

"Of course. I'll even let you use my dryer, too."

"Thanks."

"Why were you so hesitant?"

"I don't know. I didn't want to seem presumptuous."

"You're not. You never are. I don't think you ever could be."

"Thanks," Randi said.

"But you don't want to laundry right now, do you?"

"Heck, no. I'm famished. Let's go get some food."

They entered the restaurant and Randi's mouth watered.

"I love this place," she said.

"Me, too. I could eat everything on the menu."

"Not in one sitting, please. My salary isn't all that."

They laughed as they were led back to a table and then lost themselves in their menus. Randi read over each item at least twice. She was so hungry and it all looked so good. She finally decided and put her menu down. She saw Eleanor sitting there, clearly already having decided.

"Sorry," Randi said. "I was having the hardest time making up my mind."

"No worries. You're through now so we can focus on each other."

Randi fought the urge to reach across the table and take Eleanor's hands in her own. She wanted contact, to touch her, but knew that was taboo. At least for now. Hopefully, she'll come around, Randi thought. She really wanted to be open with her.

"Where did you go?" Eleanor said.

"What?"

"You seemed lost in thought. Care to share?"

Randi wondered if she should. They'd had the discussion and there was no resolution. She opted to keep her thoughts to herself.

"Just thinking how beautiful you look."

"Aw. Thank you."

"It's the truth. I love looking at you."

Eleanor blushed and Randi gushed at having made her do that. She loved Eleanor's responses to her.

The waiter came and they ordered wine and their meals. They sat sipping their wine.

"So, what's on the agenda for the weekend?" Randi said.

"I'd like to pull out all the dead shrubs along the other side of the yard, if you don't mind."

"I don't mind at all. And my arms are as good as new."

She held up her arms, showing that the scratches on her forearms were almost gone.

"Almost," Eleanor said.

"Pretty much."

Dinner came and they ate in comfortable silence. When it was over, Randi paid the check and stood. She instinctively offered her hand to Eleanor, who looked shocked. Randi slid her hand in her pocket.

"Sorry. It was just natural. I need to unlearn some things, clearly."

"I really don't mean to be difficult," Eleanor said.

"You're not. You're different, but not difficult. And I need to keep your needs in the forefront of my mind."

They got out to Randi's truck.

"I'm really sorry, Randi," Eleanor said. "You were just being your chivalrous self and I freaked out."

"Don't apologize. There's no need. I respect your wishes, baby. Honest."

"I wish I wasn't so scared."

"But you are. We can't change that. At least not right now. Now, let's just get home and enjoy our evening."

"You're the best," Eleanor said.

Randi just smiled and took Eleanor's hand.

They arrived at Eleanor's house and as soon as the door closed, Eleanor pushed Randi against it. She kissed her hard on her mouth. Randi responded in kind and finally broke the kiss.

"What was that for?" she said.

"I don't want you to doubt how I feel about you."

"I don't doubt it. I never do."

"Still, I wanted you to be sure."

"Well, thank you," Randi said. "You can remind me that way anytime you'd like."

"I'm glad you liked it."

"How about a repeat?"

Randi pulled her to her again.

They kissed for a few more minutes and this time it was Eleanor who pulled away.

"We have a perfectly comfortable couch to sit on and make out," she said.

"Make out? You make us sound like a couple of teenagers." Randi laughed.

Eleanor laughed, too.

"We act like it, don't we?"

"I suppose we do."

They moved to the couch where they continued their make out session until Randi could stand it no longer.

"I need to take you to bed. I need you out of these clothes. I need to have you. Like, now."

She stood and offered her hand to Eleanor, who this time took it. They walked to the bedroom, stripping off their clothes as they went. When they were in the room, Randi sat on the bed and stared up at Eleanor.

"My God, you're beautiful," she said. "Come here."

Eleanor moved closer until she stood right in front of her. Randi ran her hands down the length of her and watched as Eleanor shivered at her touch. She leaned forward and took a nipple in her mouth just as she reached a hand between her legs. She was wet and ready for her.

Randi dipped her fingers inside her as she continued to suckle at her breast. Eleanor had her hands on her shoulders and was gripping them for balance. Randi continued doing what she was until Eleanor cried out and fell against her.

"Please," Eleanor said. "I can't stand up any longer."

Randi withdrew her fingers and moved back on the bed. Eleanor lay next to her.

"What was that all about?" Eleanor said breathlessly.

"I needed you. I wanted you while you stood in front of me looking beautiful in your nakedness."

"Well, I'm glad you did. It felt amazing."

"Excellent."

"And now it's my turn. I won't make you stand up, though."

Eleanor felt the usual headiness she did when she looked at Randi's naked body. She was built so well and she was all Eleanor's. She vowed never to take her for granted. She kissed her and was rewarded with a dizzying kiss in return. She finally pulled away, lest she become too aroused to focus on Randi and her needs.

"You drive me crazy," she said.

"Good. Because I lose my mind when I'm around you."

Eleanor didn't know where to start. So much of Randi called to her, urged her to kiss and suck and nibble and touch. She finally decided she needed to taste her. She kissed down her body until she came to where her legs met. She slid between them and made herself comfortable. The familiar scent that was all Randi made her mouth water. She had to have her.

She took Randi's lips in her mouth and ran her tongue over them. They tasted divine. She lapped inside Randi and almost swooned at the feel of her. She finally moved her mouth to Randi's clit which she licked and sucked until she felt Randi's hand on the back of her head. She was sure she would suffocate, but she kept it up until Randi froze against her then collapsed on the bed and finally released her grip on Eleanor.

Eleanor climbed up next to Randi. She was filled with desire and needed Randi again. She kissed her hard and rubbed against her.

"So, I take it my baby needs more?" Randi said.

"Please."

Randi moved her fingers back inside Eleanor. Eleanor felt full. Just the way she liked it. She moved around and around and up and down, forcing Randi to touch all over her deep inside. Finally, Randi pressed her thumb into Eleanor's clit and Eleanor cried out again as she climaxed again and again.

Eleanor had finally had enough.

"Okay, okay. That was wonderful, but I think I'm through now."

She moved into Randi's arms and attempted to fall asleep. But she kept replaying the scene at the restaurant. Randi was just being polite, so why did it scare her so much? And how long was she going to make Randi wait to be able to be open and carefree about everything? These thoughts kept her up even after Randi was sound asleep. She told herself to turn her brain off and get some sleep, but it wasn't easy.

They slept late the following morning and Eleanor woke to Randi between her legs. She groaned a good morning and lay back, allowing herself to feel all there was to feel. She was getting close. So very close.

A phone rang.

"Shit," Randi muttered.

"What?"

"Work. I have to answer it."

Eleanor balled her fists in an effort to resolve some of the tension that had balled up inside her.

"Animal Control," Randi said into the phone.

She was silent for a few minutes.

"How big? Where?"

More silence.

"Okay. We'll be right there."

She hung up and dialed.

"Johnny?" she said. "We got a call. An alligator. Can you meet me there?"

She gave him the address, then hung up.

"Sorry for that coitus interruptus," Randi said.

"Me, too. But work is work."

"You wanna go with?" Randi said as she pulled on her uniform.

"May I?"

"Of course."

Eleanor quickly dressed and they were out the door in minutes. The drove to the outskirts of town and finally stopped at a nice house sitting on a half an acre or so. Randi pointed to Johnny's truck.

"Oh, good. Johnny's here already."

Randi got out and went up to talk to Johnny, whose window was down.

"You been up to the door yet?" she said.

"Nope. I've been waiting for you."

"Okay. Let's go."

Eleanor sat in the truck and watched them go to the door. She saw a tall, slim woman answer it. The three of them spoke briefly and Randi came back to the car.

"It's around back. We're going to follow the driveway back there."

"Sounds good."

Eleanor was nervous and excited. She'd seen Randi do this before, so she knew she was capable. But still, she was nervous. What if something went wrong? She told herself to relax. This was Randi's job, after all.

Johnny was in the Animal Control truck behind them. He pulled up even and rolled down his passenger side window.

"Do you see him?" he said.

"Yeah. Just over there at one o'clock."

Johnny looked where Randi was pointing.

"Got it," he said. "You ready?"

"Yep. You want face or body?"

"Randi, you know every time you give me the choice, I'm going to take the body."

"Fair enough."

Randi turned to Eleanor.

"You don't get out of this truck, okay? No matter what happens."

"No worries there. I'm not about to get anywhere near an alligator."

"Good answer."

Randi climbed out and she and Johnny got the tape and other implements needed to catch the gator. They walked over to it and it opened its mouth wide and chomped down mere feet from Randi.

"Careful," Eleanor whispered in the truck.

Randi tried again but met with the same result. She moved a little closer. Eleanor wanted to close her eyes but couldn't. Something was making her watch the spectacle before her.

The alligator opened its jaw wide again then snapped it shut. Randi grabbed hold of the jaw and squeezed. Johnny wrapped its jaw shut with the tape and together, they managed to pick the creature up and put it in the back of the work truck.

Randi and Eleanor followed Johnny the short distance to the Everglades where Eleanor watched, terrified, as Randi and Johnny unbound the alligator and released it into the wild.

Randi came back to the truck.

"Johnny wants to go get breakfast. You up for that?"

"Yeah. That sounds great.'

"You do know he's going to pepper me with questions once he gets me alone?"

"What? Oh, crap. I didn't really think this excursion through, did I?"

"What do you want me to tell him?" Randi said. "I can say you were just a one-night stand. I can tell him you are a friend and we were having coffee. You make the call."

"I suppose you should tell him we're friends. I hate to ask you to lie."

"I don't want to lie. But I respect your wishes. If you want me to tell him we were just out for coffee, I will."

"Thank you, Randi."

## Chapter Sixteen

Randi wasn't happy. She didn't want to lie to Johnny. Besides, she figured Johnny knew her so well, he'd see right through it. But this is how it had to be. She wished she could figure out a way to gently bring Eleanor out of the closet. But she couldn't. It had to be Eleanor's decision and Eleanor's doing. All Randi could do was wait and try to be as patient as she could be.

They arrived at the diner and Randi instinctively opened Eleanor's door for her. She refrained, however, from offering her a hand down. Eleanor climbed down a little gracelessly, but she made it.

Randi slid her hands in her pockets as they strode over to meet up with Johnny.

"All in a day's work, eh, Randi?" he said.

"Yeah. Right. Johnny, this is a friend of mine, Eleanor. We were out having coffee when the call came in so I brought her with me."

Johnny grinned and extended his hand.

"Friend, huh? Well, any friend of Randi's is a friend of mine."

Eleanor took his hand and shook.

"It's a pleasure to meet you. I've heard a lot about you."

Johnny arched an eyebrow toward Randi but didn't say anything.

They went inside and placed their orders.

"You seem really familiar to me, Eleanor," Johnny said. "Have we met before?"

"Not exactly. But you and Randi rescued an alligator from my yard not long ago."

"Oh, yeah. I remember you now. Well, great to see you again."

Eleanor was silent most of the meal while Johnny and Randi chatted away.

"So, how long do you think we'll have jobs?" Johnny said.

"I'm not really worried about it. I mean, closing the office on weekends will save some money. I don't think they'll be letting anyone go. I, for one, am glad I get to simply be on call on the weekend. It works for me."

"Yeah. It lets you have coffee and stuff."

"Exactly." Randi fought the urge to laugh. She knew Johnny didn't believe their story for a minute. She was dreading being alone with him. She knew he'd be tenacious about getting to the truth.

Breakfast ended and Johnny shook hands with both of them.

"I'll see you on Monday," he said to Randi, then turned to Eleanor. "It was great seeing you again."

"See ya," Randi said and she turned to hold the door open for Eleanor. She was about to help her up, but caught Johnny watching them through his rearview mirror. She went around and got in, leaving Eleanor to fend for herself.

When they were in the truck and their doors were closed, Eleanor was the first to speak.

"See? That wasn't so bad. He thinks we were having coffee."

"I'm not so sure about that, baby, but we'll see."

"You think he knows there's something between us?"

"I wouldn't be surprised. Look, I have a bit of a reputation, you know? Or, I did, rather. I guess I still do. No one knows about us, so people still think I'm a player. I just don't want him to think you were just another nameless woman who happened to be in my bed."

"Were you in the habit of taking your playmates out on calls with you?"

"I wasn't in the habit of bedding women when I was on call."

"Ah. I see."

"I'm not really comfortable talking about my past," Randi said.

"No? Why not?"

"I'm not really proud of it now that I have you."

Eleanor took her hand.

"But it's part of what makes you you. You wouldn't be able to be with me if you hadn't gone through those millions of women before me."

"Millions?" Randi laughed.

"Strictly guesstimating."

"I see."

They were back at the house and this time, Randi helped Eleanor out of the truck.

"You know, I'm not helpless," Eleanor said. "But I've gotten so used to you helping me, I almost fell getting out at the restaurant."

"Sorry. I wasn't sure how much chivalry would make things too obvious."

"It's okay. I managed."

"Yeah you did."

"So," Randi said. "Shall we pick up where we left off this morning?"

"That sounds wonderful."

They went to the bedroom where Randi pulled Eleanor to her and kissed her passionately while she deftly removed her clothes. When Eleanor was naked, Randi quickly stripped and stood flesh against flesh with Eleanor.

"I love the feel of your body against mine," she said.

"Mm. Yeah. Your skin feels amazing. You're so warm and inviting."

"Actually, I'm hot. Hot for your body."

"Then take me."

Randi sat on the bed and pulled Eleanor down next to her. They kissed some more then Randi lay down and moved over to let Eleanor do the same. She ran her hand over Eleanor's curves then kissed down her body and finally settled in between her legs. She stretched her tongue to lap along Eleanor's silky walls then moved it to her clit. She licked over it for a few minutes and Eleanor cried out her name.

Randi wasn't through. Eleanor tasted wonderful and Randi couldn't help herself. She licked over the length of her again and again until Eleanor came over and over. Randi finally kissed back up her body, stopping at a pert nipple. She took it in her mouth and ran her tongue over it until Eleanor climaxed again.

"I don't think I'll ever get tired of making love to you," Randi said as she took her place next to Eleanor. She held her in her arms and fought the urge to fall back asleep. They had work to do and she needed to be up for it. She kissed Eleanor on the head. "You about ready to hit the backyard?"

"After that? I'm like a wet noodle here."

Randi laughed. It made her feel good to be able to do that to Eleanor. She climbed over her and sat on the edge of the bed.

"I'll get coffee going," she said. "You get up when you're ready."

She walked over to the dresser and pulled out an old pair of jeans and a faded T-shirt. She went out to the kitchen and started the coffee. She sat at the kitchen table and reflected on her life, her past and present. She had come a long way in a very short time. One minute she'd been a freewheeling, fast-loving woman on the prowl. Now she was completely domesticated. She'd thought she'd miss those prowling days, but she didn't. She had all she needed in Eleanor. It was a strange feeling, but one that made her smile.

Eleanor padded into the kitchen to join Randi. She was still in a state of post coital euphoria, but knew Randi was right. They had things to do. She poured them each a cup of coffee and sat down across from Randi at the table.

"Penny for your thoughts?" she said.

"Just thinking how happy I am."

"Really? You don't miss a constant stream of different women in your bed?"

"Not a bit. I have you in my bed. That's all I need."

Eleanor felt all warm and fuzzy. She had the constant fear that Randi would need to get back to her womanizing ways. After all, Eleanor was only one woman and Randi was used to a smorgasbord. She was grateful she was able to keep her happy.

"So, about that yard?" Randi said.

"One more cup of coffee and I'll be ready."

They finished their coffee and went to the garage to get the tools they would need.

"Are you sure your arms are up for this?" Eleanor said. She looked at the still red lines where the mama cat had scratched Randi.

"Sure I am. Let's do this."

"Whatever happened to the kitties you rescued?" Eleanor asked. "Are they all alone at the office?"

"Oh, no. Someone from the shelter picked them up. They'll take care of them now."

"Good. I was worried."

"No need to worry. Now, let's get to work."

They spent the next two hours pulling shrubs and dragging them to the middle of the yard. It was back breaking work and Eleanor was hot and sweaty and needed a break.

"You ready for some lunch?" she said.

"Sounds good to me."

Eleanor made them sandwiches which they washed down with beer. After their break, Eleanor wasn't too enthusiastic about getting back to work.

"Shall we call it a day?" she said as she opened her second beer.

"No." Randi laughed. "There's work to be done and we may as well finish it."

"But I really don't want to."

"You really do. You don't want to leave it half done until next weekend, do you?"

"Ugh," Eleanor said. She knew Randi was right. She was tired and sore, and she knew Randi had to feel worse. If Randi was willing to keep going, there was no reason she shouldn't be.

"Come on, now," Randi said. "Let's finish pulling the bushes. I'll take them around to the front tomorrow, so we don't have to do that today."

They worked another few hours and got all the dead shrubs piled in the center of the yard. Eleanor stepped back and looked at the pile of brown. They'd been successful in their endeavors. The whole left side of the yard was open now and she would be able to plant new plants and flowers and make the yard hers.

"How are you doing?" Eleanor asked Randi.

"I'm fine. Sore, but fine."

"How are your arms?"

Randi held up her arms and showed off many new scratches to go along with the mama kitty's.

"Oh, man. You took a beating."

"You didn't exactly get away unscathed."

Eleanor looked at her arms and saw several crisscross patterns cut across her.

"Oh, well. I'll survive," she said.

"As will I."

"So, what do you say? You want to take a shower and go get a steak?'

"Sounds wonderful. Lead the way."

They stopped at the laundry room to deposit their dirty clothes in the washer, then made their way to the bathroom. While they waited for the water to heat up, Randi pulled Eleanor close.

"You're so sexy. Even when you're covered in dirt," Randi said.

"Ugh. I don't feel very sexy."

"Well, trust me. You are. Now, let's get you in that shower so I can run my hands all over your body."

They got in the shower, and true to her word, Randi lathered up her hands and washed every inch of Eleanor's body. Her touch sent tingles through Eleanor. She needed more. Craved more. She spread her legs wide and braced herself against Randi as Randi slid her soapy hands between them. She touched all the right spots, and in no time, Eleanor was fighting to maintain her balance as the orgasms cascaded over her.

They rinsed off and dried, then Eleanor took Randi by the hand. She was determined to return the favor. She took her to the bedroom and eased her back on the bed. She buried her face between her legs and used her tongue to please her. Randi took no time to get off. She must have been as ready as Eleanor was.

"You ready for some food now?" Eleanor said.

"Oh, my God, yes. I'm famished."

"We'd better get dressed, then."

Eleanor chose a long skirt and white blouse that she knew showed off her cleavage.

"You look devourable," Randi said.

Eleanor blushed.

"Thank you," she said.

Randi was wearing cargo shorts and a black golf shirt.

"You look very handsome," Eleanor said.

"Thanks. Let's get going."

They held hands in the truck in silence.

"What are you thinking about?" Eleanor said.

"Just thinking. You know, we keep showing up at these restaurants together. This is a small town, baby. People will talk."

"What are we supposed to do?" said Eleanor. "Never leave the house?"

"I don't know. I'm not trying to start a fight, baby. You asked what I was thinking and I'm telling you."

"I know you're not trying to start a fight. I'm sorry I got defensive. You're right, though. People will talk. I don't like that."

"It's the way of the world."

"Yeah. I know."

They arrived at the restaurant and the silence between them was thick. They were seated at a table.

"So, are you not speaking to me now?" Randi said.

"What? Oh, my God, no. Of course I am. Just lost in thought is all."

"Why don't we talk about it some more?"

"There's nothing more to say, really. And I don't want to talk about it in a public restaurant anyway."

"Fair enough. Well, promise me you'll relax and enjoy dinner?"

"I'll certainly try. A little wine will help, for sure." She smiled.

"Good. Then we'll order a carafe and split it."

"Sounds wonderful."

They sipped their wine and chatted about the week to come.

"So," Randi said. "Is it going to be that bad going back to work Monday?"

Eleanor rolled her eyes.

"It's going to be horrible. These kids have been out of school for a week. It's going to take at least that long to get them back in the swing of things."

"I'm sorry to hear that. Aren't your kids the brainiacs or something?"

"Yes. They're the brightest of the bright. But they're still kids."

"I guess that's true."

"And they were antsy as all heck before vacation. I anticipate it being hard to get them to settle down after it."

Dinner came and they ate in quiet conversation. Eleanor really enjoyed her time with Randi. She loved their lovemaking, of course, but there was so much more. She enjoyed being out with her. She liked sitting on the couch and drinking with her. She just really liked Randi. But Randi had been right. Soon, people would start to talk. What would she do then?

Eleanor paid for dinner and they went home, holding hands as Randi drove.

"Thank you again for all you did for me today," Eleanor said.

"No problem. I'm happy to help. And I'll haul it all to the front yard tomorrow. Just like last weekend."

"Look at it this way," Eleanor said. "At least next weekend we'll be able to do something besides tear up my yard."

"True."

They got home and each grabbed a drink and they sat on the couch together.

"What am I going to do when people start talking?" Eleanor said.

"I don't know, baby. That's your issue. You have to resolve it."

"I wish things could just stay the way they are."

"It would be nice, but I just don't see it happening," Randi said.

"Hm." Eleanor snuggled close to Randi. "Well, I'll just cross that bridge when I come to it, I guess."

"That sounds reasonable."

They finished their drinks and made their way to the bedroom.

Randi took her time with Eleanor, loving her softly and slowly. Eleanor was about to crawl out of her skin by the time Randi let her come. She returned the favor and was pleased, as usual, when Randi called her name.

Randi wrapped her arms around her and held her close. Eleanor heard Randi's breathing turn to soft snores, but sleep eluded her. Her mind was full of unpleasant thoughts and her stomach churned in fear.

Would she be strong enough to stand by Randi if people started talking? Only time would tell.

## CHAPTER SEVENTEEN

Randi woke before Eleanor and let her sleep. She hadn't heard her fall asleep the night before. Eleanor almost always fell asleep first. Randi often listened to her steady breathing to help herself get to sleep. But that hadn't happened the previous night. She didn't know how late Eleanor had lain there, so she opted to let her sleep in. She made coffee and sat at the table comparing her life with Eleanor's.

In theory, they were sharing their lives now, but in reality, each of them had a different life than the other. Randi was out, loud, and proud with no qualms about it. Eleanor had the closet door closed so tight Randi worried she may suffocate in there. Oh, well. There was nothing she could do about it.

She poured her second cup of coffee and went out to look at the yard. She didn't hear Eleanor come out there. She didn't even know she was there until she felt her arms around her waist.

"Hey, baby," Randi said.

"Hey. Why'd you let me sleep so late?"

"Late? What's late? You haven't missed anything yet."

"No. I see that. Come on in. I need coffee."

They sipped their coffee and made their plans for the day. Randi would pull all the dead shrubs to the front curb, then they would go plant shopping.

Eleanor was beside herself in excitement. She was really looking forward to making the yard her own and not the shadow of its former glory.

Once Randi was done, they took a shower together where Randi took Eleanor to several orgasms, then dried off, dressed, and headed out to the nursery.

Their baskets were full of flowering plants and greenery, as well as some annual and perennial flowers to add around the edges.

"How much do you think we'll get done today?" Randi said.

"I have no idea. But I want to get as much done as possible, obviously."

They were interrupted when a woman called to Eleanor.

"Eleanor! Eleanor! Over here."

Randi looked around the plants in her basket to see a woman about their age, with graying hair waving at Eleanor.

"Martina!" Eleanor called. She moved her basket over to where the woman stood. Randi stood briefly, unsure whether to follow. Then she decided she may as well. "How have you been? How was your break?"

"Oh, it was wonderful," Martina said. "We had more fun on that houseboat. I'm sorry you couldn't be there the whole time."

"Me, too. I had fun while I was there."

Martina seemed to finally have noticed Randi standing there, listening to their conversation. Eleanor seemed to just have remembered she was there.

"Oh, Martina," she said. "This is my friend, Randi. She's helping me with my yard."

"Nice to meet you, Randi."

"Likewise." Though Randi wasn't entirely sure she was happy to meet Martina. An uncomfortable feeling crept over her. She was feeling jealous again. How was she supposed to maintain a relationship if she felt jealous every time she met one of Eleanor's friends?

"It was good seeing you," Eleanor was saying. She motioned to the two baskets. "We need to get these in the ground. I'll see you tomorrow."

They paid for their treasures and loaded up the truck with them. When Randi had started up the truck and was making her way out of the parking lot, Eleanor reached for her hand. Randi let her take it, but left her hand limp.

"What's up?" Eleanor said.

"Did you sleep with her?"

"What? Who? Martina? Heck no. I don't even know if she's a lesbian."

"She is," Randi said. She glanced sideways at Eleanor. "Don't you have a gaydar?"

"I guess not. At least not a very good one. She was so nice to me when I first moved here. I wondered at times if she was interested, but she didn't seem to be, so I chalked it up to kindness."

"And that could be it," Randi said. "She could have just been being nice." She squeezed Eleanor's hand. "Sorry I got so jealous."

"It's okay. I kind of like you being the jealous type."

"Yeah? Well, I don't. One of these days I'm going to meet the woman you slept with and I just hope I can hold it together."

"What?" Eleanor said. "You wouldn't *fight* her, would you?"

"I don't know. I just get so angry. But I'm an adult, so I'm sure I'd be able to behave. But know it would be hard."

"I can accept that. Let me ask you a question. Have I ever met any of the women you've slept with?"

Randi thought of Veronica from the mini-mart.

"Yeah. At least one that I know of."

"Okay. And I'm okay with that. I'm sure there are many more that I haven't, but the chances of bumping into one of your former playmates is pretty good in a town this size. And I'm okay with that. It was all before us. That's what you need to remember."

"I'll try, baby. I just got all balled up inside watching you two talk."

"I'm sorry. I wish I'd have known."

"It's okay. Like I say, it's my problem."

They pulled into the driveway.

"And now, we get to forget about all this and work on making the yard a little paradise," Eleanor said.

"Sounds good to me."

Randi carried the plants and Eleanor carried the flowers out to the backyard. Randi dug the holes and poured the topsoil for the big plants while Eleanor planted border flowers. They worked until

Randi's back was about to break. Fortunately, she didn't have to throw in the butch towel.

"I'm wiped out," Eleanor said. "I can hardly move. Do you mind if we call it a day?"

"Are you sure?" Randi said. She wasn't sure she could even stand up straight at that point.

"I'm positive. Come on. Let's go inside and take a shower.

"Okay," Randi said. "If you're sure."

She dropped the shovel where she stood and didn't even bother to pick it up. She was so sore, she didn't even know if she'd be able to take care of Eleanor in the shower, though the thought was so tempting, she felt her boxers dampen.

They deposited their filthy clothes in the washing machine and headed to the bathroom. Randi ached all over. She longed to take a hot bath rather than a shower. It would help ease the tension in her muscles.

"Hey, Randi," Eleanor said. "Would you mind showering alone? I'd really like to soak in the tub."

"I'd like to join you in the tub," Randi said.

"I don't think there's enough room."

Randi knew the disappointment showed on her face.

"Okay," she said. "I'll take a shower."

She stood there, letting the hot water beat away at her sore muscles. She got out and toweled off, never taking her gaze off Eleanor in the tub.

"You want some help getting clean?" she said.

"Sure. You want to bathe my back for me?"

"Then do I get to bathe your front?"

Eleanor smiled at her and the whole room lit up. She loved Eleanor's smile, especially the smile that said everything Randi was feeling.

"Of course," Eleanor said.

Eleanor turned in the tub so Randi could reach her back. She was stiff and sore, but the bath had eased her tired muscles somewhat. She relaxed and let Randi wash her back. It was erotic the way Randi would squeeze the bath sponge and let trickles of water run down her back. It felt so good to have her rub her back and shoulders with sudsy hands.

"Okay, baby," Randi said. "Your back is clean. Let's see that front."

Eleanor rotated in the tub and sat there, breasts exposed for Randi.

"Ah, yes," Randi said. "You're so beautiful. You take my breath away."

Eleanor felt the warmth start at her chest and creep upward. She hoped the heat and steam in the bathroom would hide it from Randi's prying eyes. Randi took the soap between her hands and lathered them well. She placed her sudsy hands on Eleanor's breasts. Eleanor drew a sharp intake of breath as her body immediately responded to her touch.

Randi knew just how to touch her. She was magic with her hands. As soon as her fingers found her nipples, Eleanor knew it would be useless to resist. She rested her back against the opposite side of the tub and arched toward Randi. Randi teased and tugged on her until Eleanor could hold back no longer. She closed her eyes and let the orgasms wash over her, one after another. When she finally returned to earth, she stared at Randi, who was grinning wickedly.

"Thanks," Eleanor said. "I guess I needed that."

"I know I did."

"Good. Now, how about handing me a towel so I can get out of here. The water's getting cold."

Randi held the towel open and Eleanor stepped into it. As Randi rubbed the towel over Eleanor, Eleanor's body came to life again. She was filled with a new desire. It coursed through her and overwhelmed her. She wrapped her arms around Randi and pulled her close. She kissed her hard on the mouth.

"We need to go to bed," Eleanor said.

"Right behind you."

Eleanor fell into bed and pulled Randi on top of her.

"Easy, there, baby. I'm going to crush you."

"Never. I like the feel of your body on mine," Eleanor said.

Randi lowered herself so she covered Eleanor. She ground her pelvis into her. Eleanor was going crazy with want. She spread her legs and Randi slipped one of her own between them. Eleanor pressed into it, needing contact. Randi moved it against her, giving her what she needed. Eleanor cried out as she came again.

She was lying there, breathing heavily when Randi kissed down her body to taste the orgasm she'd just had. Eleanor pressed the top of Randi's head, urging her lower. When Randi was between her legs, Eleanor put her head back and closed her eyes. She focused only on Randi and what she was doing between her legs. Randi took her to several more orgasms before Eleanor patted her head.

"Okay. That's it. I've got nothing left."

Randi kissed up her body and lay holding her for a few moments.

"You're such a stud," Eleanor said.

Randi laughed.

"I don't know about all that."

"Mm. I do."

Eleanor lay next to Randi and couldn't resist her naked body. She ran her hand over her, stopping to cup her small breasts before moving it down over her taut belly. She slipped it between her legs and found her warm and wet.

"Someone's a bit excited," she said.

"Making love to you always does that to me."

"I like it."

She moved her fingers over Randi's slick clit to her center. She slid her fingers inside her and stroked her, urging her closer and closer to the brink. Soon, Randi could take no more and Eleanor felt her clamp down on her fingers and she cried out her name.

But Eleanor wasn't through. As soon as she could draw her fingers out, she did, and moved them to Randi's swollen clit. She rubbed it until Randi arched into her, called her name, and collapsed back onto the bed.

Eleanor climbed up next to Randi and they slept for an hour. When Eleanor woke, Randi was between her legs again.

"What are you doing?"

"I can't get enough of you."

Eleanor didn't complain, just rode out the multiple orgasms Randi gave her. When Randi was through, she lay next to Eleanor again.

"I'm starving. Let's go get some food."

"It's a good thing sex burns so many calories," Eleanor said. "Or I'd be as big as a house with all the food we're eating out."

"You've got an awesome metabolism," Randi said. "I'm not worried about you ballooning up or anything."

"Well, that's good to know."

They dressed and headed to Tony's for Italian food. The waitress that seated them made friendly conversation.

"You two are becoming regulars here," she said.

Randi laughed and Eleanor's whole body tightened. It was happening. She tried to think of some casual way of saying they were just friends, but couldn't. Her mood was gone.

## Chapter Eighteen

Eleanor was so happy when Friday rolled around. It had been a tough week, as she'd known it would be. The kids were restless after the break and the homework they'd turned in had been subpar at best.

Randi had been patient with Eleanor. She watched TV while Eleanor graded homework. She said she'd never really understood how hard it was to be a teacher. Eleanor had smiled her appreciation. The only things that kept her going was the promise of seeing Randi after work and spending their nights making love.

Friday afternoon, she dismissed her last class and collapsed into her chair from exhaustion. She really hoped the next week would be better. She hoped the kids would calm down and settle into their normal routine.

Ron popped his head in her room.

"You okay?" he said.

"Yeah. Just wiped out. What a week. How was yours?"

"About the same. I could use a drink. Meet you at the Bull?"

"You know it."

Eleanor and Randi had talked that morning about the Bull. Randi had promised to come by after work. So, Eleanor drove to the Bull and ordered her usual. She walked over to the table of teachers and her stomach knotted up. There was Haven. Why did she have to be there? She was the last person Eleanor needed to see at that moment. Then, she told herself she was being ridiculous. Haven had been nothing but friendly on the houseboat. They'd had a one-night stand. That was it. Eleanor had to put on her big girl panties and deal with it.

Everyone said their hellos when Eleanor walked up. She sat in a chair next to Martina and across from Haven.

"You look exhausted," Martina said.

"Why, thank you." Eleanor laughed. "Rough week. How was yours?"

"Oh, you know. Rowdy kids with zero attention spans. I sent two kids to the office this week."

"And yours?" Eleanor forced herself to look at Haven, who looked back with a knowing gaze.

"I'm a substitute. I never expect kids to behave," she said.

The conversation turned to what everyone had done over the break. Eleanor was having fun. She was relaxed and enjoying herself. Soon, people moved to the pool table and the games were on.

Eleanor had lost track of time and was surprised to hear Martina.

"Say, Eleanor, isn't that a friend of yours over there?"

Eleanor looked over to the bar and saw Randi leaning against it. She was looking all dapper in her cargo shorts and golf shirt. Her hair was still wet. Obviously, she'd just gotten out of the shower. Eleanor felt desire creep over her. All she wanted to do was take Randi home and have her way with her.

"Yes. That's Randi," Eleanor said out loud.

"Invite her over," Martina said.

"Are you sure?"

"Of course."

Eleanor excused herself from the group and crossed the bar to where Randi stood.

"You look wonderful," Eleanor said.

"Thanks. So do you."

"They've asked me to invite you to join us."

"Is that what you want?"

"Sure. There's no harm in it."

She led them back to the group. Martina was to her left.

"You remember Martina, don't you? We met her at the nursery last weekend?"

"Of course," Randi said. "Nice to see you again."

The others were caught up in their games and didn't seem to notice that a newcomer had approached them. Until Haven walked up.

"Haven," Randi said coolly.

"Hello, Randi. What are you doing here?"

Martina and Eleanor exchanged glances.

"She's a friend of Eleanor's," Martina said.

Haven looked from Randi to Eleanor and back again.

"Oh, yeah?" she said.

Eleanor didn't know what to do. She was worried there might be a fight the way the two women were staring at each other.

"Yeah. She's my friend, so I invited her over. We were just leaving though."

"Don't bother. I'm gone."

The group had quieted and all watched the exchange. Eleanor didn't know what kind of past the two had, but was certain she'd find out. Everyone watched Haven leave. Eleanor set down her own glass.

"Maybe we should go, too," she said.

Martina put her hand on Eleanor's arm.

"You don't have to," she said.

"I think it would be best. See you all next week."

Randi finished her beer and set her empty bottle on the table before following Eleanor outside.

"You okay?" Eleanor said.

"I will be. I just didn't expect to see her there."

Eleanor noticed her hands were balled into fists. She hit the hood of her car.

"Damn it," she said. "She's the one you slept with isn't she?"

Eleanor stood silently, unsure of how to respond. She didn't want to lie, but Randi was clearly upset. She nodded.

"Yes."

"I should have guessed. She's a teacher. She'd have a way to meet you and if she's anything, she's a master at seduction."

Eleanor struggled. For some strange reason, she felt the urge to defend Haven.

"Randi, I'm a big girl. And it takes two to tango."

"Yeah, but you didn't know what you were up against. She's like a spider. Once she has you in her web, you're a goner. And you were new to town. You were easy prey. Damn her anyway!"

Eleanor reached out and took Randi's hand. Randi pulled away as if bitten.

"What can I do to make this better?" Eleanor said.

"You can't."

"There's more to this. Sure, you're pissed that I slept with her. I get that. But we've talked about this. It was before us so doesn't matter."

"Haven is a raging bitch. I hate her fucking guts and hate that she seduced you."

"How do you know her? How come you hate her so much?"

"I was in a relationship once. Years ago. We'd been together six years. In waltzes Haven and takes my partner away from me. My partner couldn't resist her charm. She told me they'd never slept together or even kissed before we split up, but I don't know that I believe her. Anyway, Haven had her in her grasp and there was nothing I could do to change her mind. Haven kept her for a year. A measly year, before she dumped her like yesterday's trash. My ex was crushed. I've hated Haven since she took the love of my life and then broke her heart."

"Why didn't you and your ex get back together?"

"I couldn't have taken her back. I had my pride. Besides, she wasn't interested. She recoiled into herself. I see her around town once in a while. She still looks horrible, like a shell of who she used to be."

"I'm sorry, Randi. I'm so sorry."

Randi shook her head. She tried to shake off the feeling of anger and betrayal she felt. It had all come back to her. All the feelings of hatred and anguish she'd felt when Haven had first stolen her woman. And now Eleanor. She didn't blame Eleanor, though. She couldn't. She needed to pull herself together.

"It's not your fault. And I don't blame you for being sucked in by her. She's just that way."

"I was new to town and hadn't been with anyone for so long. I guess I just felt needed. And I went for it."

"That's how she works. She can smell weakness. And clearly it was a weak moment in your life. You're not the type for one-night stands. I know that. I'm surprised she let you walk away unscathed, though."

"How do you mean?"

"I mean," Randi said. "I'm surprised she didn't promise you the moon and then renege."

"Oh, no. We were both clear on the fact that it was for one night only."

"Good."

Randi moved forward and pulled Eleanor into a full body hug.

"I'm sorry," she said. "I'm sorry I freaked out."

"It's okay. I don't blame you."

They stood like that in the parking lot for a few minutes before Randi released her hold and stepped back.

"We should get going," she said.

"Yeah, we should."

"You up for steak tonight?" Randi said.

"Sure. I'll meet you there."

Randi used the time in her truck to try to lose the anger that still flowed through her. She had Eleanor. No one else did and no one was going to take her away. Least of all Haven. She shuddered as disgust washed over her once more. Why had she seen Haven? She could have gone the rest of her life without laying eyes on that lowlife scum.

Calm down, she told herself. Calm down. It finally worked and she was in a decent space when she pulled into the parking lot next to Eleanor. She got out of the truck and hugged her again.

"Are you going to be okay?" Eleanor said. "We can just go home if you'd like."

"No. I'm fine. All that anger left me starving. Let's go eat."

They walked inside where the waitress smiled in recognition and took them to a back table.

"I feel like we sat here last time," Randi said.

"I think we sit here every time. Like it's our table or something."

"That's kinda cool, don't you think?"

Eleanor was silent. Obviously, she didn't think it was cool. She had to know people were going to notice if they kept going out together. How many times had they talked about it? Randi fought to keep her temper in check. She fought the urge to lay into Eleanor about it. Her nerves were still too raw from seeing Haven. Eleanor didn't deserve to bear the brunt of them.

They sipped their wine and waited for the dinner to come. The silence between them was deafening. Randi had to break it.

"So, how was school today?"

"Not bad. Not great, but not bad. I'm just so glad this week is over."

"I bet. You work so hard. You deserve a raise."

This got a smile out of Eleanor.

"Thank you. But we don't teach to get rich. We teach to mold young minds. Although this week I've felt like the minds were more filled with mold than I was molding them."

Randi laughed.

"That bad, huh?"

"Yeah. Don't get me wrong. I teach a great group of kids. But, man, do they have a hard time settling back in after a week off."

"I bet. I'd do the same, I'm sure."

"True. I wasn't exactly chomping at the bit to get back myself," Eleanor said.

"No. You had a good week off."

"That I did."

They finished dinner and drove home. Once inside, Randi grabbed a beer and poured Eleanor a glass of wine. She felt drained after her emotional outburst earlier and had actually considered just going home to her own place. But in the end, she couldn't. She had to be with Eleanor. She was the stabilizing factor in her life. And she needed her. Physically and emotionally, she needed to be with Eleanor.

She handed the glass of wine to her and sat next to her on the couch. She rested her head on the back of the couch and exhaled loudly.

"That good, huh?" Eleanor said.

"What an evening."

"At least dinner was good."

"That's true."

"And now we're home. Alone. Just how I like to be with you."

Randi put her arm around Eleanor and squeezed her.

"I do like our little sanctuary here," she said.

Eleanor took a sip out of her wine.

"We've got a good thing, don't you think?"

"Sure I do," Randi said. Although, she thought it could be better. She'd much prefer it if she could take Eleanor out with her to the club dancing. What difference did it make being seen at restaurants and being seen at the club? It was obvious to anyone they were a couple.

"I'm so happy you came into my life."

"I'm so happy being in your life."

"You know I'm yours, right, Randi? I belong to you and only to you and nothing or no one is going to change that."

"I know this, baby. I know this."

Randi set her beer down and turned to face Eleanor.

"I need you. I need to claim you tonight. I need to brand you as mine and mine alone."

"Do it. I'm ready."

They rose and wordlessly made their way to the bedroom. Randi sat on the bed and watched appreciatively as Eleanor undressed herself. When she was naked, Randi pulled her to herself and held her tight. She never wanted to let go.

Eleanor pulled away.

"Your turn," she said.

Randi stood and quickly stripped. When she, too, was naked, she pulled Eleanor to her again.

"Your skin is on fire," Randi said.

"It's what you do to me. You start a fever deep inside me. It radiates out and threatens to consume me."

"Good. I'm going to consume you now. I'm going to take you and make you forget any woman you've ever been with."

Randi meant it, too. She still had the sour taste of Haven in her brain. She didn't want Eleanor to think of her ever again. She lay on the bed and scooted over so Eleanor could join her. She ran her hand over each inch of Eleanor's body, as if committing it to memory for the first time.

She lowered her head and gently tugged on a hard nipple. She pulled it deeper into her mouth and ran her tongue lovingly over it. She kept at it, licking and sucking, until Eleanor called out her name. That's right. It was her name on Eleanor's lips. Eleanor belonged to her.

She moved her mouth lower, nipping and sucking at Eleanor's belly. She was leaving marks, but didn't care. No one would see them but the two of them. She finally reached the spot where Eleanor's legs met. She climbed between and gazed at the beauty that was all Eleanor. She ran her tongue over the length of her before dipping it inside and lapping every inch she could reach. Eleanor squirmed on the bed. Randi licked back to her clit, which she took between her lips and ran her tongue over. Eleanor pressed her hand into the back of Randi's head, but Randi didn't stop. She couldn't. She had to make her come again and again.

Randi succeeded. Soon, Eleanor lay breathless on the bed. Randi moved up next to her and kissed her gently.

"I love you," she said.

Eleanor rolled over and looked Randi in the eye.

"Those are big words," she said.

"They are. But I mean them. And I want you to know that."

Eleanor leaned forward and kissed Randi.

"I love you, too."

## Chapter Nineteen

The next few weeks passed in easy routine. Days were spent at work and nights were spent grading papers and spending time with Randi. Until one Thursday evening when Randi answered her phone.

"Hello?" she said.

She was silent for several moments.

"Okay. No. I'm going down. I'll fly down tomorrow. No. It's not up for debate. I'll see you tomorrow."

Eleanor crossed the room and placed her hand on Randi's arm. "What's going on? Is everything okay?"

"No. My baby sister was in a car wreck. She's not doing well. I need to call the boss and let him know I won't be in until Monday at the earliest.

As Randi went into the bedroom to make her calls, Eleanor reflected that she really didn't know that much about her. She had no idea how many siblings she had or what their names were. It had never seemed important, she reasoned. But clearly it was. She wondered what else she didn't know about Randi.

Randi came out of the room and grabbed a beer.

"So, I'll be gone for a few days."

"Yeah. I got that. I'm really sorry, Randi."

"Yeah. Me, too."

"So," Eleanor said as she poured herself a glass of wine. "How many kids are in your family?"

"Four of us. I'm the oldest. My baby sister is only twenty-four."

"I hope she's going to be okay."

"Me, too. But for now, it doesn't look good."

Eleanor took Randi's hand. She felt so helpless.

"I'd better go pack," Randi said. She pulled her hand away and went back into the bedroom.

Eleanor was at a loss. She didn't know what to do.

"Is there anything I can do to help?" she said as she entered the bedroom.

"Yeah. You can run to the mini-mart and pick up some more beer. If you don't mind."

"I don't mind at all."

She grabbed her purse and headed out the door. She arrived to find the woman she'd first seen Randi flirting with working the register. She tensed up but reasoned she was being ridiculous. Even if they had slept together, it was none of her business.

She picked up two twelve-packs and made her way to the counter.

"You're Randi's girlfriend, aren't you?" the woman said.

"What?" Eleanor was stupefied. Where had this woman gotten that idea? How could she possibly have known?

"I've seen you in the truck a few times when Randi runs in to buy beer. We figured she's seeing someone since she hasn't been to the club in a while. And I just guessed it was you."

"Nope. We're just friends. Sorry to disappoint you."

She paid and left. Her stomach was churning when she got to the car. She thought she might get sick. She hoped she had played it cool enough, but knew she hadn't. She was curt, even rude to the woman. Life had been so good for so long. She'd really hoped they'd been flying under the radar. She wondered now who else had noticed.

She got home and put the beer in the refrigerator.

"Thanks, baby," Randi said.

"I saw your friend at the mini-mart."

"Oh? Veronica?"

"Is that her name?"

"Yeah," Randi said.

"She asked if I was your girlfriend."

"And? What did you say?"

"I told her we were just friends."

Randi took a beer and collapsed on the couch.

"I don't really have the emotional capacity to discuss this right now," she said.

"Oh. It's okay. I just thought I'd let you know." Eleanor sat next to her. "Did you get packed?"

"Yeah. And my flight's reserved. I'll be leaving at six in the morning."

"I'm going to miss you, Randi."

"I'll miss you, too, baby. Know I'll be thinking about you even if I can't make contact with you. I'll be most likely to call you at bedtime, though."

"That's okay. You take care of yourself and your sister, to the best of your ability."

"I will. But you'll always be on my mind."

They sat silently for a few minutes.

"My family is going to ask if I'm seeing anyone," Randi finally said.

"They don't live around here. I don't suppose it would hurt if you told them."

Randi nodded, but didn't say anything. Eleanor searched for something to say, but had nothing. She thought of her own dysfunctional family and wondered if Randi was close to hers.

"Are you and your family tight?" she said.

"Very. If I find out who hit my sister, I'm going to kill the mother fucker."

The passion in her words hit Eleanor like a ball of fire. It was hot and deadly. She didn't respond. She just wanted to take the fear and worry away from Randi. She didn't know how.

Randi drank beer after beer and finally it was late and they needed to go to bed.

"Come on," Eleanor said. "We need to get some sleep."

"I may just stay up all night," Randi said.

Eleanor looked at her pleadingly, but resolved to let her do what she wanted.

"Okay. If you think that would be best," she said.

"No. It wouldn't be. It sounds good, but would be incredibly irresponsible."

She followed Eleanor to the bedroom. When they were in bed, Eleanor felt Randi's hand skimming over her body.

"You don't have to, Randi. I know you're probably not in the mood."

"I'm always in the mood with you. Besides, I want to love you, to feel alive."

"Well, you know I'm never going to tell you no. I just want you to know I'll be okay if you want to take the night off."

"Never gonna happen," Randi said.

Randi moved her hand to cup one of Eleanor's breasts. She pinched and teased her nipple until Eleanor could hold out no longer.

"Oh, God, Randi. How do you do that?" she asked when she had caught her breath.

"You're just so easy to love," Randi said. "Your body is so receptive. I love making love to you."

"Well, you don't even have to touch me down there and I come. How is that possible?"

"Your nipples are very sensitive. I can't believe no one took the time in the past to give them the attention they need for you to climax."

"No one ever has."

"Well, it's only one way to please you. I know of several others."

She grinned and slid her hand between Eleanor's legs. Eleanor felt herself swell in anticipation. When Randi's hand slid past her clit, she arched her back, wishing Randi would pay it some attention. But Randi slipped her fingers inside her instead.

Eleanor loved how full Randi made her feel. She lifted herself off the bed with every thrust, urging her deeper. She felt her world begin to disappear. All that remained was Randi and the magic she was performing. She saw little bursts of light behind her eyelids as she reached her orgasm and gradually floated back to reality.

She didn't have time to fully appreciate the one orgasm before Randi was rubbing her clit, pressing into it, and soon Eleanor screamed again. Randi finally stopped her ministrations and Eleanor relaxed completely.

Randi kissed her softly and Eleanor felt her desire rage again. This time it was desire to have Randi, to please her as she'd just been pleased. She kissed her back, then pried her lips open with her tongue. Randi opened her mouth and welcomed her in.

As they kissed, Eleanor moved her hand between Randi's legs to find her wet and ready for her.

"I love that you're always so ready for me," Eleanor said.

"Always," Randi said.

Eleanor dragged her fingers over Randi's clit. She played over it and teased her. Randi was making soft, mewling noises.

"Please, baby. Don't leave me hanging."

Eleanor rubbed her fingers into Randi's clit then and Randi cried out Eleanor's name, which filled Eleanor with pride. She loved being the one to give Randi that kind of pleasure.

"I love you so much," Eleanor said. "I love making love to you."

"I love you, too. Now, let's get some sleep. It's going to be an early morning."

Three thirty in the morning came early. Eleanor dragged herself out of bed with Randi.

"You don't need to get up," Randi said.

"I don't mind. I'll make the coffee."

"I can just hit the road. I'm all packed."

"You'll need coffee. You're going to have a long day ahead of you."

"True, but I can make it myself," Randi said.

But she wasn't protesting too much. Eleanor could tell she liked having Eleanor up with her. Although, Eleanor knew it would mean a long day for herself, as well. She made the coffee and poured them each a steaming cup. They sat in silence at the kitchen table.

"You know I'll be with you in spirit, don't you?" Eleanor finally said.

"I know. And I appreciate that."

Eleanor didn't know what else to say or do.

"Do you want some more coffee?" she said.

"Sure. One more cup. I don't want to be peeing on the plane."

Eleanor smiled. An attempt at humor was nice.

She refilled their cups and sat back down. They finished their coffee and Randi stood.

"I need to get going. I don't want to be late."

"Okay."

Eleanor walked Randi to the door. Randi kissed her good-bye and hugged her tight.

"I love you, baby," she said.

"I love you, too. Have a safe trip."

"I will."

Eleanor went back to bed after Randi left, but found sleep hard to come by. She loved Randi. She knew that in her heart, but she didn't like people referring to her as her girlfriend, like Veronica had done. She was still not ready to come out of the closet here and didn't know how to feel. She didn't want to lose Randi, but didn't know if she'd be able to stay with her. The risks were too great.

She finally got out of bed and made another pot of coffee. She took a long, hot bath and took her time getting dressed. Finally, it was time to leave the house. She was tired, scared, and unsure of her future as she went to work.

Her day was long, but the kids were remarkably well behaved which made the day much easier. She gave a test, which left her quiet time to reflect some more on her current state. She wasn't sure it had been a great idea, but the test was scheduled, so she had no choice. At the end of the last period, she gathered up the tests and told her kids to have a good weekend. She slid the tests in her briefcase, then started out the door when Ron showed up.

"Hey, Eleanor," he said. "It's been a while since we've seen you at happy hour. Any chance you're going today?"

Eleanor was exhausted and really didn't want to go, but the chance to be out with peers beat the sound of sitting home alone.

"Sure," she said. "I'll see you there."

She walked into the Bull and walked straight to the bar. From her vantage point, she could check out who was there. No Haven. Good. She ordered her drink and walked over to the table. She sat next to Martina.

"Well, this is a pleasant surprise," Martina said.

"Yeah," Eleanor said. "I deserve an afternoon out every so often, don't I?"

"You sure do."

They all visited and soon Eleanor had forgotten her problems and just relaxed and enjoyed herself. They moved to the pool table where Eleanor even managed to win a few games. She was feeling good when Martina came over to her. She glanced over at the bar.

"Is Randi meeting you here today?" she said.

Eleanor felt cold in the pit of her stomach. She told herself to calm down, that it was a reasonable question.

"No," she said. "She won't be."

"Oh. Well, then, how about catching a bite? It's been a long time. We need to get caught up."

Again, thinking this better than the option of sitting home alone, Eleanor agreed to go to dinner with Martina. They met at the Pink Orchid. Once seated, Martina looked concerned.

"So, are things okay with you and Randi?"

"What do you mean?" Eleanor hadn't meant to sound so defensive.

"Well, it's just that the last time I saw you two together, things got pretty tense."

"Oh, yeah, well that was a while ago."

"So, you two are okay?"

"I'm not sure why you keep asking me that," Eleanor said. "It's not like we're a couple or anything."

She wondered if she'd made a huge mistake. Like, by saying that had she confirmed they actually were a couple? She froze and awaited Martina's response. Martina raised her eyebrows.

"You're not?" she said. "I'm sorry. I guess I just assumed..."

"No," Eleanor lied. "We're just friends."

Martina took a sip from her tea.

"I just figured two lesbians hanging around together that much, you had to be a couple. I apologize."

"I'm not a lesbian," Eleanor lied again.

"You're not?" Martina said. "Then I was barking up the wrong tree the whole time I was asking you out?"

She laughed uncomfortably. Eleanor squirmed in her seat. So Martina *had* been after her in the beginning. How could Eleanor have been so naive?

"I just thought you were being friendly," Eleanor said.

"I was being friendly. And testing the waters to see how friendly I could be." She laughed. "Are you sure you're not a lesbian? My gaydar is usually spot-on."

Eleanor was growing less comfortable by the moment. She really just wanted to get out of there. She needed to get home and sort things out in her mind. She felt dirty, and filled with self-loathing. Martina had been a good friend and now she was having to lie outright to her face.

"And then, you went to dinner with Haven that time," Martina was saying. "That pretty much sealed the deal for me. And then I kept seeing you with Randi, who's obviously a lesbian."

"I can have lesbian friends and not be a lesbian."

"Of course. I'm sorry. I feel horrible now for just assuming."

"It's okay," Eleanor said. She wasn't at all hungry, but added anyway, "Let's just order dinner."

"Okay. Fine. Let's do that."

Conversation was stilted during dinner. They talked about their classes, mostly, with what little conversation they had. When dinner was over, Martina reached for the check.

"I'll get this," she said.

Eleanor threw some money on the table.

"No. We'll split it. I'm not comfortable with you buying me dinner."

The last thing she wanted was for Martina to make it feel any more like a date. She left the restaurant and the tears fell. She was so upset. She didn't want people to know she was a lesbian. She'd done her best to hide it. Or so she'd thought. But clearly, she hadn't been careful enough. What was she going to do now? What if Martina and Haven compared notes? How did she know they hadn't already? Her carefully planned existence was slowly unraveling and she wasn't sure how to stop it.

## Chapter Twenty

Home alone, Eleanor sobbed hard. She needed to make some decisions. Some hard decisions. She had to decide whether she could continue seeing Randi and living in a bubble hoping never to be found out or whether she needed to cut her losses and say good-bye to Randi.

Her phone rang. She saw it was Randi. She almost didn't answer it.

"Hello?" she said.

"Hey, baby. How you doin'?"

"I'm okay. How's your sister?"

"It's not looking good. You sure you're okay? You sound funny."

Eleanor knew she was congested from all her crying. She was glad Randi couldn't see her.

"I'm fine. I'm sorry to hear about your sister," she said.

"Yeah. They're thinking she won't pull out of the coma she's in."

"I'm so sorry. Is there anything I can do?"

"No, baby. Just be there for me. I need you now like never before."

Eleanor's gut twisted. She wasn't even sure she wanted to be with Randi and here Randi was saying how much she needed her.

"I'm here for you," Eleanor said.

"Thanks, baby. So how was your day?"

Eleanor told her about school, happy hour, and even told her she'd gone to dinner with Martina.

"And Martina didn't make a pass at you?" Randi laughed.

Eleanor's stomach tightened more.

"No. It was just dinner." It came out harsher than she'd intended.

"Hey, baby. I'm just giving you a hard time. I know you're closeted at work. I was just teasing."

Eleanor didn't know what to say. She thought for a moment.

"I know."

"You know, some time we're gonna have to seriously talk about this closet you're stuck in, but not now. Not tonight. Unless maybe you want to explain to me again why it's so important to you?"

"I wish I could. I'm just afraid. Part of it stemmed from not wanting to get involved with anyone, but obviously that's not the case now. I'm still scared of the conservative air of this town and where I work. It's not as open as California. And that terrifies me."

"There's a happy medium between left wing liberalism and right wing conservatism. People can be in between, you know?"

"It just doesn't feel like a good idea, Randi. That's really all I can say."

"Okay. Maybe I'll be able to convince you otherwise sometime, but not now. I need to get back in the room, just in case there's been any change. I love you, baby."

"I love you, too."

She hung up the phone and poured herself a glass of wine. She tried to relax, but her mind was a jumble of thoughts. She poured it out and went to bed.

Eleanor spent the weekend working in her yard, trying to keep her focus on something rather than her carefully made closet that seemed to be falling down all around her. She talked to Randi in the evenings and went to bed missing her, yet not knowing if she could continue their relationship.

Monday morning, when Eleanor got to work, there was an email from Principal Ted Barret asking her to come to his office after work. Her blood turned cold. Everyone knew Ted was an extreme right-winger. What had he heard? What could he possibly want to talk to her about? Of course, she knew, but didn't want to believe it. This would be the nail in her coffin. She might as well pack up her things now. Why bother to wait until the end of the day?

She made it through her classes and left her classroom to make her way to the Ted's office. His door was closed so she took a seat in the waiting area. Her stomach was churning. She was a bundle of nerves. She only hoped she could hold it together and not fall apart in front of him when he let her go. But tears were already threatening. She swallowed hard and fought to keep them from falling.

The door to his office opened and out walked Martina.

"Hi, Eleanor," she said as if Friday night had never happened.

"Hi."

"What are you doing here?"

Eleanor wondered the same thing about Martina.

"I have no idea. I just got an email to come after school today. So, here I am." She hoped she sounded lighter than she felt.

"Weird, but I'm sure it's no biggie."

"I hope not."

Ted came out of the office then.

"Eleanor?" he said. "Come on in."

With what felt like lead in her body, she stood and followed him into his office. His office walls were covered with pictures and plaques, some education based, others not. He had a plaque honoring twenty years in the NRA and a picture of him shaking hands with Jeb Bush. There was no doubt where he lay on the political spectrum. She slipped her hands into her slack pockets so he wouldn't see her shake.

"Please," he said. "Sit down."

She sat in one of the chairs across the desk from him.

"I suppose you wonder why I've called you in," he said.

"Yes."

"Well, you've been here a few months now, and we haven't really had a chance to chat since you came on board."

Oh, God, she thought. Here it comes.

"How are you liking it here?" he said.

"I like it a lot."

"Yes? And you're making friends in the community?"

Community? Did he mean the lesbian community?

"I've made a few friends here and there," she said.

"Excellent. We like our teachers to be active in the community. That's important to us."

She nodded, wishing he would get to the point.

"Well," he said, finally sitting down in his seat and pulling out a file from his drawer. "We certainly are fortunate to have you on staff."

"Thank you, sir."

"I've been hearing wonderful things from other staff members and I just wanted you to know that doesn't go unnoticed."

Eleanor relaxed a little.

"Thank you," she said again.

"So I'd like to give you a raise. You like it here. We like having you here. It seems like the only logical thing to do."

Eleanor almost fell out of her seat. This was the last thing she expected. She was thrilled.

"Thank you." She felt like an idiot. Surely she could think of something more to say. "I hadn't expected this."

"Why else would I call you to my office?" He arched an eyebrow at her.

Why else, indeed, she thought.

"I don't know," she said. "I had no idea honestly. I thought perhaps I'd done something wrong, though I couldn't think of anything."

He laughed.

"Still the fear of being sent to the principal's office, huh? Just like when we were kids. Don't worry, though. I have heard nothing but wonderful things about you from staff and parents alike, by the way. The parents love you."

"Thank you. That means so much to me."

"You're welcome."

They discussed the details of her raise and he had her sign a new contract.

"Thank you again," she said as she was leaving his office.

"No. Thank you."

She walked back to her classroom feeling much lighter than she had in days. She put the homework she had to grade in her briefcase and headed home for the night.

Randi called her just as she got home.

"Hey, baby," Randi said. "How was your day?"

"Oh, my God. You're not going to believe this, but I actually got a raise today."

"No way. That's fantastic. In the middle of a semester? That's kind of odd isn't it?"

"I know, but he said I was doing a great job and that the other staff and parents really like me, so he wanted to extend my contract and give me a raise. I'm beside myself. I so thought I was going to get in trouble when I got called to his office."

"Why would you get in trouble? You haven't done anything wrong." She hoped her tone sounded more casual than she meant it. She still really didn't understand why Eleanor's sexuality should affect her job.

"I guess not. But you never know, you know?"

"Well, I'm glad, baby. I've seen you work long nights at home and I know you deserved that raise."

"Aw. Thanks."

"I mean it," Randi said.

"So, how are things down there?"

"Not good. She's slipping away. I can feel it."

"Oh, Randi. I'm so sorry to hear that."

"And I don't know what to do about work. So far, they're being really good about letting me take time off day by day, but I don't know how long they'll let me keep doing that."

"Oh, I'm sure they'll let you keep doing that. I can't imagine they'll make you come back."

Randi hoped Eleanor was right. When she'd called her boss and asked for another day and possibly more, he'd said to take all the time she needed. She just hoped he meant it. She'd heard he could be double-crossing and she didn't want that to happen to her.

"I hope so, baby. I really do."

Randi heard voices coming from inside her sister's room. She wished she could shake her and wake her up. This waiting was hard beyond measure.

"You still with me?" Eleanor said.

"Yeah. Sorry. I'm kind of distracted."

"It's okay. Go. Be with your sister."

"Okay. I'll call you later tonight, okay?"

"Okay. I'll talk to you then," Eleanor said.

"I love you."

"I love you, too."

Randi put her phone in her pocket and walked back to her sister's room. Her mom and younger brother were in there.

"Any change?" she asked, though she knew the answer. Her mother's eyes were red and puffy. Her nose was raw and runny. She needed to be strong for her, but the vigil was wearing on her, too. She crossed the room and took her sister's hand. It was cool and limp. She sat next to her and spoke.

"Come on, Sissy," she said. "We need you. Come back to us."

At that moment, the machines showed flat lines going across them. The nurses were in the room immediately. They pushed Randi out of the way so they could work on Sissy. But no matter how hard Randi hoped, there was nothing they could do. Sissy was gone.

Randi crumpled into the seat she'd been forced to vacate and buried her face in her hands. She wanted to scream, to cry out at the unfairness of it all, but she didn't. From what seemed far away, she heard her mother wailing in anguish. Randi took a deep breath and went over to her.

"It's okay, Mama. It's okay."

"My baby's gone," she cried. "My baby."

Randi held her while she cried. She held her until she had worn herself out and there was nothing coming out of her, but wretched sobs. Randi continued to hold her against her chest and rub her back. She loved her mother and hated this unnecessary pain inflicted on her.

Randi's sadness turned to anger and frustration that the bastard that had hit Sissy hadn't stuck around and no one had any idea who it was. Randi wished she could find him and beat the shit out of him. But she had no clue where to even start looking.

A nurse came in then and escorted the family out of the room, so they could deal with the body. *The body*. This was her baby sister they were talking about. Or what was left of her. She felt nauseous.

Her brother drove her mom and her back to her mom's house. They helped get her inside and settled. Her mom's doctor came over and gave her some sedatives to help her sleep. She took one and lay on the couch, staring off into space.

Randi, finally able to let loose, went into the bedroom she had slept in as a kid and collapsed on the bed. Tears trickled out of her eyes, but the hard sobs she'd expected didn't come. She fished her phone out of her pocket and called Eleanor.

"Hello?" Eleanor said.

"She's gone, baby."

"Oh, Randi. I am so sorry."

The tears finally began to flow in earnest.

"She's really gone. I feel like I should be doing something, you know? Starting arrangements or something, but I can't. I don't want to believe it's real."

"I don't blame you," Eleanor said. "You need to take some time to process this."

"I don't want to process it. I don't want it to be real."

"I'm sure you don't. I'm so sorry this happened. Were you with her?"

"I was holding her hand."

"Oh, good," Eleanor said. "I'm so glad you could be there for her. How's the rest of the family taking it?"

"Mama's a mess. My brother, Matt, is being a rock, but I can see it's killing him, too. My sister who couldn't be here is going to feel horrible. We haven't called her yet. Unless Matt is calling her now. I don't know."

Eleanor was silent on the other end of the line, which was fine. Randi knew there was nothing she could say that would make her feel any better. Except one thing.

"I'd really appreciate it if you could be at the funeral," Randi said. "It would mean the world to me. Do you think you can take a day off? Surely they'd understand."

There was more silence. It seemed to stretch interminably. Randi didn't say anything either this time. She just waited and gave Eleanor the time she needed to say something. Finally, she spoke.

"I'll see what I can do. I mean, I'll ask anyway."

"It would mean the world to me, baby. I really need you."

"I understand that. I'll do my best to be there. Do you know when the funeral is going to be?"

"No. We haven't talked about that yet. I suppose we should. It's just, that would feel so...final."

"I get that. I don't blame you."

"Okay. Well, I'll let you know what we decide. I'll try to get them to hold off on the funeral until Saturday. How does that sound?"

"That would be great." Randi could hear the relief in Eleanor's voice.

"Okay. I'll see if we can do that. For now, I should go check on my mama.

"Sounds good. I'll talk to you tomorrow?"

"Definitely. I sure do love you, Eleanor."

"I love you, too."

Randi slid the phone in her pocket wondering what on earth she would do if she didn't have Eleanor in her life.

## CHAPTER TWENTY-ONE

Eleanor set her phone on the table. She felt nauseous. What if the funeral was held before Saturday? Would she be able to go? She didn't think she'd be comfortable asking for the day off. She'd just have to sit tight and hope for the best.

The idea of meeting Randi's family was overwhelming, to say the least. She fought the nerves that coursed through her body. She wouldn't be there for a social occasion, she reminded herself, but still…

And what about her own feelings? What about her insecurities and all the doubts she'd been having? What if she decided she couldn't stay with Randi? Would it be fair to go to the funeral and lead her on? All these questions floated around in her head as she wrestled yet again with what she was doing with her life.

Underneath all the fear, though, was a deep felt sympathy for Randi and her family. How terrible to have lost a sister, especially one so young. Twenty-four was too young to die. Eleanor felt horrible for Randi. She knew she would try to be strong for her family. That's just how she was. And the pressure would have to be devastating. She knew she should be there for Randi. It would be the right thing to do, but could she do it?

She set about grading homework in order to take her mind off things. She finished and crawled into bed, mentally and emotionally exhausted.

Randi called her the next afternoon.

"Hey," Eleanor said. "How are you doing?"

"I'm hanging in there. This whole thing sucks. I can't believe my sister's gone. I keep expecting her to pull up in front of the house any minute now."

"I'm sure. I'm so sorry. How's your mom doing?"

"Mama's a wreck. She just keeps taking sedatives and zoning out. I suppose it's her way of coping. I'd like to get mad at her and make her talk to me about what she's feeling, but I basically know how she's feeling. Bereft beyond words. I just don't know if she's as pissed as I am, you know? I'm so almighty pissed off at the bastard that did this. I wanna find the guy and cut his balls off and shove 'em down his throat."

Eleanor shuddered at the intensity of Randi's words. She'd only seen her angry once before, she now realized. What would happen if she called things off? How angry would she be then? She brought herself back to the conversation at hand.

"I don't blame you," she said. "Not one bit. I can't believe it was a hit-and-run. It takes a special kind of coward to leave the scene of an accident."

"Yeah. So, I wanted to let you know, we're going to cremate her tomorrow and we're going to have the funeral Saturday. I figure you can fly down Saturday morning and we can fly home together Sunday. Sound good?"

Eleanor swallowed hard. She hoped she was doing the right thing.

"Sounds great. What time's the funeral?"

"It'll be at three, so if you catch a morning flight, you'll have plenty of time. Or you could fly down Friday night."

"Okay. That's what I'll do."

"And, Eleanor?"

"Yeah?"

"Thanks a lot for doing this. I miss you like crazy and really need you here with me."

"I miss you, too," Eleanor said. She thought about saying she wouldn't miss being there, but knew in her heart it was a lie. She'd rather not have to go to a funeral with a bunch of strangers for a person she hadn't known.

"Hey, baby?"

"Yeah?"

"Is everything okay with you? I've been so obsessed with what I've been going through, I haven't really checked in with you."

"Everything is fine here," Eleanor said. "Just the usual, you know. Work, homework, bed. Repeat."

Randi laughed.

"Thanks, baby. That's the first time I've laughed in I don't know how long."

"Good. I'm happy to help."

"I can't wait to see you."

Eleanor felt cold in the pit of her stomach. She wasn't sure how she was feeling, but over the phone before Randi's sister's funeral was no time to have the conversation with her.

"I can't wait to see you, either," she said. And it was true, if she thought about it. She did miss Randi. She missed their evenings and nights. She really missed their nights.

"I need to get going now," Randi said. "I'll talk to you tomorrow."

"Okay."

"I love you."

"I love you, too."

Eleanor set the phone on the table and went back to grading homework.

The rest of the week sped by for Eleanor. She wished it would slow down, but soon it was Friday and she was a tense wreck as she taught her classes. She made it through the day and was packing up her things when Ron stopped by.

"Happy hour today?" he said cheerfully.

"No. I'm not going to be able to make it today," she said. Or any other time, she thought.

"That's too bad. We'll miss you."

"Maybe some other time," she said and hurried past him out of the building to her car. She'd packed her suitcase the night before so she could drive straight to the airport. Her stomach knotted more with each passing minute.

Once on the plane, she ordered a rum and Coke in hopes it would calm her nerves. She wished she wasn't having so many doubts about Randi. She felt like a hypocrite making this trip. She should have said no, but then Randi would have known something was up. And she did still love Randi. She just didn't think she could be with her any longer.

The plane landed and she walked out into the night air, looking for the Subaru Randi had said she'd be driving. She saw it and saw Randi waving at her. She rolled her bag over and put it in the backseat.

Seeing Randi took her breath away. She didn't look good. Her fun loving Randi looked haggard and hollow. She gave Eleanor one of her crooked grins before pulling her in for a bear hug, but her eyes didn't twinkle. Eleanor felt sorry for her. She looked every bit like she'd just lost her baby sister.

They drove to Randi's mom's house.

"We're taking over my mama's room," Randi said. "It's the only room in the house with a queen bed. She's going to be in my old room."

"Oh, Randi," Eleanor said. "I hate to put her out like that."

"It doesn't matter. She's not really sleeping much these days anyway. She was fine with the switch. Plus, it's only for two nights."

Eleanor's unease only grew as they approached the house. She had been feeling a little better when Randi hugged her, but the reality of the situation hit her again. She did not want to be there.

"Well, here we are." Randi pulled into the driveway of an old two-story Victorian.

"What a cute house."

Randi shrugged.

"It's home."

Randi grabbed Eleanor's bag and took her hand.

Eleanor froze.

"What's up?" Randi said.

"I'm not…I mean…Well, this is big. I'm about to meet your family. Let me take a breath first."

"Baby, they're going to love you."

"They have so much more to worry about than me right now anyway."

"True. But they're going to love you. Now, are you okay?"

Eleanor nodded, but Randi wasn't convinced.

"We can take another minute if you need to."

"No. I'm good now."

"Okay. Let's go."

Randi's heart was swelling in her chest. She was so proud Eleanor was her woman. She couldn't wait for her family to meet her, regardless of the circumstances. They climbed the front stairs and Randi opened the door for her. Eleanor walked in, stopped, and turned toward her.

"You okay?" Randi said.

"Yeah. I guess I just need to know you're here."

"I'm here, baby."

Randi set Eleanor's bag down and took her hand. She led her into the living room where she introduced her to her mom and brother.

"Nice to meet you," Eleanor said. "Though I wish the circumstances were different."

"Thank you, my dear. It's nice to meet you, too. It's about time Randi had a nice girl in her life."

"Girl? Mama, she's thirty-three years old. She's hardly a girl." Randi laughed.

"Still," Mama said.

Eleanor looked at Randi.

"I thought you had another sibling."

"My other sister will be here tomorrow."

Eleanor nodded.

"Please. Sit," Randi said. "I'll get you a glass of wine."

Eleanor sat in a wing back chair while Randi went to get the wine.

"We have this loveseat here," Randi said. "Why don't you come sit with me? You don't have to worry about Mama. She knows how I am and she's fine with it."

Randi sensed Eleanor's unease at acting like a couple. But they were one and she needed that at the moment. She was desperate to be with Eleanor as her partner.

Eleanor moved to the loveseat to join Randi. Randi slid her arm around her shoulder and felt her tense.

"Baby, relax," Randi said. "There's nothing to be uptight about here. We're safe here."

"She's still closeted back home," Randi told her mama. "She's not used to public displays of affection."

"Oh, that's too bad. Randi's been out since high school," Mama said. "The closet was no place for her. And we're glad. We're proud of who she is, lesbian and all."

Randi could feel Eleanor relax beside her.

"You feelin' better?" Randi said.

"Yeah. Sorry. I'm just a little overwhelmed right now."

"I'm sure," Mama said. "Meeting your partner's family is always challenging."

"I just really wish the circumstances were different," Eleanor repeated. "I wish it was a festive occasion."

"Well, that can't be helped," Mama said. "What's done is done."

Randi's brother excused himself from the room.

"He's not taking any of this well at all. Actually, none of us are," Randi said.

"You seem to be."

"I think we're all putting on a brave face for you," Randi said.

"I wish you wouldn't."

"I'm just numb," Mama said. "I guess I'm in shock now."

"What a horrible thing for you guys to have to go through."

"Thanks, baby," Randi said. "Thank you so much for understanding."

She gave Eleanor a squeeze.

"It's been a long day. We should probably get to bed," Randi said.

"Yeah. I'm pretty wiped out."

Randi got Eleanor's bag and led her back to the master bedroom at the far end of the house.

"This room will afford us plenty of privacy, as well," Randi said.

"Randi," Eleanor said. "Surely you're not planning to…"

"Ah, but I am. I've missed you so much, baby. Every inch of me craves you. I can't go that long without you ever again."

"But…I don't know how comfortable I am with that."

"Come on. I need you. We're adults. We can do what normal adults do. No one will hear. They're both at the other end of the hall. We can be quiet."

She drew Eleanor to her and kissed her softly on the mouth. She felt the frozen exterior melt a little. She kissed her more passionately and Eleanor wrapped her arms around Randi's neck and pulled her closer. Randi was happy she seemed to be coming around. She needed her with every ounce of her being. She continued kissing Eleanor, their tongues frolicking.

Randi eased Eleanor back on the bed and looked down at her.

"Dear God, you're beautiful."

She watched the familiar blush creep over Eleanor.

"I don't even know where to start."

"How about we start by getting out of these clothes?" Eleanor said.

Randi unbuttoned Eleanor's blouse. She peeled it back to reveal the silky skin she'd missed so much. She bent to trace kisses over the exposed area. Eleanor tasted wonderful. Randi kissed the tops of her breasts, visible over her bra cups.

"I need more," Randi said. She helped Eleanor to a sitting position and unhooked her bra. Together, they got her shirt and bra all the way off and tossed them on the floor. Randi sat next to Eleanor and bent to take her nipple in her mouth. She lovingly ran her tongue over it, moving it around and around before flicking the tip of it. Eleanor lowered her face into Randi's shoulder to keep from crying out.

"I can't get over this. I've missed you so much," Randi said. "I can't believe you're finally here. Come on, let's get out of the rest of our clothes."

She watched Eleanor stand and step out of her slacks. She rubbed her palms on her shorts. She couldn't wait to get at those long legs and the heaven they led to. She quickly stripped out of her own clothes and lay in bed, beckoning Eleanor to join her. Eleanor lay next to her and Randi skimmed her hand over her body.

"Damn, I've missed you," she said. "I know I sound like a broken record, but it's true. It's like part of me has been gone."

"I have missed you, too," Eleanor finally spoke. "And I need you, too. Please, Randi. Please take me."

Randi kissed down Eleanor's body until she was between her legs.

"You're so beautiful," she said.

Randi lowered her face to Eleanor and licked her all over. She buried her tongue as deep inside as she could get before she moved it to her clit. She lapped at it, savoring Eleanor's unique flavor, until Eleanor shuddered on the bed beneath her.

"Finally," Randi said. "Damn. I needed that."

But Eleanor clearly had to please Randi as well as being pleased by her. She played her hand over one of Randi's breasts, stopping to pinch, tug, and twist her nipple. Randi let out a moan of pleasure.

Eleanor ran her hand lower to where Randi's legs met. She found her wet and ready. She slid her fingers inside her and Randi went crazy. She gyrated on the bed and arched to meet each thrust. Eleanor kept at it until Randi let out a muffled groan as she reached her climax.

Eleanor climbed up next to Randi.

"That was most excellent, baby," Randi said.

"I sure enjoyed it."

"We're so good together."

"I love you, Randi."

"I love you, too."

Randi wrapped Eleanor in her arms. She felt more at ease than she had in a week.

## Chapter Twenty-two

Eleanor awoke the next morning to Randi between her legs, working her magic on her. It took her no time to come fully awake as Randi's talented tongue moved over her. She clutched the sheets as the energy coalesced in her center. She held tight as the energy burst free, coursing through her body as she experienced one orgasm after another.

"Good morning to me," she said.

"Mm-hm," Randi said as she pulled herself next to Eleanor.

"I can't believe you'd be in the mood for that, what with the day it is and all."

"I needed you. I saw you laying there and had to have you. I know what day today is, but we're still alive and should live our lives."

"Then come here and let me make you feel alive."

Eleanor kissed Randi and ran her hand down her body. She placed it between her legs and entered her with ease. She moved them in and out.

"More, baby. I need more."

Eleanor slipped another finger inside and thrust them as deep as they could go. She pulled them back out and entered her again. Randi moved underneath her, arching to take her as deep as she could. Eleanor found the special spot inside her that she knew would do the trick and rubbed it.

Randi bit her lip to keep from crying out as she came.

"Thanks, baby," she said. "I needed that.

"I'm glad I could help."

They lay in each other's arms and dozed for a little while. When Eleanor woke up later, she was all alone in bed. She was immediately uncomfortable. She didn't know her way around and was upset that Randi had left her alone. She pulled on some shorts and a shirt and went looking for her.

She found her in the kitchen talking to her mom. Randi crossed the room and took her in her arms.

"Good morning, sunshine."

"Hi. It was weird to wake up alone."

Eleanor wanted to tell her how rude she thought it was but didn't want to make a scene in front of her mom.

"You looked so cute sleeping there. I didn't want to wake you. Sit. I'll bring you some coffee." She motioned to a small kitchen table.

Eleanor sat down and gratefully took the cup of steaming liquid.

"How are you this morning, my dear?" Randi's mom asked her.

"Fine. The question is, how are you doing?"

She watched as Randi's mom's eyes filled with tears. She dabbed at them with a tissue.

"Not so good, I guess."

Eleanor got up and hugged her. Randi's mom buried her head in Eleanor's shoulder and sobbed. Eleanor looked over her head to Randi who stood watching. She finally moved over to them and took her mom away from Eleanor and held her in her own arms. Eleanor moved back to the table.

"It's okay, Mama," Randi said. "We'll get through this together."

"One should never have to bury one's child," her mom said.

"No, they shouldn't," Eleanor agreed. She took a sip of coffee and imagined just how hard a day this was going to be. It would be hard on her, but that would be nothing compared to what Randi and her family would be going through. Eleanor had to put her own misgivings aside for the day and just be there for them.

Randi's mom tried to pull herself together.

"How'd you sleep last night, my dear?" she said to Eleanor, who blushed slightly.

"I slept like a log. Your bed is very comfortable."

"Oh, good. I'm glad it wasn't too soft for you."

"Not at all. And thank you again for letting us sleep there. I do hate to put you out."

"No need to thank me. It's the least I could do. I'm so glad you came down here to be with Randi for this."

"It's the least I can do. I can't imagine what you all are going through."

"It's horrible, to say the least."

"Who wants breakfast?" Randi piped up.

"I don't think I could eat," her mom said.

"I think you should eat something. You need your strength. I'll make you some toast. What about you, baby? Sausage and eggs?"

Eleanor was famished after their lovemaking the previous night and that morning.

"That sounds wonderful. Thank you."

"No problem. It's better for me to stay busy anyway, you know?"

"So does that mean you don't need any help?"

"That's exactly what that means."

Randi's mom sat at the table with her while Randi made breakfast. Eleanor searched her mind to find something to say but came up empty. It was going to be a long, hard day for everyone. She wished she could relax. Randi's family was very accepting of their lesbian daughter, and, by extension, her. She didn't need to be ashamed of what she was here. Not that she was ashamed of what she was at home either, really. She just didn't want anyone to know about her. It didn't make a lot of sense to her as she sat at the table watching Randi.

Randi. She was so gorgeous and so easy to be around. And so in love with her. Why had Eleanor been having all these second thoughts? So far from home, it seemed so easy. But of course, there were no prying eyes. No busybodies. No über conservative school principal. Just Randi's family who accepted her so easily.

Randi finished frying and set a plate in front of Eleanor before setting the toast in front of her mom. Then she sat down to join them.

"Dig in," she said.

Eleanor didn't have to be told twice. She wanted to devour everything at once, but took her time. She didn't want to look like a pig. Randi's mom picked at her toast.

"Mama, you need to eat. It's going to be a long day. You need something in your stomach."

She watched as her mom took a nibble.

"But, dear, I'm really not hungry."

"Please eat," she said as she dug into her own food.

Randi's mom managed to eat one piece of toast and finished at the same time Randi and Eleanor did. Randi took the plates and Eleanor got up to help with the dishes.

"I've got these," Randi said. "Why don't you go take a shower and get ready?"

She kissed Eleanor and Eleanor followed the hall back to their room. She laid her clothes out on the bed. Her black pencil skirt and black blouse. She'd be warm, but it was a funeral, after all.

She took her shower and came out of the bathroom wrapped in a towel. She found Randi sitting on the bed.

"You okay?" she said.

Randi looked up with red eyes.

"I will be."

"Oh, Randi." Eleanor sat next to her and took her hand in her own. "What can I do? Is there anything I can do to ease the pain?"

"Just be here for me."

"I'm here. I'm here."

Eleanor wanted to add she'd always be there, but couldn't make herself. She didn't know if that was true and the last thing she wanted to do was lie to Randi at that moment.

Randi took Eleanor in her arms and held her as the tears flowed. She was so grateful to have Eleanor in her life. She couldn't imagine any day without her, let alone this, the hardest day of her life. She pulled back and wiped her eyes on her sleeves.

"I need to pull myself together," she said.

"No, you don't. You need to feel what you're feeling. That's not a crime."

"No. I mean, I get what you're saying and all, but I need to be strong for the family."

"Well, I'll be here being strong for you."

"I appreciate that. I should get in the shower now."

"I won't keep you." Eleanor stepped out of the pathway to the bathroom.

"I will say, you sure look tempting right now."

"How can you go from crying to horny in a split second?" Eleanor laughed.

"You weren't standing here half naked when I started crying. And now, looking at you. I think I have to have you again."

She pulled Eleanor's towel off her and brought her closer. She leaned forward and took one of her nipples in her mouth.

"You taste good. All clean and whatnot."

"I'm glad you think so." Eleanor held firmly to Randi's shoulders.

Randi continued to suckle her until Eleanor came for her. She stood up and gestured to the bed. Eleanor lay down and Randi climbed between her legs. She ran her tongue all over her, savoring the flavor that was all Eleanor. She dipped it inside her, licking as deep as she could. Eleanor moved on the bed.

"Oh, God, Randi. Oh, yes. That's it. Oh, please. Oh, God. Yes." She cried out as the orgasms washed over her.

Randi moved up her body and kissed her, sharing her flavor with her.

"You're delicious, you know that?"

"I'm glad you think so."

"I do. I need to hit the shower now. I'll let you get dressed."

Randi came out of the shower to find Eleanor sitting on the bed in her somber outfit.

"You look great," Randi said.

"Thanks?"

"I mean, given the occasion and all. You look very nice."

"What are you going to wear?" Eleanor said.

"You'll see. It's pretty basic. But nice."

Randi dropped her towel and stared hard at Eleanor. She needed her again, but knew no matter how much she kept putting off the inevitable, they'd have to go to the funeral soon. She dressed in black slacks with long-sleeved black button down shirt and a purple tie. She stood in front of Eleanor.

"Well?"

"Very nice. And appropriate."

"Thank you."

Eleanor straightened Randi's collar for her and Randi felt the warmth radiating from her. She wrapped her arms around her and pulled her in for a soft, sensuous kiss.

"There's no time for that right now," Eleanor said.

"I know. But I needed it. I can't help it."

They walked hand in hand to the living room where Randi's sister had just arrived. Randi broke away from Eleanor and embraced her sister. They stood together for what seemed an eternity. Randi could feel the sobs racking her sister's body. She finally pulled back and offered her the handkerchief from her pocket.

"I don't want to dirty your handkerchief," her sister said.

"It's okay. I've got more."

Randi watched as she dried her eyes and blew her nose. She suddenly remembered Eleanor. She stepped to her and put her arm across her shoulders.

"Cindy, this is my partner, Eleanor. Eleanor, my sister Cindy."

Cindy reached out a trembling hand and took Eleanor's.

"It's nice to meet you," Eleanor said. "Though I'm sorry for the circumstances."

Cindy just nodded.

Randi walked over to her mom.

"How're you doing, Mama?"

Her mom just nodded, her eyes wet and lips trembling.

Randi's brother came into the room then. He hugged Cindy and thanked her for making the trip.

"I had to be here," Cindy said.

"I think it's time to get going," Randi said. She walked over and helped her mom off her chair.

"I've got her," her brother said. He led her to the mantle where Sissy's ashes were kept and handed them to her.

"Thanks," Randi said. She moved back to Eleanor and grabbed her hand. She squeezed it tight. She didn't know what she would do without her.

They arrived at the nondenominational church Sissy had attended and were met by the pastor. He shook everyone's hand in turn, taking both of Randi's mom's.

"I'm so sorry this has happened," he said. "Sissy was a favorite of everyone here. We're all going to miss her."

He led them into a packed church.

"Holy shit," Randi whispered to Eleanor. "I had no idea there would be this many people here."

"She must have been truly loved."

"She was such a wonderful kid. You'd have liked her."

"I'm sure I would have."

Randi's brother set Sissy's urn on the altar then joined the rest of the family in the front row. Randi draped her arm over Eleanor's shoulder, grateful for the closeness. She tried to maintain her composure as person after person got up to extol Sissy's virtues. She missed her so much, it was like she was punched in the gut with every new speaker.

When the pastor spoke, Randi lost it. She had tried to hold it together, to be strong, but it was too much. The pastor spoke of how God always seemed to call the ones who were too good for this earth home to him and Randi knew it was true. Sissy had been too good for this earth.

Next it was Randi's turn to speak. She got up and cleared her throat, but no words would come. She took a deep breath. She started speaking and her voice cracked. She tried again and finally realized how hard this was going to be. Eulogizing Sissy was going to be pure hell. She took one more deep breath and let the tears flow as she spoke.

When she was through. She sat again next to Eleanor and pulled her close. What would she have done without her? She sat with tears streaming down her face as the pastor stepped forward again and invited the congregation to join the family at the inurnment service.

They arrived at the inurnment wall and Randi at once wished they'd made it a family only event. She loved the fact that so many people had loved Sissy. She felt the love these people were pouring out to her. But it felt like it should have been private. Putting Sissy away for good should have been just the few of them. But it wasn't. She held Eleanor in one arm and her mama in the other until the pastor handed her Sissy's urn. Then she stepped up to the wall and slid the urn inside. The pastor said a prayer and closed the door. Sissy was gone.

## CHAPTER TWENTY-THREE

Eleanor sat quietly at the reception while Randi made the rounds. She thought how strong Randi was. How resilient she was. She wished she could be more like her. Randi made her way to her through the throngs.

"Hey, baby. How're you doin'? Can I get you anything?"

"I'm okay. Just kind of observing everything. Your sister certainly was loved."

"Yeah. She was. I wish you would have known her."

"Me, too."

Someone came over then and spoke to Randi. Eleanor watched as Randi easily engaged in conversation. Her long body seemed at ease, even in these circumstances. Eleanor looked at her longingly. She knew it was inappropriate, but she couldn't help it. The sight of Randi turned her on. There was no denying it. She loved her. This, too, was a fact. But what would happen when they got home? Would she be able to keep seeing her?

That morning, Randi had introduced her as her partner. That sounded so serious. Eleanor still considered them just seeing each other. She'd never even been to Randi's house. She knew she was trying to minimize the relationship to make a possible break up easier, but she couldn't help it. No matter how she felt about Randi, she had her own mental well-being to think about.

As the crowd thinned out, Randi was back by her side.

"Come on, baby. You need food."

Eleanor realized how hungry she'd become.

"Yeah. Food sounds good," she said.

She allowed Randi to lead her to the food table, where she helped herself to the hors d' oeuvres. She piled her plate, giving in to her hunger.

"You want something to drink?" Randi said.

"I'll have some water."

"We have wine," Randi said.

"Okay. I'll have a glass of wine."

She took her plate and found a place to sit. She tried not to devour her food again. She ate slowly and felt like a fish out of water. She was the only person in the room who hadn't known Sissy. She was very self-conscious. She was grateful when Randi came back and handed her a glass of wine. She took a sip.

"This is good," she said.

"Thanks. Mind if I sit with you for a while?"

"Not at all. How are you holding up?"

"Well, I've got to keep a brave face and I'm doing my best. But I'm tired, baby. This is wearing me out."

"I'm so sorry all this has happened."

"Yeah. Me, too."

Another person came up to talk to Randi. She stood and talked to them for a while. The conversation died and they stood there in awkward silence. Eleanor just watched. She wanted the person to leave so Randi could sit back down with her. The person finally left and Randi collapsed next to her. She took a piece of food off her plate.

"Do you want me to make you a plate?" Eleanor said. "You haven't eaten, have you?"

"There's not really time. How long do you think these people will stick around? What's the time frame for a funeral reception?"

"I've no idea. I can't imagine it will last much longer."

As if they heard their conversation, one by one and in groups, people started leaving the house. Finally, it was silent. The family sat alone in the living room. The caterers came in and cleaned everything and the family was alone again. Randi's mom, eyes still wet, excused herself and went into Randi's room. The siblings sat there silently. Eleanor felt like an outcast, even with Randi sitting next to her.

"I don't feel like Sissy would want us to just sit around and mourn," Randi's brother said.

"I'm not sure I have the energy to do anything else," Cindy said.

"I think we should go out. Let's get some drinks," her brother said.

"I'm up for that," Randi said. "Eleanor?"

"I'll do whatever you want."

"Great," Randi said. "Let's take a cab in case we have too much to drink."

They piled into a cab with Eleanor in the middle of the back seat. She scooted as close to Randi as she could get. She felt immensely uncomfortable going out with virtual strangers, but she was there for Randi and if this is what Randi needed, then so be it.

They arrived at a nondescript bar on the east side of town.

"This is where Matt and I used to hang out when we were younger." Randi motioned toward her brother. "It's nothing fancy, but the drinks are strong and cheap."

"Sounds good to me," Eleanor said. She needed a drink. And a strong one sounded wonderful.

The group found a booth and Randi went up to buy the first round. She came back and handed Eleanor her rum and Coke. Eleanor took one sip.

"Holy Jesus," she said. "That's strong."

"Told you," Randi said.

Along with their drinks, Randi had brought them each a shot of tequila. She held hers up.

"To Sissy," she said.

"To Sissy," they all said then downed the amber liquid.

It burned going down, but tasted great. Eleanor couldn't remember the last time she'd had a shot of tequila. She set her shot glass down and sipped her rum and Coke.

Matt went to the bar to get more tequila. Eleanor told herself to pace herself. She didn't need to get sick or say or do anything that would make a fool out of herself in front of Randi's family.

When they had done their second shot, Randi piped up.

"So let's everyone tell our favorite story of Sissy."

Eleanor sat back and listened to the adventures of a woman she'd never know. She found herself laughing along with the others as they recounted some of the antics of Sissy. It was an easy group to be with. It helped that Randi had her hand on Eleanor's leg under the table. It offered her a sense of comfort.

After another shot of tequila and another drink, Eleanor was completely relaxed. She was beginning to think of Matt and Cindy not as Randi's siblings, but as friends. She hoped they were thinking the same thing about her, though she wasn't really contributing much to the conversation.

"You doin' okay?" Randi asked her.

"Yeah. I'm having fun. I mean, is that okay? After today and all? To have fun?"

Randi just looked at her. She loved her so much. She saw the honest concern in Eleanor's eyes.

"Of course it's okay. That's the purpose of us all going out. To let loose. To blow off steam. It's all good, baby."

She squeezed Eleanor's leg to let her know everything was fine.

"You need another drink?" She motioned to the empty glass sitting in front of Eleanor.

"Sure. Maybe just one more."

"Good." Randi stared at Eleanor before she got up. She wanted to kiss her right then and there, but knew that wouldn't be wise. The neighborhood was not known for being gay friendly. Resting her hand on her leg under the table was one thing. Out and out kissing her could cause trouble. So she just stared hard into her eyes, hoping to convey all she was feeling and desiring in her look.

She came back with drinks for the table. The group had suddenly become quiet.

"Hey," Randi said. "What happened to the party?"

"I don't know," Cindy said. "I guess I'm feeling melancholy now."

"Yeah," Matt said. "I think reality is setting in again. Let's finish these drinks and head home."

They did just that. When they got home, Matt and Cindy said good night and went to their rooms. Randy pulled Eleanor to her in a tight embrace.

"How you doin'?" she said.

"I'm okay. A little tipsy, I suppose, but overall okay. What an exhausting day this must have been for you."

"It was rough. I'll admit that. But I'm holding up."

"Good."

"I want a beer though. You want a glass of wine?"

"I guess. What would it hurt at this point?"

They sat on the couch sipping their drinks.

"Thank you again so much for coming down for this," Randi said. "I don't know that I would have made it without you."

"You have a strong support system in your family. I'm sure you'd have been fine."

"True. My family is the best, but they're not the same as you, you know?"

Eleanor didn't say anything. Randi pulled her close.

"You're my rock," she said.

"I don't know about all that."

"I do. I had a really hard day, but it would have been so much worse if you hadn't been here."

"I'm happy I could be here for you," Eleanor said.

Randi kissed Eleanor then. It was a soft, tender kiss. She needed to show Eleanor how important it had been for her to be there. Words didn't seem to be conveying it. She hoped the kiss would.

"That was nice," Eleanor said.

"There's plenty more where that came from."

She kissed her again as she held her tight and pressed against her. Her need to consume her threatening to overwhelm her.

"You're awfully amorous," Eleanor said.

"I can't help it. I love you and want you and need you. Let's finish these drinks so we can get to bed."

They got to the bedroom and Randi pulled Eleanor to her again. She looked into her eyes.

"My God, you're beautiful."

"Thank you. You're not so bad yourself."

Randi laughed.

"I'm glad I'm not so bad."

"You're hot and you know it."

"As long as you think I'm hot," Randi said. "That's all that matters."

"Well, I do."

"Thank you."

Randi unbuttoned Eleanor's shirt and slid it to the floor. She unhooked her bra and tossed it aside. She held her breasts in her hands and ran her thumbs over her hardening nipples.

"I love your breasts," she said.

"They certainly love you."

"I love how responsive they are."

"You're driving me crazy and you know it."

"Wait until I suck on them. Then I'll make you scream my name."

"There'll be no screaming tonight. Not here. Not in this house."

"Okay," Randi said. "You don't have to scream, but you'll be fighting not to."

She bent and took one of Eleanor's puckered nipples in her mouth. She ran her tongue over it, enjoying how it felt. She pressed it to the roof of her mouth and moved her tongue along its underside. All the while, she kept on sucking, pulling it as deep as she could get it.

Eleanor groaned and collapsed onto the bed.

"Oh, yeah," Randi said. "Now we're getting started."

She eased Eleanor onto her back and climbed up next to her. She took her other nipple in her mouth and repeated the process. Eleanor curled her fingers in Randi's hair and held tight as Randi took her to another orgasm.

Randi ran her hand up Eleanor's smooth leg to her soft thigh. She could feel the moist heat radiating from her. She wanted her so badly. She had to touch her, to taste her. She helped Eleanor out of her skirt and panties until she was laying naked for her.

"Please, Randi," Eleanor said. "I need to feel you on me. Please, take off your clothes."

Randi did as she was instructed, hurriedly removing her shirt and slacks, her undershirt and boxers. She stood looking down at Eleanor who looked back at her with glazed eyes. Randi lay down so her body covered Eleanor's.

"That's it," Eleanor said. "I love the feel of your weight on me."

Randi kissed her passionately as she ground her hips into Eleanor's pelvis. Eleanor wrapped her legs around Randi and pulled her to her. Randi didn't know how much longer she could wait. She wanted to be inside her. She needed to be. She ground into her for a few more minutes before she slid off her.

"I need to have you now," she said.

"Take me, then. Take me now."

Randi skimmed her hand over Eleanor's body until she found where she needed to be. She easily slid inside her and rubbed her fingers along Eleanor's silky walls. Randi moved lower on the bed until she could put her mouth on Eleanor's clit. The combination worked wonders. Eleanor pressed her hand into the back of Randi's head. Randi could hardly breathe. But what a way to go.

She heard Eleanor mewling as she moved against her. She knew she was getting close. She struggled for air as she continued to love her. She felt Eleanor rise off the bed and freeze, then collapse back down. When Eleanor released her, Randi climbed up next to her.

"Thanks, baby," she said. "I needed that."

"Apparently, so did I."

"Yeah?"

"Yeah. And now it's my turn to take care of you. Let's see if we can relieve some of the tension of the day."

"Sounds excellent to me." Randi was swollen and wet and ready for Eleanor. She was craving her touch.

Eleanor kissed Randi. It was a kiss that made Randi's toes curl. She felt herself drip. She needed Eleanor desperately. Eleanor moved her hand between Randi's legs and Randi spread them wider to grant her easier access. Eleanor slipped her fingers inside and Randi gasped in pleasure.

"That's it, baby," she said. "That's what I need."

Eleanor kept moving her fingers in and out until Randi was writhing on the bed.

"Oh, God," she said. "Oh, dear God. That feels so fucking good."

Randi closed her eyes and focused all her attention on the feelings Eleanor was eliciting. Nothing mattered in those moments but Eleanor's fingers stroking deep inside her. She felt a ball of energy forming in her very core. It burned hot and fierce. The more Eleanor fucked her, the hotter it burned until finally, the ball burst open and sent the heat coursing throughout her body.

"That was incredible, baby," she said.

"Mm. Yeah it was. You want to let go of my fingers now?"

"Sorry."

"It's okay. I can wait."

Randi kissed Eleanor and slowly relaxed. Eleanor was able to retrieve her fingers.

"I can't get over how hard you clamp down on me when you come," Eleanor said.

"Sorry," Randi said again.

"Oh, don't be. It's hot."

"It's getting late," Randi said. "We should probably get some sleep."

Eleanor moved into Randi's arms. Randi fell asleep feeling loved.

## Chapter Twenty-four

Once back home, Eleanor began to feel the doubts creeping back in about her relationship with Randi. She knew she had become distant and untouchable. Except at night. She gave herself willingly to Randi every night. She felt like a hypocrite. Either she was going to stay with her or not, but she couldn't keep using her for sex.

One Friday after work, Randi called her on her way home.

"Hey, baby, are you going to happy hour today?"

Eleanor still hadn't told her about her last happy hour and how it had ended up with Martina trying to out her. She hadn't been to one since.

"No," she said. "I'm just heading home."

"I'd sure like to go out for drinks after work today. Can I meet you at the Bull a little later?"

"Like what time? I really don't feel like socializing with my coworkers."

"Why not? That used to be the norm."

"I don't know. It just doesn't appeal to me right now."

"Okay. I'll try to think of someplace else. I'll come home after work and we'll decide where to go then. Sound good?"

"Sounds great."

Eleanor tossed the phone back on the passenger seat. She wasn't sure she wanted to be seen in public with Randi. She'd been careful to have dinner cooked every night so they didn't have to go out. Even though a few restaurants already thought of them as a couple.

She just couldn't take it. She wanted to keep her relationship with Randi confined to the walls of her house. And now Randi wanted to go out? She had no excuse to tell her no. Randi deserved to be able to blow off steam. So did she. She just hoped they didn't run into anybody they knew.

Randi got home and pulled Eleanor into a tight embrace.

"Hey, baby. It is so good to see you," Randi said.

"It's good to see you, too. Rough day at work?"

"You could say that. Johnny got bit by a cottonmouth. It was pretty scary. He's gonna be okay, but it was a terrifying experience. Hence, the need for a drink or three."

"Oh, my God. I'm glad he's going to be okay."

"Yeah. He's a tough son of a bitch. That's for sure."

"Well, I can certainly see why you need a drink. You want to take a shower? I can run to the liquor store while you do and we can drink here."

She hoped she didn't sound as desperate as she felt.

"Ah, thanks, baby, but I really need to go out. We haven't been anywhere in a while. I'm going a bit stir crazy."

"Okay."

"You okay, baby?"

"Yeah. I'm fine."

"Okay. Just checkin'. I'll be out of the shower in a minute."

Eleanor sat in the living room and waited for Randi to get out of the shower. She really didn't want to go anywhere. The now familiar knot in her stomach was back. She felt nauseous. She really couldn't take any chances of being seen in public. She told herself to relax. It was only for a drink.

Randi came out of the shower with a towel wrapped around her waist. The sight took Eleanor's breath away. There was no doubt she was attracted to Randi, even loved her. So, what was the big deal? Maybe it was time to come out of the closet and live in peace. No, her brain screamed. That wasn't going to happen.

"You know," Randi said. "I was thinking we could go to Joni's. It'll be quiet there this early on a Friday evening. We can get a couple of drinks. It'll be fun."

"Joni's?" Eleanor said.

"Yeah. The women's bar I've told you about. It won't be crowded with people. I know you worry about that."

"But, Randi. What if someone sees me going in there? That's not a chance I'm willing to take."

"Baby, honestly. I don't know what you're so afraid of."

"Yes, you do. I'm afraid of being outed. We've gone over this. Now, choose somewhere else."

Randi let out an exasperated sigh and left the room. Eleanor almost felt bad. But she couldn't. How dare Randi even suggest a women's bar? She knew Eleanor couldn't go in there. Not in a million years.

Randi emerged from the bedroom dressed in shorts and a T-shirt.

"Okay then. Let's go to the Bull. Most of your coworkers should be gone by now."

Eleanor checked the big clock hanging over the mantle. It was six o'clock. Randi was right. The coast should be clear by then.

"Sounds good," she said.

They climbed into Randi's truck and drove to the bar.

"Drive around it once so I can check for coworkers' cars," Eleanor said.

Randi shot her a look.

"Are you serious?"

"Yes."

Randi drove around the building. Eleanor didn't see any car she recognized.

"Okay," she said. "We can go in."

They walked in and took a couple of barstools. Randi ordered a beer with a shot of tequila and Eleanor ordered a rum and Coke. Randi tossed back her head and downed her tequila.

"God, I needed that," she said.

Eleanor sipped her drink.

"I'm glad. I'm sorry you had such a rough day."

Randi ordered another shot and took a long pull off her beer.

"So, what's going on?" Randi said. "You seem more paranoid than usual today."

"You don't know what happened while you were gone," Eleanor said. "It scared me and I am doubling my efforts not to appear gay."

"So tell me. What happened?"

"I went to dinner with Martina."

"Oh, so you went on a date and didn't feel the need to tell me?"

"It wasn't like that and you know it. I went to happy hour rather than go home to an empty house. After, she asked if you were meeting me and I said no. She asked if I wanted to grab a bite to eat. It all seemed so innocent."

"But it wasn't?" Randi signaled for another shot.

"She started asking questions about us. Asking if everything was okay between us. I told her we were just friends, but I could tell she didn't believe me. Then she told me she was a lesbian and that all the time I thought she was being nice, she was actually feeling me out."

"I told you that," Randi growled. "I knew she was into you. But no, you wouldn't believe me."

"So, I had to keep insisting I was straight. It was hard, but I think she finally believed me."

"So now you're even further in the closet than before."

"And then I got called into the principal's office."

"For a raise," Randi said.

"Right. But I didn't know that. And I walked into his office. Randi, he's a member of the NRA. He has a picture of him with Jeb Bush. He's ultra-right wing. I can't have him find out about me. I just can't."

Randi heard the fear in Eleanor's voice. She tried to muscle up some sympathy, but couldn't. She had given herself heart and soul to a woman who would deny their very existence as a couple. The idea enraged her.

"Are you ashamed of me?" she said.

"I'm not, Randi. It's not you. It's all me."

"Well, I have to say, I think you're treading on thin ice right now."

"What?"

Randi called for another shot of tequila, enjoying the liquid courage it provided.

"I think it's time for you to decide which you love more. Me or the closet."

"Randi, please. Don't make me make that choice."

"I don't think I can live in the bubble you've built around us. At first, it was great. You know, just the two of us. But I miss my friends. And most of them are gay. And they would love you, but you're terrified of meeting them. I miss Joni's, my hangout. And lately, we haven't even left the house for dinner or anything. All because you insist on staying firmly in that stupid closet. You need to come out or say good-bye."

"Randi, please."

"No. I've tried to understand. I've been patient, but I can't do it any longer. I don't live in a closet. You knew that when we met. I'm out, loud, and proud. And I plan to stay that way."

"But, Randi, I love you."

"Then show me. Go places with me. Don't be scared of what other people think. This isn't the Stone Age. People don't give a rat's ass who you sleep with these days. They just want you to be happy."

"I am happy with you, Randi."

"But I can't be happy living the life we've been living," Randi said.

"I can't be out, Randi. My livelihood depends on me remaining in the closet. I do still think this area thinks it's the Stone Age. I don't believe people don't care. They do. And I believe they'd crucify me if they knew."

"It's all in your head, Eleanor. It's not real, but you've got yourself convinced. Come on. I'll take you home."

Eleanor placed her hand on Randi's arm. Randi looked down at it then up to Eleanor.

"You sure you should touch me like that in public? People might talk."

Eleanor's eyes glistened with unshed tears.

"This isn't how I thought it would go," she said.

"No? So you've thought about it then."

"I worried it might come to this."

"And just how did you think it would go?" Randi said.

"I never wanted to hurt you."

"And you think not wanting to be seen with me would make me feel good? Come on. I mean it. I'm leaving. Do you want a ride or not?"

Once in the truck, the tears trickled down Eleanor's cheeks. She swiped away at them at first, but they kept coming. Randi looked over at her and wondered what she was expected to do. She should be the one crying. She was losing a partner. But she was too pissed off. She'd been as patient as anyone could have expected her to be. Still, it hurt her to see Eleanor crying. She handed her a handkerchief.

"Here," she said.

"Thanks," Eleanor said. She looked over at Randi with giant doe eyes. "I'm really sorry Randi. I wish it hadn't come to this."

"No more than I do."

"Will we be able to work through this?" she said.

"Not as long as you stay in the closet."

They pulled into Eleanor's driveway. Randi got out.

"What are you doing?" Eleanor said.

"I'm going to get my things. I'm not leaving them here. I won't be coming back."

She grabbed her overnight bag from the closet and packed her clothes in it. She threw the bag over her shoulder and headed to the front door.

"Randi?" Eleanor said.

She turned around, but Eleanor said no more.

"Good-bye," Randi said and let herself out.

Alone in her truck, Randi slapped her hands on her steering wheel. She felt frustrated, angry, sad, and betrayed. She'd been a good partner and she'd been patient and hadn't pushed Eleanor. Until today. And, now that she had, they were over. She couldn't believe Eleanor had chosen her precious closet over her.

Randi drove to Joni's. She knew it was early, but she needed to be in a women's bar, surrounded by women like her, women who weren't afraid of their sexuality. She pulled up a stool at the bar.

"Hey, stranger," the bartender said. "Long time no see."

"Yeah. I was out of commission for a while, but I'm back now."

"Well, it's good to see you. You want a beer?"

"Yeah. And a shot of tequila, please."

Randi had already had three shots. This would have to be her last or she'd black out or puke or do something she might regret. But she could handle her beer and planned on having quite a few of them. She handed the bartender her card.

"Keep it open," she said.

She turned on her stool to watch as the crowd trickled in. Slowly but surely, the place filled up. She saw many familiar faces and a lot she didn't recognize.

"Hey there, hot stuff," someone whispered in her ear.

She turned to see Veronica standing there.

"Hey yourself," Randi said. "How've you been?"

"Good. How about you? You disappeared for a while. I thought you had a girlfriend, but when I asked her about you, she said you were just friends."

"Yeah, well, that's a complicated story. Can I buy you a drink?"

"Sure."

Veronica sat on the open stool next to Randi. Randi ordered her a drink and herself another beer.

"So, you want to tell me the story?" Veronica said.

"Huh?"

"The complicated story. I'm all ears."

Randi opened her mouth, but couldn't make the words come out. Pissed though she was, she couldn't open Eleanor's closet door. She'd have to do that on her own. She wanted to tell Veronica everything, but shook her head.

"I'd rather not talk about it," she said.

"Fair enough. How about a dance then?"

"That I can do," Randi said.

She followed Veronica to the dance floor and watched as she moved and flowed with the music. She admired her form as she moved along with her. The music slowed and Veronica moved into Randi's arms.

Randi held her loosely, not ready to hold a woman tight yet. She felt guilty at first and then remembered she was as free as a bird and she could do what she wanted. When the dance ended, they walked back to their seats.

"That was fun," Randi said. "Thanks."

"I know what would be more fun." Veronica smiled seductively.

"So do I. But not tonight. Maybe another time."

"Bummer."

"Sorry."

Randi paid her tab and left the bar. The night was warm and still. It pressed in on her, adding to her depressed state. She drove home and sat in her dark living room as she replayed the events of the day. What a fucked up day it had been. She hadn't thought it could get any worse after Johnny got bit, but she had been wrong. She had been so wrong.

She walked back to her bedroom and climbed into bed. She didn't like the idea of sleeping alone, but knew she had to get used to it. She had no doubt Eleanor's closet wasn't opening any time soon.

## Chapter Twenty-five

Eleanor woke up Saturday morning and instinctively reached out for Randi. She woke fully when she didn't find her. The previous evening came back to her in a gush of memories. She felt the tears forming again. She tried to blink them away, but it was no use. They fell in full force. She sobbed until she had nothing left in her. She took a deep breath and thought about the situation.

Randi was gone. She was alone. There would be no more humorous talks. No more working together in the yard. And no more loving at night. That was reality. But there was a flip side to things. She no longer had to live in fear that someone would call her a lesbian. Not being seen in public with Randi could only help her reputation. So, she took a deep breath, life was going to be much better. If only her heart believed her.

The week went by with Eleanor still licking her wounds, but trying to convince herself all was well. Friday afternoon arrived and Ron poked his head into her room.

"Hey, stranger. It's been a while. Happy hour today?"

"No, thanks. I think I'll just head home."

"Are you sure? You look like you could use a night out."

Eleanor laughed.

"I'm not sure how to take that. But I really think I'd rather just go home."

"Suit yourself. You're missing out."

"I know, Ron. Have fun."

"Will do."

Eleanor went about gathering the homework she would take home to grade over the weekend.

"I don't suppose you're going to happy hour?" she heard someone say.

She looked up to see Martina. She felt her stomach grow cold. They hadn't really spoken since the last time they'd had dinner. Martina taught in a completely different wing at school and Eleanor hadn't engaged her at lunch at all.

"What are you doing in this wing?" Eleanor said.

"I came to talk to you."

"What about?" Eleanor held her breath. She didn't want a big scene.

"I've been watching you in the lunchroom this past week. You look like a little kid who's lost her puppy. I've been worried about you. Are you okay?"

"I'm fine." Eleanor wasn't about to go into it with Martina.

"Look, I wanted to apologize, also. I mean, I didn't really do anything wrong. Just misread signals. And I'm sorry for that. I didn't mean to make you uncomfortable around me."

"No," Eleanor said. "It was fine. You didn't do anything wrong. You're right. And I'm not really uncomfortable around you. I just haven't felt like socializing much."

"Well, how about going out this afternoon and blowing off some steam? I'm sure it'll be good for you."

"I don't know." Eleanor wasn't in the mood, really. But she had no reason to go home. Home was empty and lonely.

"You don't have to stay long. We won't even make you play pool." She smiled.

Eleanor felt the knot in her stomach loosen.

"Sure. Why not?" she heard herself say. "I'll meet you there."

After Martina left, Eleanor told herself she still didn't have to go. Who cared if she let Martina down? But she knew it would be good to socialize. She just hoped Randi didn't show up. But why would she? She was probably somewhere filled with a bunch of other out lesbians all celebrating their lesbianism and frowning on anyone in the closet. She felt anger coursing through her for the first time since Randi had dumped her. She'd been so busy feeling bad for hurting Randi that she'd never stopped to think how Randi had hurt her. And now that she thought about it, she was pissed.

She picked up her briefcase and headed for her car. Her heart was pounding. She was livid. How dare Randi simply cast her aside because she had certain needs? If Randi had truly loved her, she would have honored her desire to keep her sexuality private. It was no one's business who she slept with anyway, she thought.

She walked into the Bull and went straight to the bar to get her drink. She took her drink to the table and almost turned away when she saw Haven sitting there.

Shit.

"Have a seat." Haven moved over one seat and motioned to the one she'd vacated. Eleanor sat down uncomfortably. She sat up straight and sipped her drink.

"It's okay to relax," Martina said. "You're among friends."

Eleanor wished it was true. Being this close to Haven brought up feelings she didn't need to be having. She had just gotten out of a relationship, but there was no denying the heat she could feel radiating from Haven and the warmth in her eyes. She made it a point not to look at her.

"I'm relaxed," Eleanor said. "Or I will be after a couple of these."

"Good," Haven said. "You look like you need them."

"Jesus," Eleanor laughed. "Do I really look that bad?"

"Yes," Haven and Martina said in unison.

"Wow. I had no idea."

"You've been moping around for a week now. Every time I see you in the lunchroom, I want to try to cheer you up but you definitely give off the vibe that you want to be left alone," Martina said.

"And I'm just looking at you now. You look hollow. Nothing like the woman I first met," Haven said.

"I had no idea I was so transparent," Eleanor said.

"So, do you want to talk about it?" Martina said.

"No. I want to drink and forget about it."

"Fair enough."

The afternoon passed and soon people were getting up to play pool. Haven hung back at the table with Eleanor.

"Hey, you know, seriously, if there's anything I can do to help, just say the word," she said.

"I appreciate that, but I really am okay."

"Sure. After a few drinks. But what happens after that? You wake up tomorrow and have to deal with it, whatever it is. I'm a good listener. Why don't you let me take you to breakfast tomorrow?"

"I don't know, Haven…"

"Why not? I even promise to keep my hands to myself."

Eleanor had to laugh. She appreciated the offer. And she didn't need to hide anything from Haven. She already knew she was a lesbian. Maybe it would feel good to talk to someone.

"Sure," she said. "Why not?"

"Great. I'll pick you up at nine."

"Sounds good. And, Haven?"

"Yeah?"

"Thanks."

"No problem. I really do hate to see you this way. Now, how about some pool?"

Eleanor shot a couple games of pool, then excused herself for the evening. She stopped by a fast food joint and picked up a greasy meal to eat when she got home. The food tasted good. It was comfort food. As she ate, she contemplated her date with Haven the next day. No, she told herself. It wasn't a date. It was just a friend taking her to breakfast. A very nice looking lesbian friend she'd slept with. She sighed. What had she gotten herself into?

Sleep escaped her much of the night. She tossed and turned, second-guessing herself. She finally fell into a restless sleep and felt horrible when she woke up in the morning. She was exhausted. Her shower helped. She stood in her bedroom wondering what to wear. She finally decided on a pair of shorts and a T-shirt. She checked herself out in the mirror. Were the shorts too short? Would Haven take them suggestively? No, she thought. Haven wasn't looking for anything from her.

At exactly nine o'clock, there was a knock on her door. She opened it to see Haven standing there in cargo shorts and a loose T-shirt. She looked good. Eleanor shook her head. She didn't need to be checking anyone out. Least of all, Haven.

"You okay?" Haven said.

"Yeah. Sorry. Sometimes I get lost in my head. Let's get going."

They were seated at the restaurant sipping their coffee when Haven spoke.

"So, you wanna talk about it?"

"I don't really, but I guess I should."

"Well, I'm all ears. But if you've changed your mind, we can always talk shop."

Eleanor laughed.

"No. I feel like I can talk to you. Because, as far in the closet as I want to be publicly, you know for a fact that I'm a lesbian."

"Yes," Haven said. "I do know that for a fact."

She grinned at Eleanor who blushed.

"So, does this funk you're in have to do with a woman?"

Eleanor nodded and took another sip of coffee.

"Well, what's the story?" Then her face fell. "This wouldn't have anything to do with Randi Hansen would it?"

"Oh, shit," Eleanor said. "I forgot there's bad blood between you two. Maybe this wasn't such a good idea."

"No." Haven took a deep breath. "I'll try to keep an open mind. Go on. What happened?"

"We were an item, as you no doubt figured out."

"Right. I suspected."

"Now, I know you don't like her Haven, but she was wonderful to me."

"Good. That makes me happy. You deserve to be treated well. So, what was the problem?"

"Haven, I'm terrified of anyone finding out I'm a lesbian. I mean *terrified*. When I found out Martina was on the trail, I freaked out. I hadn't spoken to her since until today."

"I'm sorry. Martina's a safe person."

"Yeah. I'm sure she is. But she asked if I was a lesbian and if Randi and I were an item and I blatantly denied it."

"May I ask you," Haven said. "What's with this great need to stay in the closet? It's so confining there."

"This place is so much more conservative than what I'm used to. I just don't feel comfortable in my own skin here. I feel like I'd be tarred and feathered if anybody knew."

Haven smiled gently at her.

"It's not that bad down here. I mean, I get your unease, but it shouldn't be sheer terror."

"Maybe not, but it is."

"Okay, so you and Randi were an item and then what? Don't tell me she hurt you?"

"Actually," Eleanor said. "I think I hurt her more."

"Yeah? So, what happened?"

"She told me to choose between her and my closet."

"And you chose the closet?" Haven's eyebrows shot up.

Eleanor simply nodded, not trusting her words. Her eyes teared up. She didn't want to cry. Not in public and certainly not in front of Haven.

"Eleanor. Are you serious?"

Eleanor took a deep breath. She blinked away her tears, though one slid down her cheek. Haven reached across the table and wiped it away.

"Yes, I'm serious. Haven, I can't be out. I just can't."

"Did you love her?"

"Yes." She answered quietly, almost afraid of her own answer.

"And she loved you?"

"Yes."

"And you threw that away?" Haven said.

"I know. I know. I know how it sounds, but Haven, she wanted me to go to a women's bar with her. She wanted us to be out together. I can't imagine stepping foot in a women's bar. What if someone saw me?"

"What if they did?"

"What if Principal Barret did? I could lose my job."

"Eleanor, you can't lose your job for being a lesbian. It doesn't work that way."

"Prove it to me. Prove to me I wouldn't be fired for some trumped up reason when the real reason was because I'm gay."

"I can't prove it to you and you know that. Didn't you two ever go anywhere together?"

"For a while we did. We'd go out to dinner and stuff. But pretty soon the wait staff from different restaurants started to recognize us as a couple. So, for the last few weeks, I've made sure to cook dinner at home so we wouldn't have to go out."

"Wow. Randi's a very social person. That must have been killing her not to go anywhere."

"Yeah, so I agreed to go with her to the Bull. We had a few drinks and then all hell broke loose. That's when she told me to choose. And I chose the closet. And I know I did the right thing, but I feel like I lost my best friend."

"That's because you did," Haven said softly.

Eleanor nodded. The waitress delivered their meals and she wondered if she'd be able to eat anything. She took one bite of her omelet and it was delicious. It was warm and cheesy and just what she needed.

Haven took a bite of her pancakes. She chewed slowly, then took a swallow of coffee.

"So," she said. "The only way to get Randi back is to leave your closet behind. I'd be happy to do that with you."

"No. I'm too scared. You don't understand."

"No, I don't. But I know if you want Randi back you're going to have to figure out how to bust that bad boy wide open."

"I don't know that she's worth it. I don't know that anyone's worth that price."

"What can I do to convince you it's not that conservative here?"

"I don't think you can. If Randi couldn't, how could you?"

"Do you know we have a lesbian city councilmember?"

"Like openly so?"

"Like openly so," Haven said. "She actually used it as part of her campaign, hoping to get the liberal vote. And it worked."

"Well, I suppose that's a start."

"Good. I think you need to go home and read over your contract. I think you'll see the non-discrimination clause."

"I'm sure there's something in there, but like I said, they can fire me for something else, you know?"

"Then you threaten a wrongful termination suit."

"No. You don't understand, Haven. That's not my style."

"Eleanor," Haven said. "If you stay in that closet, you're going to suffocate. I can't believe you got Randi Hansen to settle down, but if you did, it must have been something pretty special. I can't believe you're willing to throw it all away. You need to think long and hard about what I've said. We don't live in the dark ages around here. It's okay to be gay. Trust me."

"I wish I could."

Breakfast was over and Haven paid the bill. She walked Eleanor out to her car.

"Do you feel any better?" she said.

"I don't know. I'm still so conflicted. But maybe coming out slowly wouldn't kill me. I just don't know."

"Well, you think about our talk, okay? And if you need to talk some more, you just call me."

She took Eleanor's phone and entered her number.

"Thanks," Eleanor said. "For everything."

"No problem. What are friends for?"

Eleanor rode home pondering all that Haven had told her. She felt a headache coming on.

## CHAPTER TWENTY-SIX

Saturday morning, Randi woke up with a sore head and achy body. She'd been on call the night before, but it had been a slow night. Still, she hadn't been able to go to the club. She'd stayed home, just in case. That didn't stop her from drinking too much tequila. She didn't know what she would have done if she'd gotten a call. In retrospect, it hadn't been the most responsible night of her life.

Her body ached from all the weights she'd been lifting. Her workouts had all but disappeared while she'd been with Eleanor. She'd spent every hour possible with her, leaving virtually no time to lift. Sure, she snuck in a workout once in a while when Eleanor had been at happy hour, but even those sessions had been abbreviated. So she'd pushed herself hard the night before. Too hard. And now she felt like shit all over.

She made a pot of coffee and sat down on her patio to wait for it to brew. It was going to be a very warm day, the kind she loved. She looked around her yard and thought she could do a little work on it. But yard work reminded her of Eleanor and she didn't want to think about her.

She poured her coffee and sipped it slowly. She again had to fight to keep thoughts of Eleanor out of her head. She seemed to be all she thought about lately. Damn her! How could she have chosen the closet over her? Randi had made her happy. She'd loved her. Why hadn't Eleanor chosen her?

Fuck her, Randi thought. She was going to go out that night, have a few beers, and dance the night away. Maybe she'd even find some nice warm body to fill her bed with. The thought made her smile. She needed to get back in her groove.

Saturday evening rolled around. Randi treated herself to dinner out, then drove to Joni's, ready for some action. When she arrived, the place was still fairly quiet. She took her usual spot at the bar and ordered a beer.

"You want a tequila with that tonight, sugar?" the bartender said.

"No, thanks. No tequila tonight."

She sipped her beer and looked around. There were slim pickings so far. There were some nice looking ladies there, but none of them really called to her. She turned back toward the bar and drank her beer.

She ordered another one and turned around again to survey the room. It was filling up nicely. The music finally started and she tapped her toe in time. She sized up all the women and her gaze finally landed on a petite redhead sitting at a table. There were several women with her. She wondered if she was taken. There was only one way to find out.

Randi approached the table full of women and, as she did, her gaze met the redhead's. The redhead smiled. This was a good thing. Randi sidled up next to her.

"So," Randi said. "Is one of these women your girlfriend, partner, or wife?"

The redhead laughed.

"None of the above," she said.

"Would you like to dance?"

"Sure."

Randi led her to the center of the floor where she released her hand and started to move to the music. They danced several dances and then a slow song came on.

"I should get back to my table," the redhead said.

"Okay. Maybe we'll dance more later?"

"Maybe."

That didn't sound too promising, Randi thought. But by then, the place was packed and she had her pick of women. She scanned the room and saw a tall brunette. She started to approach her, but was too late. Someone else had just asked her to dance. Randi sat back down. She ordered another beer and watched the brunette move on the floor. She swayed as one with the music and looked sexy as hell. Randi's palms itched. She couldn't wait to take her turn.

The song ended and the woman walked back to her table. Randi decided to make her move. She crossed over to her.

"Would you like to dance?" Randi said.

"Sure," the woman said.

They danced on the edge of the dance floor, since the floor was so crowded. They danced well together and, when the song ended, Randi offered to buy her a drink.

"That would be nice," the woman said.

Randi went to the bar and ordered herself another beer and a martini for the woman. When she got back to the table, the woman was back out on the dance floor. Randi sat down and nursed her beer as she waited for her to get back.

The song ended and the woman was back. She sat across from Randi.

"Thanks for the drink," she called over the music.

"You're welcome. I'm Randi, by the way."

"I'm Melissa."

Randi extended her hand and Melissa took it in hers. Her hand was soft and warm. Randi didn't want to let go, but she did.

"So, tell me about yourself, Melissa."

"I'm a teacher at the high school."

Randi felt like she'd been punched in the gut. She wished Eleanor was there to see that another teacher was there having fun, not worried about being seen. Damn it, she thought. Get Eleanor out of your head.

"Are you okay?" Melissa said. "You look like you've seen a ghost. Did you have a horrible high school experience or something?"

"Oh, no," Randi laughed. "Nothing like that. It just seems like that would be a challenging job."

"You have no idea. And what do you do, Randi?"

"I work for Animal Control. Nothing exciting about that."

"No? You don't have any stories to tell?"

"Oh, you know," Randi said. "There's the occasional alligator to wrassle. Or stray cat or dog to rescue. That's about it."

"You've really wrestled an alligator?"

Randi's mind went back to the alligator she wrassled at Eleanor's house. That was the first time they'd met. They'd gone out to dinner after that. Randi knew then she was into her. She brought herself back to the present.

"Sure have. My partner and I have it down. I take the mouth. He takes the body. Together, we get it done."

"Wow," Melissa's eyebrows shot up. "I hope I never have a run in with an alligator. That's my greatest fear living in these parts."

"Well, if you ever see one, just call us and we'll come get it for you." Randi handed her her card.

"Thanks."

"Did you want to dance again?"

"Sure."

Randi took her to the center of the floor this time, where there was hardly any room so they were pushed close together. The music was fast, but that didn't matter. She liked the feeling of Melissa so close to her that she rubbed against her when she moved. A slow song started and Randi held out her arms to invite Melissa in. Melissa moved into her arms and they danced a provocative dance. Randi felt things stirring inside her that hadn't stirred in a week.

When the song ended, Melissa pulled Randi down for a kiss. Randi closed her eyes and braced for the electricity she knew was coming. Melissa was hot and obviously into her. But when their lips met, there was nothing. No reaction at all.

Melissa opened her mouth, urging Randi in, but Randi had no desire to continue. She pulled away. She couldn't take Melissa home. No matter how attractive she was and no matter how badly Melissa wanted her, she just couldn't do it.

"I think I should get going," Randi said.

"Are you serious?"

"Yeah. I'm sorry. Maybe I'll see you here some other time."

She left Melissa on the dance floor, staring at her incredulously. Randi didn't know what was going on. She had no explanation for it, but she knew she had to get out of there. She got home, stripped, and climbed into bed. Alone. What had she been thinking? Melissa had been a sure thing. She closed her eyes and tried to sleep, but sleep eluded her. She allowed her mind to drift to thoughts of Eleanor and she fought the urge to cry herself to sleep.

❖

Eleanor watched the news that Saturday evening. It was an election year and it seemed like every other commercial was about one candidate or another and their view on social issues. It seemed so many of them were against gay rights. Eleanor wrapped her arms around herself. She wasn't surprised. And one of them would likely get elected, she thought. And everyone who was out, loud and proud, now would be scurrying for the closet. She was just ahead of the trend.

Sure, the news showed gay rights rallies, too, but she knew they were fighting for a useless cause. People hated homosexuals in small, underdeveloped areas. Sure, it was different in a city like San Francisco. They openly accepted anyone. But this wasn't San Francisco. It was a small town with small-minded people. And nothing anyone could tell her would convince her otherwise.

She turned off the television and poured herself another glass of wine. She decided to grade homework. It would be less stressful. She worked until ten then climbed into bed. It was when she was in bed that she missed Randi the most. She missed the warmth of her body and the limitless passion they shared.

Eleanor lay thinking of Randi and placed her hands on her breasts. She loved how Randi had made her feel just by teasing them. She pulled and twisted her nipples as she thought of Randi's mouth on them. She was becoming aroused. She didn't care. She hadn't come in what seemed like forever.

She continued tweaking her nipples and finally she had a small orgasm. It was nothing like the gut wrenching climaxes Randi gave her. She moved her hands down her body to where her legs met. She played her fingers over her clit, urging it to stand taller. She was already wet, but not as swollen as she usually got for Randi. She moved her hand lower and slid her fingers inside herself. She moved them in and out as she stroked herself. She thought of Randi and her powerful fingers. She closed her eyes and pictured her gorgeous eyes and strong body. She bit her lip as she came.

Eleanor dragged her fingers back to her clit and rubbed it. She rubbed hard and fast and forgot everything as a powerful orgasm washed over her. Satiated, she closed her eyes and dreamed of Randi.

The rest of the week dragged on for Eleanor. She was still miserable, but knew in her heart she had done the right thing. Friday afternoon finally rolled around and she went to happy hour with the gang. This time, she was almost sad that Haven wasn't there. She'd been so nice when they'd had breakfast together.

As usual, Eleanor bought her drink then joined the raucous crowd at the table.

"What's going on?" Eleanor said as she sat down. It was then that she noticed a strange woman sitting next to Martina. She was short, with thick dark hair that fell to her shoulders. She was very pretty.

"We're celebrating," Ron said.

"So I noticed. What are we celebrating?"

"Someone's finally captured Martina's heart," he said.

"Oh yeah?" Eleanor arched an eyebrow.

"Hi, Eleanor," Martina said. She put her arm around the other woman. "This is Sondra."

"Wow," Eleanor said. "Congratulations."

"Yep. We're officially a couple now."

Eleanor didn't ask what made that official. She knew she and Randi had officially been a couple, but couldn't have said when exactly that happened. She was happy for Martina. She was positively beaming. But Eleanor couldn't help but be scared for her at the same time. She was risking her job being so open about her new relationship.

"Sondra is going to move in with me this weekend," Martina said.

"That's great," Eleanor said. She tried to put on a happy face, but was terrified for Martina.

"And what do you do, Sondra?" Eleanor said.

"I work at the middle school. Isn't that great? We'll have the same time off and everything. It's perfect."

"That really is wonderful. How'd you two meet?"

"We actually met on the houseboat," Sondra said. "I was a friend of a friend. We hit it off immediately and have been dating since then. We finally decided it was time to move in together. I'm so excited."

Eleanor fought hard to be happy for the couple, but was too scared. Soon, people got up and started playing pool. Eleanor excused herself from the happy couple and played pool with the others. As the evening was winding down, Martina approached her.

"Hey, Eleanor, we're going to go get food. We'd really like you to join us."

Eleanor tried to think of why that was a bad idea, but came up empty.

"Sounds great. Where shall we go?"

"Tony's. Sondra loves Italian."

"Okay. I'll meet you there."

Eleanor got to the restaurant before the happy couple. She hoped they behaved. She didn't want people to talk. She didn't want to be embarrassed, or, worse yet, kicked out of the place. As she sat in the entryway, she saw them walk up holding hands. She felt like they were just asking for trouble.

When they were inside, Eleanor stood behind them as Martina asked for a table. She was amazed and appalled that they were still holding hands. Didn't they realize they were in public? They were led to a table and Martina and Sondra sat on one side of the booth and Eleanor sat on the other.

"Don't you two worry about being in public?" Eleanor said.

Martina looked from Sondra to Eleanor.

"Worry about what?"

"You're in public. People will see you."

"So?"

"So, what if they try to beat you up or something?" Eleanor said.

"Are you serious? Sister, what year do you think you live in?"

"I know what year it is, Martina. And I know things like that still happen in small towns like ours."

"Our town isn't that small, honey," Sondra said. "People are accepting. People don't judge. Not around here. They're not like that."

"I don't believe you. And what if the principals of one of your schools finds out? Then what?"

"Then they find out. Who cares?"

"Aren't you worried you could lose your jobs?" Eleanor said.

"No. I'm a damned good teacher. I've got nothing to worry about," Martina said.

Eleanor shook her head.

"I'm sorry. I mean, I'm really happy for you two and all, but I really think you need to be more careful."

"Nonsense," Martina said. "We're happy. We deserve to be happy and I don't care who knows about it."

They tabled the conversation as they ate.

"So, Eleanor," Sondra said. "Are you not seeing anyone?"

"Nope. I'm free as a bird."

"It's no wonder, I guess, huh? What with the fear you live with?"

"How do you mean? It's different with me."

"How so?" Sondra said.

"I'm straight."

"Oh. My bad. I guess my gaydar is off. I apologize."

Eleanor flushed.

"It's okay. Apparently, it happens a lot." She looked pointedly at Martina.

"Yeah," Martina said. "I was trying to put the moves on Eleanor when she first got to the school. I soon found out I was barking up the wrong tree."

"Lucky for me," Sondra said.

"Yeah." Eleanor made herself smile. "Lucky for you."

As she followed them out of the restaurant, Eleanor tried to hang back, lest she be seen with them and labeled a lesbian.

## CHAPTER TWENTY-SEVEN

Eleanor drove home from dinner with her head swimming. She had so much to think about. She just wanted to get home and forget about Martina and Sondra. But she got home and they were still on her mind. She poured herself a glass of wine and pondered their open happiness. She wondered what that would be like? Sure, she'd had it in the Bay Area, but that seemed a long time ago in a galaxy far away.

She questioned whether her makeshift closet had ruined her one true shot at happiness in her new life. Was it possible to be out down here? Martina and Sondra sure seemed to think so. But their relationship was new. People didn't know about it. That's not true, she thought. She'd spent how many hours at the bar with several coworkers who not only knew about them, but were happy for them. Perhaps she had been viewing this town as more conservative than it truly was.

Still, she couldn't help the feeling in her gut and that feeling told her that it wasn't safe to be in an openly gay relationship there. Maybe she'd just watch Sondra and Martina and see what happened. That seemed like the logical thing to do.

She missed Randi. She couldn't deny that. She wanted to be able to hold her hand in public, to be able to relax if Randi slid her arm around her at a bar. But she couldn't. Deep down, she couldn't. And now that she'd built this closet, would she be able to come out of it? Would she be okay telling Martina that she had lied to her?

She didn't know what to do, but she knew she didn't want to be alone with her thoughts any longer.

She picked up the phone and dialed. It was answered on the first ring.

"Eleanor?"

"Hi, Haven."

"Is everything okay?"

"Yeah. I just don't want to be alone and I couldn't think who else to call. Am I interrupting anything?"

"No," Haven said. "I'm just chillin'."

"Do you want to come over? Or maybe meet somewhere for a drink?"

"I'm up for either. Which would you prefer?"

"Why don't you come on over?" Eleanor said. "I have wine."

"Okay. I'll be there in a few."

Eleanor put her phone on the table and poured a glass of wine for Haven. She got butterflies in her stomach as she poured. What was she doing? Was this okay? She didn't want to give Haven the wrong idea. She didn't want her to think she was into her. She just needed someone to talk to. She probably should have specified that on the phone. She hoped she wasn't leading Haven on.

She heard a knock on her door and opened it immediately. Haven stood there with a look of concern on her face.

"Come on in," Eleanor said.

Haven stepped inside and pulled Eleanor into a giant bear hug.

"You okay?" she said. "It was quite unexpected, getting a call from you."

"I don't know. I'm so confused. And the more I think, the more confused I get. I couldn't think of anyone else to call to get me out of my head, so I called you. I hope that's okay."

"Of course it's okay. I'm happy to be here for you."

Eleanor handed her a glass of wine and invited her to sit in the living room. She sat on the couch and Haven took the loveseat.

"So, you wanna talk about it?" Haven said.

"I don't know. I guess. Otherwise, why would I have called?"

"Yeah. I didn't think this was a booty call," Haven smiled. "What's going on?"

"I had dinner tonight with a lesbian couple."

"Let me guess. Martina and Sondra? Aren't they a great couple?"

"Yeah. I guess."

"What? What's wrong? I think they're great together."

"I'm scared for them."

"Scared? They're solid, Eleanor. There's no reason to be scared for them," Haven said.

"But they walked up to the restaurant holding hands. Holding hands, Haven. In public."

"And?"

"And then they sat on the same side of the booth. It was awkward."

"Why?"

"What if someone hassled them? Hurt them, even? I don't think they realize the risks."

Haven crossed the room and sat next to Eleanor.

"Eleanor. I keep trying to tell you. It's not like that here."

"How can you be sure?"

"I've done my share of dating. I've never felt uncomfortable. Let me ask you something. Were you nervous having dinner with me that time? Or breakfast?"

"Not really."

"And we were clearly two lesbians. Or maybe it's easier for me because I couldn't pass for straight if I tried. You could. And you do. But you're not being true to yourself. It's not healthy."

"I don't know," Eleanor said. "Part of me wants to believe that. A big part of me now. But part of me is still worried."

"Well, I say you don't listen to that little part. It could keep you from happiness."

"That's another thing I'm scared of. I just threw away a perfectly good relationship out of fear. Will I get another chance? I don't plan on moving away. Do I plan on living alone for the rest of my life?"

"Those are hard questions, Eleanor. And only you can answer them."

"I'd ask what you'd do if you were me, but I already know that answer."

"Yes, you do."

They sat there in silence for a few moments. Eleanor took a sip of wine.

"But after what I've done, do you think Randi would take me back?" she said.

Haven sat back against the couch.

"You said she loved you?"

Eleanor nodded.

"Then why wouldn't she take you back?"

"I don't know."

"You worry too much, Eleanor. I'd hate to see you worry yourself out of happiness."

"But what if she's found someone else?" Eleanor said.

"I wouldn't worry about that. She's not the settling down type, to be honest."

Eleanor let out a long sigh.

"I wish I could just make up my mind."

"Well, I think you're getting close, Eleanor."

"Yeah. I am."

"You want me to be here when you call her?"

"No. That won't be necessary."

"Okay. I'll say good night then. But, Eleanor?"

"Yeah?"

"Promise me you'll call her?"

"I promise."

She walked Haven to the door.

"And I promise you being out isn't anywhere near as scary as being in the closet," Haven said. She took Eleanor in her arms again. "Be strong."

Randy was working out when she heard her phone go off. She set the bar down and checked the read out. Eleanor. What the hell? Why would she be calling? She tossed her phone down and went back to working out. She tried to focus on what she was doing, but it was no use. She gave up and went inside. She took a shower. When she was drying off, her phone rang again. It was Eleanor again.

"Hello?" Randi barked.

"Randi?"

"Yeah. What's up?" She knew her voice was cool, but what did Eleanor expect? She'd ripped her heart out of her chest and torn it to shreds. Did Eleanor think she'd be happy to hear from her?

"Can we meet tomorrow to talk?"

"What about?"

"Us."

"There is no us."

"Please, Randi," Eleanor said. "It's important."

"Okay. Fine. Where do you want to meet and when?"

"Can we meet for breakfast?"

"I don't plan on being up early enough for breakfast. Let's get a pizza at Tony's for lunch. Say one o'clock?"

"One o'clock? Okay. I can do that."

"Okay. I'll see you there."

Randi tossed her phone on the couch and went to the kitchen to get a beer. She wasn't on call that weekend, but hadn't been in the mood to go to Joni's. She took a long pull of her beer. What the hell could Eleanor want to talk to her about? She searched her brain. Had she left something there that Eleanor found and wanted to return? That must be it. There was certainly no "us" to talk about. Eleanor had made damn sure about that.

Randi finished her beer and grabbed another. She turned on the TV, but nothing held her attention. Just hearing Eleanor's voice had her feeling all sorts of things she didn't need to be feeling. No matter how pissed she was at her, her insides got all watery at the sound of her voice. Her heart skipped a beat. She finished that beer and thought about getting another, but opted not to. She wanted to go to bed. To sleep. To escape all these thoughts.

But when she was horizontal, sleep escaped her. She kept thinking about Eleanor and all the good times they'd had. But that was over now. She couldn't, wouldn't, live in a closet, and Eleanor wouldn't come out.

She finally fell asleep and night was filled with erotic dreams of Eleanor. Eleanor in the shower, Eleanor in bed. Her soft, silky skin under Randi. Randi woke around nine in hormonal frustration. And that was the last thing she needed if she was going to meet Eleanor. She needed to keep her head. She needed to stay calm and cool and not crumple at the sight of her.

She showered and contemplated a beer. No, it was too early. Even for her. Even on a day she was going to meet Eleanor. She drank coffee and basically sat around waiting. She should have agreed to breakfast. That way they could have gotten this over with sooner. Instead, she sat there, all sorts of scenarios running through her head and she had no idea which, if any, was accurate.

Finally, it was time to leave. She put on a pair of cargo shorts and an old, faded T-shirt. No reason to try to look nice. Not for Eleanor. She pulled up at Tony's at one and saw Eleanor's car in the parking lot. Her stomach knotted. Maybe she should just leave. Just blow her off. She didn't owe her anything. But as much as she hated to admit it to herself, she was really looking forward to seeing Eleanor. She missed her, damn it.

She walked in and saw Eleanor sitting in the waiting area. She stood when she saw Randi.

"You came," she said.

"I said I would."

"Thank you."

"What's this all about?"

"Let's wait until we're seated," Eleanor said.

They were shown to a booth and ordered their pizza.

"So, what's going on?" Randi said.

Eleanor took a deep breath. She looked hard at Randi.

"Yeah?" Randi said.

"I want to try again," Eleanor said.

"It won't work."

"Please, Randi. Hear me out."

"I'm listening."

The pizza arrived and Randi took a piece, welcoming the opportunity to look anywhere but at Eleanor. Her stomach still had a cold fist in it, but she managed to take a bite of pizza and, chewing it slowly, swallowed it.

"I love you, Randi. You must know that."

"I don't think our feelings for each other were ever in question," Randi said.

"No. But, well, the issue of the closet?"

"Yeah. That would be the issue."

"Randi," Eleanor said. "I'm willing to come out. I'm tired of living in solitary confinement. I want to be with you and I want the world to know I'm with you."

Randi felt the cold inside begin to melt. It sounded good, but could she trust her?

"Look, Eleanor, that sounds wonderful. If you could do that. But I'm not convinced. I don't want to give my heart to you only to have you go running back into the closet, closing me out forever."

Eleanor reached across the table and took Randi's hand.

"I'm not going back in the closet, Randi. I still have my insecurities, but with your help, I truly believe I can overcome them. I believe I can be out. And I want to be out with you."

Randi felt Eleanor's hand in hers. It was soft and warm. Damn it, she'd missed her so fucking much. It hurt. She wanted to believe they could be together, but she was scared. She took her hand back and took another bite of pizza. She chewed slowly.

"So, what's prompted this about-face?" Randi said.

"A lot of things. I've been doing a lot of thinking and a lot of talking to a friend."

"A friend? What friend might that be? Who knows you're a lesbian?"

"Randi, if I tell you, you have to promise not to be pissed."

Pissed? Who could she mean?

"Haven," Randi said it as her cocky face appeared in her mind.

"There was no one else for me to talk to. Please understand."

Randi nodded. She didn't like Eleanor having anything to do with Haven, but Haven was the only person beside her who knew she was a lesbian. Naturally, Eleanor would turn to her.

"Yeah," she said. "I guess that makes sense."

"And I went to dinner with a lesbian couple last night. They were so happy. And so open. And no one said anything to them or was mean to them."

"Who do you know besides Haven and me who's a lesbian?"

"Martina."

"Oh, really?" Randi raised an eyebrow.

Eleanor nodded.

"I didn't know she was in a couple," Randi said. "I thought she was hitting on you."

"She was, but I didn't know that. And that was a long time ago. She met a woman on the houseboat. They're moving in together this weekend. She brought her to happy hour and everything. She's so happy. And everyone is so happy for her."

"So, you thought you could be that happy."

"We could. Yes."

Randi leaned back against the booth and let out a sigh. It was what she wanted. It was what she had wanted all along. So, what was making her hold back?

"Please, Randi. Say something."

"I'm going to need proof," Randi said. "It sounds wonderful and we could go back to your place right now and celebrate, but I need proof."

"Anything. What do you want me to do? Just say the word."

"Go with me to Joni's tonight."

"Joni's?"

"The women's club."

Randi saw the color drain from Eleanor's face, but then return.

"Sure," Eleanor said. "That would be great. I'd love to go dancing with you."

"Okay then. I'll pick you up at eight. We'll get there in time for a couple of drinks before the dancing starts."

"Sounds fun."

Randi had the rest of the pizza boxed up.

"You want this?" she said. "You didn't eat a bite."

"No, thanks. I'm too nervous to eat."

"Don't be nervous. If you're really fine being out, then getting back together should be a breeze."

"Thank you, Randi. Thank you so much for giving me a second chance."

Randi saw the unshed tears glistening in Eleanor's eyes. When they were in the parking lot, she pulled Eleanor to her.

"It's going to be okay," she murmured. "Everything is going to be fine."

"I know. I believe that. I'm just so glad you're willing to take me back."

A tear broke loose and Randi brushed it away.

"I still love you, Eleanor. I've never stopped."

"Oh, Randi. Thank you. Thank you so much. I love you, too."

Eleanor turned her face up and Randi looked into her beautiful eyes. They were deep and dark and called to her. She knew Eleanor wanted a kiss as badly as Randi wanted to kiss her. But it would have to wait. It would all depend on how things went at the club that night. Randi half expected Eleanor to chicken out at the last minute. Randi took a step back.

"So, I'll see you at eight?"

"I'll be waiting," Eleanor said.

Randi drove off with a smile on her face, feeling lighter than she had in weeks.

## Chapter Twenty-eight

Eleanor was beside herself when she got home. Lunch had taken two hours so she still had five hours to kill before she got to go out with Randi. Randi was going to take her back. Of course, it was contingent on her going to Joni's, but she didn't think that would be a problem. She'd already agreed to go. And although her stomach got a little queasy at the idea that someone might see her walk into a women's club, the benefits far outweighed the downside.

She needed to do this. She needed to prove to herself and to Randi that she could be out. This was just the first step. Besides, she was actually looking forward to being around a whole bunch of lesbians. She hadn't done that since she moved here and she missed the synergy that came with those occasions.

As the time to leave got closer, she made herself a sandwich, finally able to eat. Then, she soaked in a bathtub filled with lavender oil. She felt soft and sexy when she got out. She put on a short red leather skirt and a white button-down blouse. She slipped on a pair of red flats and she was ready to go. She checked herself out in the mirror and was certain Randi would like what she saw.

She poured herself a glass of wine and sat down. She was jittery, nervous. But she was also excited. She was going out on a date with Randi and it had been too long. Even when they'd gone out to dinner, though, back when they were seeing each other, she'd never really considered that a date. It was just Randi and her going to get dinner. This was a date. Randi would pick her up and take her to the club.

The club. She would walk in to an all-women's club escorted by a handsome, obviously gay, woman. And, damn it, she'd do it proudly. Who cared who saw? She was a grown woman with grown woman needs, and if those needs required a woman to take care of them, then so be it.

She lost track of time and almost jumped when she heard the doorbell. She answered it and there stood Randi, looking exquisitely dapper in cargo shorts and a green golf shirt. Eleanor wanted to take her to bed right then.

Randi gave her the once over and let out a low wolf whistle.

"Damn, Eleanor," she said. "You look amazing."

"Thanks." She blushed. "Did you want to come in for a beer before we go?"

"Sure."

It was awkward having to invite her in. She wanted Randi to walk in, help herself to the beer, then come join her. She wanted things to be like they used to be. Soon, she told herself. Soon they would be.

Eleanor went to the kitchen to grab Randi a beer. When she walked back to the living room, Randi was seated in the loveseat, although Eleanor's wine glass was in front of the sofa. Eleanor handed her her beer and sat down across from her.

"You sure about this?" Randi said.

"Don't I look sure?"

"You do. I've gotta admit, I like what I'm seeing. But I still wonder if you'll have second thoughts."

"No. Not me. As a matter of fact, I'm even looking forward to this."

"You are?" Randi arched an eyebrow.

"I am. It'll be fun to be in the company of so many lesbians."

"I hope you don't plan on checking any of them out."

"No. I only have eyes for you. And, you? Will you be dancing with all the hot ladies there?"

"Nope," Randi said. "I plan to focus all my attention on you."

"Good. I'm glad that's settled."

They finished their drinks and Randi stood.

"Come on. I'd like to have you there before the dancing starts. We can get a good seat to watch everyone and we can keep chatting while we wait."

"Sounds good."

They drove to the club in silence, but it wasn't uncomfortable. Eleanor would occasionally get nervous, but she mentally talked herself out of it. She was going to have fun. She was determined to.

The club was still mostly empty when they arrived.

"Dancing doesn't start until nine," Randi said. "Most people will get here after that."

She escorted Eleanor to a table just off the dance floor and went to the bar to get them drinks. When she came back, Eleanor smiled widely at her. Randi looked delicious. She had her swagger on and exuded sexuality. Clearly, she was in her element. And so was Eleanor. She looked around the room at the women that were there. There were mostly couples so far. And they all looked so happy. She felt a sense of calm settle over her. Things really were going to be okay.

The place was filling up and Randi pointed out a few of the regulars as they came in. The music started and they turned around to face the dance floor. They were watching people move when Eleanor heard a voice in her ear.

"Straight, huh?"

She turned to see Martina standing there with Sondra. She blushed a deep red. She got up and hugged first Martina then Sondra.

"It's so good to see you," she said. "This is my first time here. Martina, you remember Randi, don't you? Sondra, this is Randi. Randi, Sondra."

Randi shook hands with Martina and Sondra. Martina looked back at Eleanor.

"So, you just figured out you're a lesbian? Honey, I've known all along."

"I knew, too," Eleanor admitted. "I just never planned on coming out down here."

"Why?"

"Stupid reasons. Fear mostly. But you two showed me it's okay to be out. People not only don't treat you like crap, they're happy for you."

"Well, good. I'm glad you're out now. Feels good, doesn't it?"

Eleanor nodded and pulled up two more chairs.

"Do you want to join us?"

"Sure."

Randi stood and walked over to Eleanor.

"I hate to break up this happy scene, but I really would like to dance with you."

"Of course," Eleanor said. They excused themselves from the table and made their way to the center of the dance floor. It still wasn't crowded, so they had plenty of room to move.

Randi felt good to get her groove on and she loved the way Eleanor danced. They'd never danced together and this was quite a treat. Eleanor just let the music flow through her as she swayed to and fro on the floor. They danced song after song and finally a slow song came on. Randi opened her arms and Eleanor immediately moved into them.

Randi wrapped her arms around Eleanor and held her tight as they moved as one to the music. It was so familiar and so right to hold Eleanor this way. She was so proud of her and so happy that she was willing to live her life as a free woman and not some second-class citizen.

The song ended and Eleanor looked up at her. Randi watched her lips part and saw desire in her eyes. She wanted Eleanor as much as Eleanor wanted her, but she wasn't ready. Not yet. She took her hand and led her back to the table. She went to the bar to get more drinks.

She needed a minute to regain her composure. She wanted Eleanor so badly it hurt. But she was afraid to kiss her. Afraid that once she started, she wouldn't be able to stop. And that, she was saving for later. For when they got back to Eleanor's and she got that sweet, form-fitting skirt peeled off of her and could enjoy her completely. She wasn't ready to leave just yet, though. She wanted to dance some more.

Randi got back to the table and handed Eleanor her rum and Coke.

"Are you okay?" Eleanor said.

"Yeah. I'm having a blast. You?"

"Yeah. I'm having fun. I just thought, well, that maybe I'd done something wrong."

"Oh, no, baby. You're doing everything right. You're quite a dancer."

"Thanks. So, why didn't you want to kiss me?"

"I do, baby. And I will. When the time is right, I'll kiss your socks off."

"I look forward to that," Eleanor said.

"Me, too. Now, come on. Let's dance some more."

She led Eleanor back to the dance floor where they danced until they sweat. Then they went back to the table and sipped their drinks. Randi draped her arm over Eleanor's shoulders. Eleanor moved close to her. Randi was happy. She had Eleanor back and Eleanor seemed perfectly comfortable there at the club. This was a good thing, since Randi had her mind made up that they would be going there as frequently as they could.

The night wore on and another slow song played. This time, when it ended, Eleanor looked up at Randi and Randi was unable to resist. She saw her soft lips parted slightly and knew it was no use trying to deny herself. She lowered her head and brushed her lips against Eleanor's. The feeling of electricity shot through her body. She pulled her closer and pressed their bodies together. She pulled back and saw Eleanor's nipples, hard under her blouse. She longed to take them in her mouth and make Eleanor come. She could barely stand.

"Let's get out of here," she whispered hoarsely.

They said good night to Martina and Sondra and left the club. They held hands as they drove to Eleanor's house. Once inside the house, Randi took Eleanor in her arms again and kissed her hard on her mouth. Their tongues met and Randi felt the icy hot shivers flow through her body. She needed Eleanor and soon. She had to have her. To prove to herself that Eleanor was hers again. Hers and hers alone.

She led Eleanor to the bedroom, feeling once again like this was her place as well as Eleanor's. She sat on the bed and pulled Eleanor to her. She slowly unzipped the form fitting red skirt and lowered it so Eleanor could step out of it. She rested her head on Eleanor's belly. She was warm and soft. Randi's heart raced with the need she was feeling. She slowly unbuttoned Eleanor's shirt and slid it off her shoulders.

Next, Randi unhooked Eleanor's bra. She held her breasts in her hands and ran her thumbs over her nipples. She bent forward to take one in her mouth. She sucked greedily at it, pulling it as deep into her mouth as she could. She could feel Eleanor trembling as she held her in place with one hand on either side of her head.

Randi kept licking and sucking until Eleanor cried out and collapsed against her.

"Let's get these panties off you," Randi said. She peeled them down and off Eleanor. She rested her face on Eleanor's thigh. She could smell her from there. Her mouth watered. She wanted to taste her. She needed to enjoy her wholly.

Randi stood and quickly undressed. When she was naked, she eased Eleanor down onto the bed and lay next to her. She climbed on top of her and reveled in the feel of skin on skin. She ground her pelvis into Eleanor's and Eleanor wrapped her legs around her. Randi could feel the wet heat from Eleanor's center. She couldn't wait any longer.

She got off Eleanor and kissed her way down Eleanor's chest to her other breast. She sucked on that nipple until Eleanor dug her fingernails into Randi's back to let her know she'd climaxed.

Randi kissed lower on Eleanor, stopping to kiss and nibble her cute little belly button. She finally came to where her legs met. She climbed between them and inhaled deeply. She smelled like Eleanor. Salty and musky and sweet and savory. Eleanor. She ran her tongue over her and relished the flavor that was Eleanor's alone. She dipped her tongue inside her and lapped at her walls, drinking in as much of her as she could. She moved her mouth to Eleanor's swollen clit. She sucked it between her lips and flicked it with her tongue. That's all it took. Eleanor cried out Randi's name and shook all over as she came.

Randi moved up next to Eleanor and kissed her, then took her in her arms, content to hold her while she slept.

"You're not serious, are you?" Eleanor said.

"Hm?"

"I'm glad you're all relaxed and stuff, but I haven't had my turn yet. I need to reclaim you as mine just like you did me."

"If you're up for it," Randi said.

"Oh, yeah. I'm up for it."

Randi rolled over onto her back and spread her legs. Her stomach fluttered. She was aroused beyond words. She was ready for and needed Eleanor's touch. Eleanor's hand was magic as it teased her nipples and skimmed down her belly. She arched her back to urge her hand lower. She needed to feel her in her center.

Eleanor finally ran her hand between Randi's legs, leaving no spot untouched. She slipped her fingers inside Randi and stroked her, easily coaxing her to an orgasm. Next, she rubbed her fingers over her rock hard clit that was slick with Randi's obvious arousal. She rubbed it hard and fast and Randi screamed her name as she came.

Randi wrapped her arms around Eleanor again and fell into a deep, contented sleep. She awoke the next morning to an empty bed. She put on her boxers and undershirt and walked out to find Eleanor sipping coffee at the kitchen table.

"I didn't like waking up without you," Randi said.

"Sorry. I couldn't sleep anymore."

"You look awfully serious. You got something on your mind?"

"I do."

Randi's stomach melted. Was she having second thoughts? Had last night been a one-shot deal? She hoped not.

"So, what's on your mind?" Randi said.

"Well, let me get you some coffee first."

She poured Randi a cup, then sat back down.

"You're scaring me, baby. What's going on?"

"Well, what I have to ask you might scare you, too. It's kind of scaring me, if you want to know the truth."

"Just tell me," Randi said. "It can't be that bad."

"Okay." She took a deep breath. "Randi, I was thinking that we should move in together. I mean, you're always over here anyway. Or, rather, you were before we split up. I have to believe you will be again now that we're back together."

Randi stood there, not knowing how to respond. She eased herself down into a chair.

"Are you sure?" she said. "Living together is a huge step."

"But don't you think it's the right step? Don't you think we're solid enough to make it work?"

Randi thought about her house. It wasn't much, but it was hers. Was she willing to give it up? But then, if she didn't, what was she doing? What was the end goal with Eleanor? She really did spend all her time there. It actually did make sense.

"Say something, Randi. You're scaring me."

"I had to think about it, baby, but I think you're right. I think I should move in with you. It's only logical."

"Oh, Randi, are you serious?" Eleanor leaped from her chair and wrapped her arms around her.

"Never more," Randi said.

She took Eleanor's hand and they went down the hall to celebrate their new beginning.

# About the Author

MJ Williamz was raised on California's central coast, which she left at age seventeen to pursue an education. She graduated from Chico State, and it was in Chico that she rediscovered her love of writing. It wasn't until she moved to Portland, however, that her writing really took off, with the publication of her first short story in 2003.

MJ is the author of fifteen books, including three Goldie Award winners. She has also had over thirty short stories published, most of them erotica with a few romances and a few horrors thrown in for good measure. She lives in Houston with her wife, fellow author Laydin Michaels, and their fur babies. You can reach her at mjwilliamz@aol.com

# Books Available from Bold Strokes Books

**Exposed** by MJ Williamz. The closet is no place to live if you want to find true love. (978-1-62639-989-1)

**Force of Fire: Toujours a Vous** by Ali Vali. Immortals Kendal and Piper welcome their new child and celebrate the defeat of an old enemy, but another ancient evil is about to awaken deep in the jungles of Costa Rica. (978-1-63555-047-4)

**Holding Their Place** by Kelly A. Wacker. Together Dr. Helen Connery and ambulance driver Julia March, discover that goodness, love, and passion can be found in the most unlikely and even dangerous places during WWI. (978-1-63555-338-3)

**Landing Zone** by Erin Dutton. Can a career veteran finally discover a love stronger than even her pride? (978-1-63555-199-0)

**Love at Last Call** by M. Ullrich. Is balancing business, friendship, and love more than any willing woman can handle? (978-1-63555-197-6)

**Pleasure Cruise** by Yolanda Wallace. Spencer Collins and Amy Donovan have few things in common, but a Caribbean cruise offers both women an unexpected chance to face one of their greatest fears: falling in love. (978-1-63555-219-5)

**Running Off Radar** by MB Austin. Maji's plans to win Rose back are interrupted when work intrudes and duty calls her to help a SEAL team stop a Russian mobster from harvesting gold from the bottom of Sitka Sound. (978-1-63555-152-5)

**Shadow of the Phoenix** by Rebecca Harwell. In the final battle for the fate of Storm's Quarry, even Nadya's and Shay's powers may not be enough. (978-1-63555-181-5)

**Take a Chance** by D. Jackson Leigh. There's hardly a woman within fifty miles of Pine Cone that veterinarian Trip Beaumont can't charm, except for the irritating new cop, Jamie Grant, who keeps leaving parking tickets on her truck. (978-1-63555-118-1)

**The Outcasts** by Alexa Black. Spacebus driver Sue Jones is running from her past. When she crash-lands on a faraway world, the Outcast Kara might be her chance for redemption. (978-1-63555-242-3)

**Alias** by Cari Hunter. A car crash leaves a woman with no memory and no identity. Together with Detective Bronwen Pryce, she fights to uncover a truth that might just kill them both. (978-1-63555-221-8)

**Death in Time** by Robyn Nyx. Working in the past is hell on your future. (978-1-63555-053-5)

**Hers to Protect** by Nicole Disney. High school sweethearts Kaia and Adrienne will have to see past their differences and survive the vengeance of a brutal gang if they want to be together. (978-1-63555-229-4)

**Of Echoes Born** by 'Nathan Burgoine. A collection of queer fantasy short stories set in Canada from Lambda Literary Award finalist 'Nathan Burgoine. (978-1-63555-096-2)

**Perfect Little Worlds** by Clifford Mae Henderson. Lucy can't hold the secret any longer. Twenty-six years ago, her sister did the unthinkable. (978-1-63555-164-8)

**Room Service** by Fiona Riley. Interior designer Olivia likes stability, but when work brings footloose Savannah into her world and into a new city every month, Olivia must decide if what makes her comfortable is what makes her happy. (978-1-63555-120-4)

**Sparks Like Ours** by Melissa Brayden. Professional surfers Gia Malone and Elle Britton can't deny their chemistry on and off the beach. But only one can win... (978-1-63555-016-0)

**Take My Hand** by Missouri Vaun. River Hemsworth arrives in Georgia intent on escaping quickly, but when she crashes her Mercedes into the Clip 'n Curl, sexy Clay Cahill ends up rescuing more than her car. (978-1-63555-104-4)

**The Last Time I Saw Her** by Kathleen Knowles. Lane Hudson only has twelve days to win back Alison's heart. That is if she can gather the courage to try. (978-1-63555-067-2)

**Wayworn Lovers** by Gun Brooke. Will agoraphobic composer Giselle Bonnaire and Tierney Edwards, a wandering soul who can't remain in one place for long, trust in the passionate love destiny hands them? (978-1-62639-995-2)

**Breakthrough** by Kris Bryant. Falling for a sexy ranger is one thing, but is the possibility of love worth giving up the career Kennedy Wells has always dreamed of? (978-1-63555-179-2)

**Certain Requirements** by Elinor Zimmerman. Phoenix has always kept her love of kinky submission strictly behind the bedroom door and inside the bounds of romantic relationships, until she meets Kris Andersen. (978-1-63555-195-2)

**Dark Euphoria** by Ronica Black. When a high-profile case drops in Detective Maria Diaz's lap, she forges ahead only to discover this case, and her main suspect, aren't like any other. (978-1-63555-141-9)

**Fore Play** by Julie Cannon. Executive Leigh Marshall falls hard for Peyton Broader, her golf pro...and an ex-con. Will she risk sabotaging her career for love? (978-1-63555-102-0)

**Love Came Calling** by CA Popovich. Can a romantic looking for a long-term, committed relationship and a jaded cynic too busy for love conquer life's struggles and find their way to what matters most? (978-1-63555-205-8)

**Outside the Law** by Carsen Taite. Former sweethearts Tanner Cohen and Sydney Braswell must work together on a federal task force to see justice served, but will they choose to embrace their second chance at love? (978-1-63555-039-9)

**The Princess Deception** by Nell Stark. When journalist Missy Duke realizes Prince Sebastian is really his twin sister Viola in disguise, she plays along, but when sparks flare between them, will the double deception doom their fairy-tale romance? (978-1-62639-979-2)

**The Smell of Rain** by Cameron MacElvee. Reyha Arslan, a wise and elegant woman with a tragic past, shows Chrys that there's still beauty to embrace and reason to hope despite the world's cruelty. (978-1-63555-166-2)

**The Talebearer** by Sheri Lewis Wohl. Liz's visions show her the faces of the lost and the killers who took their lives. As one by one, the murdered are found, a stranger works to stop Liz before the serial killer is brought to justice. (978-1-635550-126-6)

**White Wings Weeping** by Lesley Davis. The world is full of discord and hatred, but how much of it is just human nature when an evil with sinister intent is invading people's hearts? (978-1-63555-191-4)

**A Call Away** by KC Richardson. Can a businesswoman from a big city find the answers she's looking for, and possibly love, on a small-town farm? (978-1-63555-025-2)

**Berlin Hungers** by Justine Saracen. Can the love between an RAF woman and the wife of a Luftwaffe pilot, former enemies, survive in besieged Berlin during the aftermath of World War II? (978-1-63555-116-7)

**Blend** by Georgia Beers. Lindsay and Piper are like night and day. Working together won't be easy, but not falling in love might prove the hardest job of all. (978-1-63555-189-1)

**Hunger for You** by Jenny Frame. Principe of an ancient vampire clan Byron Debrek must save her one true love from falling into the hands of her enemies and into the middle of a vampire war. (978-1-63555-168-6)

**Mercy** by Michelle Larkin. FBI Special Agent Mercy Parker and psychic ex-profiler Piper Vasey learn to love again as they race to stop a man with supernatural gifts who's bent on annihilating humankind. (978-1-63555-202-7)

**Pride and Porters** by Charlotte Greene. Will pride and prejudice prevent these modern-day lovers from living happily ever after? (978-1-63555-158-7)

**Rocks and Stars** by Sam Ledel. Kyle's struggle to own who she is and what she really wants may end up landing her on the bench and without the woman of her dreams. (978-1-63555-156-3)

**The Boss of Her: Office Romance Novellas** by Julie Cannon, Aurora Rey, and M. Ullrich. Going to work never felt so good. Three office romance novellas from talented writers Julie Cannon, Aurora Rey, and M. Ullrich. (978-1-63555-145-7)

**The Deep End** by Ellie Hart. When family ties become entangled in murder and deception, it's time to find a way out... (978-1-63555-288-1)

**A Country Girl's Heart** by Dena Blake. When Kat Jackson gets a second chance at love, following her heart will prove the hardest decision of all. (978-1-63555-134-1)

**Dangerous Waters** by Radclyffe. Life, death, and war on the home front. Two women join forces against a powerful opponent, nature itself. (978-1-63555-233-1)

**Fury's Death** by Brey Willows. When all we hold sacred fails, who will be there to save us? (978-1-63555-063-4)

**It's Not a Date** by Heather Blackmore. Kade's desire to keep things with Jen on a professional level is in Jen's best interest. Yet what's in Kade's best interest…is Jen. (978-1-63555-149-5)

**Killer Winter** by Kay Bigelow. Just when she thought things could get no worse, homicide Lieutenant Leah Samuels learns the woman she loves has betrayed her in devastating ways. (978-1-63555-177-8)

**Score** by MJ Williamz. Will an addiction to pain pills destroy Ronda's chance with the woman she loves or will she come out on top and score a happily ever after? (978-1-62639-807-8)

**Spring's Wake** by Aurora Rey. When wanderer Willa Lange falls for Provincetown B&B owner Nora Calhoun, will past hurts and a fifteen-year age gap keep them from finding love? (978-1-63555-035-1)

**The Northwoods** by Jane Hoppen. When Evelyn Bauer, disguised as her dead husband, George, travels to a Northwoods logging camp to work, she and the camp cook Sarah Bell forge a friendship fraught with both tenderness and turmoil. (978-1-63555-143-3)

**Truth or Dare** by C. Spencer. For a group of six lesbian friends, life changes course after one long snow-filled weekend. (978-1-63555-148-8)